To Jenni

Best wishes

Clutie Brooks.

GW00808254

A Quiet Village

Christine Brooks

authorHOUSE®

AuthorHouse™ UK Ltd.
500 Avebury Boulevard
Central Milton Keynes, MK9 2BE
www.authorhouse.co.uk
Phone: 08001974150

© 2009 Christine Brooks. All rights reserved.

No part of this book may be reproduced, stored in a retrieval system, or transmitted by any means without the written permission of the author.

First published by AuthorHouse 10/13/2009

ISBN: 978-1-4490-2461-1 (sc)

ISBN: 978-1-4490-2461-1 (sc)

This book is printed on acid-free paper.

Acknowledgements

Lots of people to thank, my lovely and long suffering husband Paul. My fantastic daughter Kate who is a constant source of advice and encouragement - yes I know as her mother it should be the other way around but Kate is one in a million. My super son Tim and his beautiful wife Emma, for their love and support and special congratulations on their wedding - I couldn't wish for a more wonderful daughter in law. My dearest and "longest standing" (happy now Chops?) friend the real Shelagh Veitch who isn't a policewoman but is a fabulous cook and an even better friend. Thanks mate you know I'd be lost without you. My friend Lorraine who helped me so much when my first book came out - and gave me the tip about drinks bubbling over! Special thanks to Steve Dunn for all the proof reading and patience with me and to Terry Richards for providing the cover picture and giving me the urge to kill. My friends in Spain some of whom I used as names in this book but only with their permission and they are nothing at all like their characters. Mum and Dad, my family and friends, I can't list you all but you know who you are. You mean the world to me and a simple thank you doesn't cover it but I really do appreciate you all.

Finally I'd just like to say that all the characters in this book are totally fictitious so if you think you recognise yourself .....trust me, your secret is safe!

The principle characters in order of appearance

Robyn 'Bobby' Collins. Former secretary now wife, to successful architect Simon.

Debby Sherman married to local estate agent Nick.

Melanie Richards married to Darren they have two children Jack and Lucy.

Joanna Baines, doctor's receptionist married to Jim who runs his father in law's company.

Karen Matherson commutes to the city daily, married to Terry who works for Jim Baines.

Prologue

*J*t was a bitterly cold day. An optimistic winter sun tried in vain to penetrate the gloom but was quickly dismissed by the foreboding grey clouds that blanketed the tiny village church. William Owens, the parish rector, shivered in his robes as he stood at the doorway greeting the mourners. Endlessly the sombre stream filed past him. The church was packed to capacity and beyond. He couldn't help wondering how many were present merely to avoid missing the latest instalment of the juicy scandal.

"Morning, Vicar." A local man mumbled as he awkwardly shook hands with the cleric. "Dreadful isn't it?" he continued, before shuffling onwards into the church.

"Yes indeed," replied Bill, wondering if he had been referring to the weather or the recent tragedy. He was accustomed to mourners feeling lost for words at such events but this funeral was certainly unique in his experience. He pictured the unfortunate woman in his mind. Young, vivacious and quite beautiful as he recalled. Some people had thought her hard and calculating but with his usual optimism he had always found her very charming. He sighed deeply. How could she possibly have done such a terrible thing as to take her own life? He forced a sympathetic smile on his face as a middle-aged lady approached him. She ran the village post office and was well known as a font of all knowledge.

"Morning Father," she said primly, pursing her lips in obvious disapproval as she looked at the gathering crowds. "Quite a gathering I see. I really didn't realise she was so popular." She sniffed disdainfully towards an approaching group of the deceased friends. "Shameful carryings on from what I hear. Of course you know I would rather tear off my lips than repeat gossip but well… as the Good Book says 'God pays debts without money'"

"I'm not sure I'm quite familiar with that text," replied Bill with mild reproach. "Though I do well recall the lines 'Judge not lest yea be judged.' Good morning Miss Evans, perhaps you'd better be getting in out of the cold." he continued smoothly. He glanced after the departing woman with an air of exasperation. Miss Evans approached a pew where she was welcomed by a group of like-minded friends. Together they perched like a flock of old crows in their unrelieved black and avidly watched the door anxious to see the drama unfold.

Shaking his head the village priest turned his attentions to the approaching group. There was no mistaking their obvious grief. He could see the array of emotions crossing their faces. Bewilderment, grief and perhaps even guilt as they all remembered their friend and the part she had played in their lives. He had expected such feelings. It was usual in cases of suicide for the bereaved to feel such conflict. Nick Sherman stared ahead, white-faced and trembling. He still couldn't believe it had happened.

"Why do you think she did it Bill?" he asked, quietly despairing. "We could have worked things out. What made her do it?" Part of him hated the woman they were here to mourn.

Bill shook his head sadly. "I can't give you answers Nick. I wish I could. I'm here for you though, if ever you want to talk."

He glanced across at the rest of the group of friends. Compassion and concern on his face as he surveyed them.

Another poor soul seemed almost on breaking point. Her shoulders heaved as she clutched a handkerchief to her face and openly sobbed.

"Try to be strong my dear," he murmured. "Remember her suffering is over now. Try to imagine her looking down on us all from a far better place."

The woman merely nodded and, supported by her friends, she moved into the welcoming gloom of the old village church.

Oblivious to the curious onlookers they walked to the reserved front pew and sat lost in their own thoughts.

Terry Matherson stared at the coffin. He glanced with embarrassment across at his sobbing friend and awkwardly patted her hand.

"Umm she wouldn't want you to remember her like this," he murmured.

"I'll bet she wouldn't!" she thought triumphantly. "I'll bet she's looking down and reaching for the thunderbolts at the injustice of it all. Everyone thinks she killed herself. Everyone thinks she was barking mad and finally cracked. It's just amazing no one knows it was me. I killed her and no one knows. It's all just so incredible!" She pressed her handkerchief into her face again to smother her laughter.

"But I got away with it and now it is over. Life will eventually return to normal, and Linwood will once again become, just a nice quiet village."

CHAPTER 1

*I*t's a funny thing deciding to kill someone. Really kill them. What makes an ordinary suburban housewife from a sleepy country village decide she is actually going to calmly and clearly commit murder? Love? Hate? Or just the quiet realisation that it was the only solution. Shame really, that winter had started out so well......

It was Halloween in the small Berkshire village of Linwood. Robyn better known as Bobby spun around in front of the mirror. Looking good! she thought happily. All the effort at the gym had certainly paid off. Mind you, considering what I spent on this dress I had better be looking good! The dress in question was certainly eye-catching. Bright red, short and sparkling with hundreds of sequins, it was close fitting to just below the waist then gently flared to swirl around her hips when she danced. The back was cut low to show off her tanned back – Fake! she thought laughingly - and revealingly low at the front to show off her cleavage - genuine! she added mentally. It was not the sort of outfit you wore to church, but then again it was supposed to be a "Saints & Sinners Night" and there certainly wasn't any misunderstanding her chosen category. She'd spent hours in the hairdressers so that her hair looked a sheer blonde smooth curtain, onto which she placed a thin hair band with two sequined horns.

1

Bobby Collins - you are going to knock 'em dead tonight! she said to herself, delighted with the overall effect. She winced as she put on the impossibly high heels, which were only worth the agony because they looked so good. You'd better appreciate these Jim, she groaned as she thought of her lover. Then smiled and shrugged. The price you pay for vanity she thought to herself, as she contemplated how her feet would feel after an evening in such torturous contraptions. The shoes - naturally - matched the dress perfectly. They were bright red patent leather flimsy looking creations, consisting of a few narrow straps with tiny gold buckles. Very sheer stockings, with just enough Lycra to give her legs a shimmering tanned look completed the picture.

Simon came into the room just as she was putting the finishing touches to her make-up. He was a tall man, with slightly greying hair which he was vain enough to keep 'slightly greying' by artificial means, as he felt that any more would make him look old, and any less would be less distinguished. A regular golfer, he kept in trim by endless hours on the course and regular games of squash.

"How do I look?" she asked. She stood for his inspection and twirled around teasingly in front of her dressing table. The huge mirror showing her from every angle. She didn't really care for his opinion. The ensemble was not for his benefit but she couldn't resist the opportunity for a compliment.

Simon stood at the door and slowly looked her up and down as if looking for any tiny flaw. Finally he spoke.

"You look like a tart," he said thoughtfully. "A very attractive tart. Maybe even an expensive tart - but definitely a tart," he added, but there was no malice in his voice. Actually, he was rather proud of her, she looked very sexy - but he was wise enough to know she would soon grow to despise a man who fawned over her.

Deliberately he turned his back on her and walked over to his own dressing table to consider his array of expensive colognes. They had an easy going marriage. Bobby was pretty sure he knew of her extra marital affairs but he had the grace to ignore them. Theirs was not a torrid love match but it was an amicable enough arrangement. Simon was considerably older than his wife. He was quite satisfied to regard her as an expensive ornament provided she maintained their unspoken agreement that she was at least publicly discreet.

Bobby herself had no illusions of their domestic bliss. Simon was wealthy and generous and their arrangement suited her perfectly. She glanced idly around the room at the framed pictures that spelled out her life. Their wedding picture. Bobby immaculately dressed in a designer suit at the Registry office. Simon appearing somewhat less impeccable as this was prior to her tasteful intervention in his style. His recent divorce had meant a church wedding would perhaps seem a little distasteful under the circumstances hence the civil ceremony. There had been few guests she recalled. His family had not approved of him unceremoniously dumping his mousy first wife in favour of his glamorous secretary.

In a modern steel frame was the original architectural drawing of his greatest work. The stunning modern construction built mainly in green glass and steel and called the Emerald Plaza. It was built in the local town and housed the headquarters of the Inland Revenue. She sighed as she recalled how many times he'd bored her with the story of its design and his pride in procuring so many Government contracts. She often felt like joining in when he once again trotted out his stock phrase; "There's no chance of the taxman going out of business."

"What's it in aid of tonight?" his voice jolted her out of her reverie.

They lived in a small village and usually attended village functions with the same group of friends. The local Memorial Hall was frequently used by a variety of charities for social events and fun-raising evenings. Generally attended by the same people on each occasion often the guests would have little or no connection with the charity concerned. It was a mutually beneficial arrangement, local people enjoyed themselves without having to travel too far and local charities enjoyed the profits.

"Scouts I think." Bobby shrugged; it was of little interest to her. "Mel was selling the tickets and I think her son is about that age isn't he?"

"Guess he must be by now. I suppose all the usual crowd will be there then?"

"As far as I know, Debby said she and Nick would probably get there first and get us all a table. Joanna and Jim will probably be late - as usual. Mel and Darren were having trouble getting a baby-sitter but they have to be there, and Karen and Terry have got her mother staying, so they'll be eager to get away from her for a while."

"Sounds very cosy - I suppose you girls will all be comparing outfits... and husbands. I hope you're not going to give Joanna a hard time." He loved his wife but had no illusions about her rather cruel streak, especially where other women were concerned.

"I don't know what you mean, we only have a laugh together," she replied defensively, painting her immaculately manicured nails a bright scarlet colour and blowing on them gently to dry the varnish.

"At her expense!" he retorted. He rather liked Joanna, who was a gentle sort, who brought out his latent sense of chivalry.

"Can I help it if she makes it so easy? Anyway, you're very concerned about Joanna aren't you? Perhaps I ought to watch you with her." She was confident enough to know she could see a mouse like Joanna off with no trouble.

"Joanna would never be unfaithful to Jim, you know that. She really is devoted to him. He's a lucky man. It's just a shame he doesn't appreciate her," he persisted, starting to feel slightly irritated by his wife's condescending attitude.

Bobby picked up on his change of tone. Looking up at him she frowned, surely he wasn't interested in Joanna? He had played the 'married to the little woman type' game, she had rescued him from all that, and he had always seemed most grateful. Surely he could remember how boring life was then? Still, perhaps she ought to watch her step for a while; this conversation was getting a bit too serious.

"Hey, what's all this? We're going out remember? Let's not argue now" she smiled at him and tried to gently tease him back into his former good humour. "You wouldn't want me to waste an outfit like this now would you?"

"I'm not looking for a fight, I just feel sorry for her, that's all," he said with an air of finality. He had no intention of starting an argument either, the evening would be ruined if they started out on bad terms, and he certainly didn't want to give Bobby any excuse to find comfort elsewhere if they were not on speaking terms by the time they arrived. He had his suspicions about what went on when he was at work, but he had no intention of being made a fool of publicly.

"Aren't you going to get ready?" she asked, changing the subject and looking him over as he stood before her, dressed as a vicar. "Oh sorry - is that your costume? I thought you'd just put your shirt on back to front. You are a little forgetful these days, after all you're not as young as you once were - are you darling? Lucky for you I've always gone for the sugar daddy type!" Bobby used her sexiest voice and blew him a seductive kiss.

"Bitch", he said with an amused drawl, "By the way - just who is the lucky target tonight? I rather think you've lost Jim to Debby you know, perhaps you're losing your touch." Despite his good intentions of not upsetting her, he knew just how to get under her skin, and he wanted her to know that he was not completely blind to her little games. She should learn to exercise a bit more discretion.

Bastard, she thought, but replied in an exaggeratedly sweet voice "Darling, you know I only ever dress to please you."

"Ah, but for whom do you undress?" He leant over and kissed the back of neck, to show there was no spite intended.

She ignored him and turned to her jewellery box. To her annoyance she found her fingers were trembling as she chose a sparkling ruby choker. She struggled to keep her lighthearted mood. She wasn't worried about their brief argument - she knew it didn't mean anything, but Simon had hit a nerve when he mentioned Jim to her. He was a bit too close to the mark in his off-hand comment about Debby. Bobby had indeed been having an affair with Jim for a few weeks, but just recently he had seemed a bit cool, and she was furious.

Simon wandered off in the direction of their bathroom to finish getting ready, while Bobby sat at the dressing table staring thoughtfully in the mirror.

It's one thing to go back to your wife, but to start another affair so quickly is downright tacky! she thought angrily. After all I do for him, she glanced down at the tortuous shoes. A bit of loyalty wouldn't go amiss, she thought, deliberately ignoring the irony of her thoughts.

She wondered how far things had gone between Jim and Debby. Perhaps he was only flirting with her to keep Bobby's interest. Maybe she was reading more into it than was there. No, that couldn't be true, not if Simon had noticed too. It seemed the only person who never noticed anything was Joanna, but then they do say the wife is always the last to know. Damn him! she thought. Damn both of them! She was not about to made to look a fool. If there was any replacing to be done she would be the one doing it. First I'll get his undivided devotion, and then I'll dump him! The trouble was that she rather liked Jim. He was charming and fun, a little arrogant perhaps, but although a pushover to seduce, he was a challenge to hang on to - and she did love a challenge! Still, a girl had her pride, and as the old saying went - it had been fun while it lasted. She would teach that bitch Debby a lesson too! She would never be able to show her face at the club again if Debby stole her latest conquest right from under, or should it be over, her.

As Simon came back from the dressing room she stood up and smiled graciously at him. Glancing back at the mirror she smoothed her hair and mentally prepared to do battle for her errant lover's attention.

"All set for the fray?" enquired Simon as if reading her thoughts.

"Totally prepared," Bobby replied smoothly. She swept out of the bedroom door ahead of him.

Together they went downstairs, they were running late. Bobby was starting to feel the thrill of anticipation of a fight, and was very anxious to let battle commence, but of course Simon couldn't know that, so they still had to go through the usual routine. Leave some lights on, others off, check the doors and windows, set the alarm. Oh God, he's so predictable, thought Bobby Boring! Boring! Boring! Perhaps he really is getting too old for me. "You can't be too careful you know," remarked Simon, "This house is quite a prestigious target." Bobby stifled a scream. For Christ's sake let's just go. She silently ranted. She knew Simon was immensely proud of his architectural masterpiece but there was little crime in the village of Linwood.

"We are only going around the corner darling; we are not back packing up the Amazon for six months," she said through gritted teeth.

Simon merely smiled; he was certainly no fool when it came to home security. Knowing how it irritated his wife that he was so meticulous made him all the more so. Some had commented that it was a shame he didn't make sure his wife was as secure as his house.

They had already decided he would drive, he was extremely proud of his car, the latest model Mercedes in midnight blue with leather upholstery and a music system which could rival a professional sound studio. It had a personalised number plate - S.P.C. 1 - Simon Philip Collins. He rarely let anyone else drive it, and was not really bothered if it meant he couldn't have a drink. It was sometimes quite interesting to be the sober one at a party, he often mused. It was not a sentiment that endeared him to his wife however. She would have preferred him being a little less observant and perhaps a little less 'in control'.

He helped her into her coat. "Always the gentlemen aren't you?" she said sarcastically. "Well, my sweet" he replied, "if you're going out dressed to kill, the very least I can do is keep the ammunition dry."

CHAPTER 2

Across the village, at the home of Debby and Nick Sherman, Debby was also getting ready. She wondered what the others would be wearing. Bobby will be over the top as usual, but of course with her money she can afford to be, she thought maliciously. Joanna will try, but she can't compete. Mel always looks good, but then she's not in the running, so who cares, likewise for Karen, really. She mentally checked off all her friends and potential rivals. So that meant Bobby was her only worry. Fortunately, she knew Bobby was wearing red. It would have been too humiliating if they had turned up in similar costumes, especially as Bobby's would have been obviously more expensive. The last thing she wanted to look like was a cheap copy. Luckily Joanna had unwittingly played right into her hands over coffee that morning.

"Bobby's bought a lovely red dress," Joanna had said. "She always looks so nice in bright colours doesn't she? She did tell me to keep it a surprise - I think she wants to make an entrance tonight - but I'm sure she won't mind me telling you," she prattled on good-naturedly.

Was Joanna really that stupid? She must realise that Bobby had been having an affair with her husband for weeks now; no one could be that nice or that dumb. Still, at least it meant that she had an insight as to what Bobby was wearing - red - okay. No problem there – Debbie's outfit was black, no contest. It was bound to be short, low cut and sexy, but again Debbie was pretty confident she had the upper hand - no man could resist black stockings, and black stockings with a red dress would look sleazy - and if there was one thing Bobby could not be accused of, it was looking sleazy. If the situation called for it she could look tarty (but sexy with it), but she would never, never look sleazy, so she was safe there. Of course, there was her trump card, dealt to her, ironically enough, by Joanna herself. What was it she had said? Oh yes, now she remembered, Joanna had poured the coffee and they had chatted about men and how predictable they were. Debby had been very skilful she thought at bringing the subject around to Jim, and of course Joanna was always so keen to extol the virtues of her wonderful husband. According to Joanna, Jim was perfection personified, but he was perhaps a bit old fashioned and predictable in his schoolboy attitude.

"I mean," she'd laughed, "show him a bit of black leather and he's anyone's!"

They had both laughed, but Debby had mentally filed that snippet of information away. She felt the odd pang of guilt at trying to steal her confidant's husband, but there was an old saying about love and war, wasn't there? Anyway, it wasn't as though he was exactly as faithful as a bird dog - more like a dog for the birds! She laughed aloud at her own wit.

"What's the joke?" asked her husband Nick, surprised at her sudden burst of laughter. There hadn't been much laughter in their house for some time.

"Oh, I was just thinking of something Joanna said earlier, you wouldn't see the funny side of it, it was a woman's type of joke" she added, dismissively.

"Oh really" replied Nick, "I've never thought of Joanna as being a comic, perhaps I ought to pay more attention to her. I enjoy a good joke"

You are a good joke, she thought wearily, but she didn't bother to answer him.

Like Bobby and Simon, Nick and Debby had also been married for about five years. Unfortunately, unlike Simon, Nick had no intention of turning a blind eye to his wife's infidelities. They had both been guilty of seeking attentions outside of their marriage, but illogically, Nick found infidelity unforgivable in his wife. Their relationship had been deteriorating for some time now, and was virtually in the death throes at the moment. Neither one however, was quite ready for the final coup de grace. They had no children to keep them together, although they had once both wanted them, which probably had quite a lot to do with the current state of animosity. Both blamed the other for their lack of conception, neither wanted to suffer the indignity of tests to determine the problem.

Nick was a partner in a firm of estate agents in the village, and had seen his business suffer greatly recently. The property market had slumped, and although they had been extremely comfortable when they had first married, they were now finding things very difficult. The large house that they had bought when it had been considered a snip at the price was now in negative equity. They both realised that even if they did decide to divorce they simply couldn't afford to. A situation that added significantly to the frustration Debby felt in being stuck in a marriage of which she was rapidly tiring.

Debby was also very keen not to lose face in front of her friends, a problem Nick didn't appreciate to the same extent. She did not want to be the deserted wife, and was not about to leave her husband until she had lined up a replacement. She knew that with no children she was unlikely to get much in the way of alimony, not that Nick was earning much at the moment anyway. Her job as a secretary in a firm of solicitors - although not poorly paid, was not enough to keep her in the manner in which she would like to be kept. She had seen enough miserable women coming through the office to know she did not want to join their ranks.

Debby started on her make-up, tonight she could go completely over the top, whoever decided on 'Saints & Sinners' should really be congratulated, she thought. It gave everyone the chance to fulfil whatever secret fantasy they (or whomever they wanted to impress) desired.   Tonight she would really teach Bobby a lesson, she'd show her who was queen in the seduction stakes. She was really looking forward to it. Naturally, she was sorry that Joanna would be hurt, but still, she must realise that she couldn't hold on to Jim forever. After all, everyone knew what Jim was like, and surely she must be expecting something like this to happen eventually. Still, she had to be clever, it wouldn't do to create a martyr of Joanna, and cast herself in the role of the evil marriage breaker.

Nick continued dressing. He too, was going as a 'sinner'; a card sharp in a riverboat gambler costume, which he secretly thought, made him look pretty good. His black fedora had a couple of aces tucked conspicuously into the hatband, and he wore satin waistcoat covered with a pattern of playing cards. For further effect, he carried a small pistol that he had bought from the local novelty shop.

"What do you think?" He still hoped in some ways they could get back to how they had been not that long ago.

"Very nice," she didn't bother to turn around from the dressing table, where she was painting her nails.

"You might at least turn around and look Debby. I'm only going to this stupid thing for you. You're the one who likes dressing up!" It didn't take much to rile him these days, and she certainly was not making any effort to make things any easier between them.

"You wanted to go too - any excuse to flirt with your friends' wives, and besides, why should I inspect the costume? You've spent long enough in front of that mirror to know exactly how it looks!" She didn't want to make him so angry that they wouldn't even get to the event at all, but she couldn't resist the jibe.

"I'm a flirt! I like that! You spent so much time hanging over Jim at that last do, everyone thought you were newlyweds! It was disgusting, especially with his wife right there!" He remembered the last event they were all at when Debby had made a very obvious play for Jim.

And his mistress, thought Debby with smug satisfaction. "I'm surprised you noticed you seemed rather more interested in Bobby than me." Using the old adage that the best form of defence is attack, she turned on him.

"I was just trying to calm her down, she seemed quite upset about something, I was only being a friend! Perhaps she and Simon are having troubles..." The idea rather interested him.

Debby finished painting her nails and stood up. She was wearing a black leather mini dress, stockings and thigh high boots. In her hand she held a long leather whip. She had hired the costume from the fancy dress hire shop at the local town, and she knew it really was completely outrageous, but at least she knew she'd be noticed.

"Don't get your hopes up darling, Bobby would never leave Simon, she is far too fond of his wallet. Besides my little love bug, you've already got a wife, remember?" Her sarcasm however, was wasted on him, as he turned to face her, she groaned as she saw the look in his eye.

"How could I forget? Especially when she looks like that!" He looked at Debby appreciatively, "You look too sexy to fight with, why don't we forget tonight's event and make a little music of our own?" He grabbed at her, but she wriggled free.

"Careful! You'll mess up my make-up! Forget it my head is throbbing. You can't be serious about missing tonight, not after all the trouble I went to get our costumes? No way! Anyway, I'm looking forward to it, it'll be great for us all to be together again, should be quite a laugh! It's about time we had some fun."

Reaching into the bedside drawer she rummaged around among empty packets and found a couple of Paracetamol.

"I thought you saw the doctor about those headaches – you take those bloody things like sweets." Nick snapped.

"The doc said it was stress – any bloody wonder being married to you?" She swallowed the tablets and reached for her handbag.

"Are we walking up with Mel and Darren?" asked Nick, abandoning his brief attempt at seduction.

"No, they said they might be a bit late, something about a babysitter. At least that's one problem we don't have." she gave a small bitter laugh "Anyway, I said we would get there early and make sure we had a good table. We'll probably all walk home together."

If I don't get a better offer! she mentally added, wondering if she ought to put a toothbrush in her handbag just in case. Morning breath was such a turn off.

Chapter 3

The preparations for the evening were going on at various homes around the village. In a small cul de sac near the Memorial Hall Melanie and Darren Richards were in process of getting their children settled before the arrival of their babysitter. Mel was dressed as a French prostitute in a tight black satin skirt, fishnet tights and a clinging striped top. Heavily exaggerated make-up and a black beret securely clipped to her shiny dark bobbed hair completed the picture. Darren was dressed appropriately for his large physique in a Friar Tuck costume consisting of a long brown robe tied at the waist with a cord belt. He wore a small flesh coloured skull cap for authenticity and considered himself lucky not to need the uncomfortable looking padding which the hire shop had thoughtfully provided. Their children stood staring in wide-eyed wonderment, as their usually sensible parents seemed to be getting ready to go out looking very strange.

"Mummy looks beautiful." whispered Lucy, "But why is Daddy wearing a dress?"

Her brother just stared mutely at them unable to offer any explanation.

"I hope they're going to behave. It's not easy getting a reliable sitter," Mel said anxiously as she eyed her two angelic looking children. Jack was eight and his sister Lucy was six. Both looked cherubic in their pyjamas. "Look at them. You'd think butter wouldn't melt in their mouths. How do they turn into monsters at bedtime?" she laughed. Darren came over and rested his arm along her shoulder.

"Must take after you," he grinned. "Me? I'm always perfect!" He dodged as his wife aimed an indignant elbow at his ribs. "Bed! You horrible little monsters before I set your Mum onto you," he roared with mock terror at the prospect. The children screamed with laughter and ran towards their bedrooms.

"Terrific! You wind them up just as we're going out! You're a big help!" She went after them and made sure they had got into bed before returning to finish getting ready.

"I wonder if the sparks will fly tonight between Debby and Bobby," Mel contemplated as she wrote a few brief notes for the babysitter.

"You don't think there's anything really going on between Jim and Bobby do you?" replied Darren as he struggled to tie the belt to his costume.

"You must be blinder than Joanna!" exclaimed Mel. "Of course there is! Bobby told me yesterday she'd have to cancel our lunch as she was going into town to have her legs waxed…"

"Oh well that proves it then," interrupted Darren laughing, "Anyone who is daft enough to want that done must be daft enough to be knocking off Superstud!"

"Pillock! You haven't heard the point yet, and don't call him that. You wouldn't want Joanna to hear you. Anyway the point is that she had her legs done last week." Seeing Darren's confused expression she patiently explained. "You only go about once a month at the most. She'd have to be a gorilla to need to go twice in one week!"

"I certainly can't see Bobby as a gorilla. Perhaps she is monkeying around!" He chortled at his own joke.

"You're terrible I don't know why I bother explaining these things. Anyway…" she continued, trying to finish the story. "Yesterday Joanna said that Jim was meeting a client and would be out all day, then when I took Andrew to the dentist I passed the Silver Birch Hotel and lo and behold there were both their cars.

Discreetly parked at opposite ends of the car park but since there were hardly any cars there and let's face it they both drive flashy things don't they? Well it was pretty obvious!"

"Only to a woman's suspicious mind!" Darren replied loftily trying to maintain his dignity while still wrestling with the uncooperative belt. "Besides I really can't see what all you women see in him."

"Hey don't include me!" Mel retorted. "If he were mine I'd strangle him in his sleep, if he ever does sleep! Mind you he must have something going for him. He certainly plays away quite a bit. Here let me do that. You're all fingers and thumbs."

She took the tie cord belt from Darren and stretching her arms around him she swiftly looped it around his waist.

"You know you really ought to try and lose some of this tum," she patted his stomach light heartedly.

"Perhaps I ought to take up more exercise. You know I could start 'playing away' a bit myself." He pretended to consider the idea.

"You try it and you'll lose more than your tum!" she admonished in a mock warning tone. "Give us a kiss but don't smudge my lipstick."

"Very passionate!" grumbled Darren lunging for her he stopped suddenly as the sound of the doorbell interrupted them.

"Save it for later, unless of course I've been tempted away by what did you call him? Oh yes 'Superstud!'" Still laughing Mel went to open the front door.

The teenage daughter of one of the teachers at the village school stood patiently awaiting a reply. Clutching a battered school bag she looked with astonishment at her employer for the evening.

"Hello Kate, Thank you for coming. Come on in." Mel led the way through into the living room. "We're only up at the Memorial Hall if you need us. The 'Saints and Sinners Night' you know?"

"Oh yes, yes of course. Well you look very…um…nice?" mumbled the embarrassed girl.

"The children are in bed but I doubt they'll be asleep yet. We won't be late." Mel was still giving last minute instructions as Darren practically dragged her out the door.

"Come on Kate knows all that. Look we might even be early for a change."

They walked up through the village towards the hall.

"You know if you were to hang around here for a bit you'd probably make enough money to pay for a decent night out," suggested Darren teasingly.

"I might even get a better offer than you," Mel warned shivering in the evening chill. "Come on, speed it up a bit. I'm freezing in this! My legs feel like ice and these heels were not designed for much walking. I think I'll stick with my day job!"

Laughing they crossed the road and walked up the pathway to the small, brightly lit hall.

Chapter 4

*I*f Joanna Baines even suspected she was the object of so much sympathy, she certainly didn't show it. She hummed happily to herself, as she got dressed. She, too, was speculating on what the others would be wearing. She knew she couldn't compete if they all dressed as 'Sinners', so she didn't try, and if she said so herself, she was looking pretty good.

"Nearly ready darling? It's getting a bit late you know." Jim was notorious for taking forever to get ready, and it would be nice to be on time for a change. Joanna adored him, but even she had to admit he was rather vain. He did have cause to be, of course. He was tall and blond with lovely blue eyes that crinkled at the edges when he smiled. She suspected, accurately, that he practised that smile in front of the mirror. She had worshipped him since they were both at college, and had spent ages doing his washing, and cooking his favourite meals, until finally he had realised just what a good thing he was on to, and had married her. He had been captain of the college cricket team, and at one time had hoped to be a professional, but a twisted knee injury had put paid to those hopes. When Joanna's father offered him a job in the family printing firm he had gone into the printing trade. Not that he was just the boss's son-in-law. He had a good head for business, and had built the company up to the thriving concern it was today. He was a charming man, and people liked doing business with him. He got more orders than all the rest of the reps combined, and had genuinely worked his way up to management.

They had a harmonious life. Jim liked to be the centre of attention, and Joanna liked him to be just that. She knew she was a feminist's nightmare, but she was happy. She worked as a receptionist at the local doctors' surgery in the village, where she was popular for her caring and compassionate attitude. If people thought she was treated badly, she didn't care. So what if Jim flirted? She was the one that he always came back to. She knew he would never really be unfaithful to her. When they had married they had both said how much their vows meant to them. They had a proper Church wedding, in the true old-fashioned way. Joanna had lived at home until her father, who was delighted with her choice, had given her away at the altar. If she had not quite been worthy of wearing the white dress she looked so radiant in; at least she could honestly say there had been no other man than her husband in her life.

Jim finally finished dressing, and turned to Joanna.

"You look lovely, but then you always do." He loved his wife, unfortunately, he also loved quite a few other men's wives, but he justified his actions by telling himself that he never hurt Joanna, and that he was always a good provider. She never went short of anything, including affection. He just liked to know that he could still attract the girls if he wanted to.

"Jim, you really are a smoothie, aren't you? No wonder all the girls fancy you!" Joanna teased, as she brushed on the blue mascara that made her eyes look even larger. She was a pretty woman, a little on the plump side perhaps, but not excessively so, and at least she didn't look anorexic like so many today, she reassured herself. She had long blonde hair, which she often felt like cutting because it got in her way, but which Jim loved, so she kept it long.

"You know I'm not interested in anyone else. As the old joke goes I'm like a dog chasing cars - I wouldn't know what to do with one if I caught it!" Jim loved to tease her. He was supremely confident that she would never find out about his various mistresses, as she was not, it had to be said, the brightest of people. Where he was concerned she was totally gullible.

"Well just you mind you don't get your nose squashed if one stops too suddenly. Some of those drivers can get quite annoyed you know!" There had been the odd occasion when an irate husband had taken exception to Jim's attention to his wife.

They both laughed, and Joanna relaxed. It was going to be a perfect evening. All the crowd together, lots of laughs and a great start to the forthcoming festive season. She knew Jim would be flirting with every female in sight, but it was just his way, she was sure there was nothing in it really. He loved her; he was always telling her so.

"Is everyone going to be there tonight?" Jim enquired, casually. He wanted to ask if Debby and Bobby would be there, but that was a bit obvious - even for Joanna. He had been having a bit of a fling with the ever so sexy Bobby for a few weeks but recently Debby had caught his eye, and he was thinking of finding a way to let Bobby down gently and pick up with Debby. He realised he was a bit of a bastard where women were concerned, but his enormous ego helped him to view it all as an incredible game. No one knew, so no one got hurt. It was just a bit of fun.

"I think so, Mel did mention they were having trouble getting a babysitter, but I should imagine they've sorted something out by now, they wouldn't want to miss the first event of the season. Oh, and Debby said she and Nick would try and get there early to get us a good table. Isn't that nice of her?" Joanna paused in putting on her pale pink lipstick to answer him.

"Yes she's okay, I just hope she and Nick don't argue all evening like last time, I don't fancy refereeing all night!" Jim frowned as he remembered the last social event they had all been at. Debby had been delightful in her attentions to him, but had turned into quite a shrew where her husband was concerned. Perhaps he had better reconsider that one after all. He didn't need the hassle.

"I hope they are going to be all right. You don't think there is anything really wrong between them, do you?" Joanna asked anxiously. She had felt quite uncomfortable at the last event when Debby and Nick had started fighting, and although Debby had made quite a blatant pass at Jim she felt sure she was only doing it to get at Nick.

"No of course not. They're just going through a rough patch, that's all. They'll work it out." Jim was not exactly keen to discuss his latest interest's marital state. "Anyway, I thought we were running late - we haven't got time to discuss joining the marriage guidance club. You really are so soft-hearted, you worry about everyone!"

"No, we are doing fine for time, I only said that to get you moving, you know what you're like getting ready! They say women take a long time in the bathroom! I still think since Debby and Nick are such good friends of ours we should try and help. I'm sure if we had any problems they would be only too happy to help us." insisted Joanna.

Jim groaned inwardly, if only she knew just how 'helpful' Debby wanted to be! Mind you, she was a sexy little thing and very seductive, if only he could rely on her discretion.

"What about Karen and Terry? Actually, I wouldn't mind if he wasn't coming, I hope he is not going to talk shop all night" he remarked gloomily. Terry worked in the same printing firm, as an accountant. A grave man, he and Jim had little in common apart from work, and as a result, Terry tended to stick to work matters as a safe topic of conversation.

"Don't be mean. At least he is conscientious, and after all, you are going to be his boss one day. He probably worries about making the wrong impression."

"Oh come off it! We have known him for years; he hardly needs to worry about impressing me. Anyway, his work is fine, it's just that work is all he seems to want to talk about - hasn't the man got any other interests?"

"Well just be nice. I like them both, and it's embarrassing when you start teasing him. Just because he doesn't play the Don Juan game like you. Mind you," she laughed "Karen would kill him if she ever thought he even looked at another girl!"

"Yes, I'll bet she can be a right dragon - you can tell who wears the trousers in that household!" he shuddered at the thought.

Joanna checked her appearance once more in the mirror. She had never been a vain person, but naturally she wanted to look good tonight. She certainly didn't want to disgrace Jim either. He always looked the part. Actually, that vicar's outfit rather suited him. It made him look dignified yet caring.

"You look good in that outfit; perhaps you've missed your vocation! I can just imagine you chatting up all the old ladies at the W.I.!" She pictured him at a tea party handing around the iced buns, and charming the entire blue rinse brigade.

"I think I would be the sort of vicar you read about in the Sunday papers if I ever took Holy Orders, love! Somehow I don't think I'd last very long!" Jim laughed as he contemplated the same scene as his wife, but his scenario ended up with him in bed with the curate's wife, or someone equally willing to ease the heavy burden of responsibility of a country vicar's life.

"Oh I don't know - I think I quite fancy being a vicar's wife, I'd keep you on the straight and narrow, and I've managed so far, haven't I?" The cosy image stayed in her mind as she imagined herself making scones for choirboys or flicking around the church with a feather duster.

"Of course my love," he lied smoothly "but you know how tempting those old ladies can be, and a man has to be made of pretty strong stuff to resist surgical stockings you know!"

"Idiot! Now come on, or we really will be late, and I'm looking forward to seeing what everyone else will be wearing. It should be quite fun".

"Yes, I'm rather looking forward to it too, should be quite entertaining." Mentally he thought, I enjoy a bit of juggling, and keeping Bobby and Debby both 'in the air' would be riskier than juggling flaming torches, and far more exciting!

Across the village Terry Matherson stared gloomily at his reflection in the mirror. "I look ridiculous," he complained "I don't know why we are going to this stupid thing; you know how I hate dressing up!" Actually, his costume rather suited him, as he was a quiet, serious type of man who often wore grey and disliked bold colours, especially on himself.

"You don't look ridiculous, everyone will be dressed up and let's face it, you look far more sensible than me!" Karen laughed as she came up beside him and caught sight of her own reflection. "Besides," she went on "It'll be fun. I think it's a great idea, now the nights are drawing in it's gloomy enough at night, come on, loosen up." She tried to coax him into a more cheerful mood.

"I bet I get stuck next to Jim or Joanna." Terry muttered "I hate it when Joanna asks me how this meeting or that meeting went, or tells me how late poor Jim has to work, especially when he hasn't been near the place! One of these days she's going to catch him out, and if I'm the one who drops him in it, I'll be for the chop."

"Oh for goodness sake, don't start that again, Jim and Joanna aren't that bad, they are always very friendly to me." She was starting to get annoyed with him, but the last thing she wanted was him sulking all night. "Look, we have said we are going, so let's just make the most of it and enjoy ourselves. I am looking forward to seeing everyone and catching up."

Karen worked full time up in the City. As she commuted every day she didn't see as much of the girls as the others did, so she was glad of an opportunity to meet up with them for a decent chat. She was a pretty, vivacious redhead, who was a perfect foil to her more sombre husband, although most people thought them particularly ill matched, they were in fact very content together.

"And I bet Jim tries to flirt with you," Terry continued grumpily. He knew of his prospective boss's well-earned reputation, and was always a bit anxious where Karen was concerned.

"Jim flirts with everyone," Karen stated cheerfully. " You don't honestly expect me fall for his lines, I've heard them all before. Now, give us a kiss and let's go forth and sin!"

Chapter 5

*T*hat was the night she decided to kill Debby. Not one of those "Oh I could murder her" thoughts but a calm accepting that she had no choice. It seemed a bit drastic, but there was just too much at stake. She was not going to lose everything. Debby was not going to give up - that much was obvious, and she realised that although Jim was weak where women were concerned, she knew she loved him too much to let him go. Once the decision had been made she felt remarkably philosophical about it all. The question really was how to do it without getting caught? She wanted it to look like an accident - or perhaps suicide, but how? She didn't know enough about cars or mechanical devices to tamper with Debby's brakes, and anyway, didn't policemen always spot that sort of thing? No, she would have to be cleverer than that. She would find a way - she had to. After that night it was obvious how far things had gone.

The evening had started well enough. Debby and Nick had, as promised, arrived early and secured a table. It was quite near the dance floor, but far enough from the band to enable them all to carry on some conversation without having to shout. Mel and Darren had arrived next. Darren made everyone laugh with his Friar Tuck costume.

"Bless you my children," he boomed "I hope you don't mind me bringing along this fallen woman tonight, but I'm trying to save her - actually, I'm saving her for later - if you know what I mean!" He winked lewdly as they all laughed.

"Well, I'll go and get a couple of bottles of Holy water for starters. I expect the others won't be long." He disappeared towards the small bar set up in the kitchen of the Memorial Hall.

"You look great Mel; perhaps I ought to ask Darren to save one like you for me too," leered Nick, trying rather obviously to peer down the front of her top.

"Thanks Nick, you look good too, and at least if the evening gets dull we can all play cards, though somehow I don't think I'd win!" Mel liked Nick, he'd had some bad luck recently, and it was pretty obvious things were not right between Debby and him. She felt quite sorry for him. Debby could be a real bitch.

"Perhaps we had better play strip poker then!" Nick wanted to show Debby that he was still attractive to women, so she'd better watch out if she wanted to keep him.

"Okay you two, that's enough. We have only just got here and already you've forgotten me! Did you manage to get a sitter all right then?" Debby wasn't bothered by Nick's efforts at flirtation; she only wanted to spare Mel the embarrassment of having to fend him off.

"Yes - eventually! Love your costume Debby - that whip looks lethal...oh look, here come Joanna and Jim." They all looked up as Joanna, wearing a full-length cape over her costume, accompanied by Jim, looking deceptively benign as a vicar, approached the table.

There was a general confusion while everyone exchanged greetings and found their seats. Debby managed to engineer a seat next to Jim, while Joanna went to hang up her cape.

Never one to miss an opportunity, Debby leaned over towards Jim.

"I want you for the first dance, I do hope I won't have to force you into submission" she whispered seductively, fingering the handle of the long leather whip she carried.

"I wouldn't dare disappoint you." His previous misgivings fled as Jim ogled at Debby's blatantly sensuous outfit.

"Oh I don't think you'll disappoint me" she smiled.

"Hi Debby, great costume, what are you? Miss Whiplash?" Bobby arrived just in time to interrupt the cosy moment. Her eyes narrowed as she saw her rival make her move.

Seeing Debby coming on to Jim, she suddenly realised, much to her surprise that she really did care about him. The game had taken on a new twist, perhaps it was just because Simon had been so boring earlier, but she started to picture a more permanent arrangement with Jim, and realised she liked what she saw. Where Joanna would fit in she didn't know, but one problem was immediate - she had to get rid of Debby.

"Hi Bobby, yes, well - you sin your way, and I'll sin mine." She winked at Jim, delighted at Bobby's obvious discomfort.

"Well naturally, I'll have to bow to your far, far greater experience," replied Bobby sweetly.

"Now now girls, let's play nice!" interrupted Jim, thoroughly enjoying the exchange. "What are you drinking - wine? Or perhaps a couple of saucers of milk?"

"Oh, you know what I like, darling," purred Bobby, not about to give in.

"Along with half the rest of Berkshire!" Debby retorted, with a saccharine smile.

Joanna arrived back at the table just in time to diffuse the situation. She was dressed in a long flowing white dress trimmed with silver, with a shining silver halo. Her make-up was subtly done to accentuate her big blue eyes, she really looked beautiful. Suddenly the two main combatants looked rather tawdry beside her. Bobby's mood darkened further, she had to get a grip of herself, she was not a schoolgirl with a crush. If she wanted a man, she got him.

"Oh look everyone - it's Saint Joanna!" Debby exclaimed, not realising that belittling Joanna would not endear her to Jim at all. Bobby was quick to take advantage.

"You look lovely Joanna," smiled Bobby "That dress does wonders for your figure."

"I've always thought your wife would have to be a saint, Jim," laughed Simon "but I never realised just how gorgeous she would look as one!"

"Oh don't be silly Simon, it's just that I knew I could never manage to look as convincing a tart as Bobby and Debby," Joanna replied innocently.

"Ouch! I think she's got you both beaten hands down, " whispered Simon to a furious Bobby. "I don't think our Joanna is quite the simpleton you imagine!" He was pleased to see Joanna finally getting her own back; perhaps she was at last going to fight back.

"Drinks everyone," said Jim quickly, he had been quite enjoying the sharp conversation, but he didn't want it to get sharp enough to actually cut anyone!

Karen and Terry were the last of their usual crowd to arrive. Karen was dressed as a mini-skirted nun, while Terry had opted to be yet another vicar. He looked decidedly uncomfortable as they approached the table.

"Right!" proclaimed Darren. "The gang's all here - let the festivities commence!"

"Isn't it splendid that everyone's dressed up? It makes a welcome change and really builds atmosphere." Joanna was starting to enjoy herself.

"We seem to be remarkably well off for vicars tonight, we'll all have to be careful girls, or we might take the wrong one home," commented Karen.

As the evening wore on and the wine flowed, everyone danced. Jim was, as usual, the life and soul of the party; he managed to dance with all the ladies, some notably closer dances than others.

"You know you really look sexy in that nun's outfit, Karen, sort of forbidden fruit. Perhaps I could help you with your vows?" Jim chuckled lewdly.

"No thanks Jim, I think you've got quite enough in your fan club. If I wanted to join a harem I'd find a rich Arab!" Karen laughed, but she wasn't offended. It was just Jim's way.

"Ah, there's always room for one more!" offered Jim.

"You had better watch out - not everyone likes to share their toys you know," she warned.

"No problem, I can handle it, or should I say, them?" he boasted.

"Don't let Joanna hear you talking like that. One of these days she's going to be after you with the rusty scissors - and I don't mean to cut your hair!" She could never understand why Joanna put up with Jim's ways.

"Joanna trusts me." He protested his innocence. "I'm a model husband. After all, there are not many men who would be so nice to all their wife's friends!"

The music ended and Jim returned Karen to her seat with a small bow.

"Thank you Sister, that was wonderful!"

Karen laughed, he really was incorrigible! Terry looked gloomily into his glass; he had known Jim would try it on with Karen. "One of these days that chap will get what's coming to him." he thought darkly.

Simon danced with Joanna, he looked at her appreciatively, and she really did look radiant in that dress. Suddenly he felt very protective towards her.

"You do look lovely in that costume Joanna, sort of pure and virginal," he murmured in her ear as they danced closer.

"After all these years with Jim I could hardly be described as 'virginal'" Joanna replied smiling, holding him slightly further away from her.

"After all those years with Jim you could certainly be described as 'saintly'!" He knew he was wasting his breath, but he felt it only right that he try and warn her.

"Oh Jim's all right - you just have to know how to take him, that's all. " She hoped Simon wasn't coming on to her, she always felt slightly uncomfortable about that sort of thing.

"Seriously Joanna, I hope you know that I'm always here if you ever need a friend. I would hate to see you hurt." He spoke earnestly, trying to convey his genuine concern for her well-being.

"Thanks Simon, I know I could always rely on you and Bobby, but honestly, there is nothing to worry about. Come on, it's a party, remember? Lighten up!" She tried to shake him out of his suddenly serious mood.

Simon smiled back at her, but somehow his smile didn't quite reach his eyes. He had cringed inwardly when she mentioned Bobby to him. He was pretty sure Bobby and Jim were having an affair, and while he wasn't overly concerned for himself, he was sure Bobby would tire of Jim quickly enough; he knew Joanna would be devastated if she ever found out. He liked Joanna, perhaps even more than liked, but she was blind where Jim was concerned.

"Why is it you girls always go to the ladies room in pairs?" grumbled Darren. "Why doesn't one of you stay here with me - and we could explore each other's habits?" He grinned wickedly.

"I'm sure you've got some very dirty habits Darren," replied Bobby "and I don't just mean the one you're wearing! Come on Joanna, let's freshen up." She dragged Joanna off towards the ladies room at the back of the hall. She was getting quite alarmed now about Debby's obvious plays for Jim, and wanted to recruit Joanna as an ally - albeit an unwitting one.

Once inside the ladies room, both girls set about repairing make-up and tidying their hair. The room was small and rather basic in its amenities, but as there was never room for more than a couple of ladies at one time, it was the ideal place for an intimate chat.

"Debby looks good like that, doesn't she?" Bobby commented casually, applying fresh lipstick.

"Yes, she always really enters into the spirit of things. I hope she and Nick are okay tonight though, things have been a bit strained between them recently."

"Personally I think she's on the prowl for a replacement. You had better keep her away from Jim." There, that should sow a little seed of doubt.

"Don't be silly. Debby wouldn't do that. She's just flirting to make Nick jealous, that's all"

"Oh God, Joanna - don't be so naive!" said Bobby in exasperation. "I wouldn't be so sure. She's got another side to her, and I wouldn't trust her if I were you. I have heard she broke up another marriage some time ago, and you know how badly Nick's business is doing. You must admit Debby is not one to find it easy economising," Bobby warned. If she had to spell it out she would. In fact she had no idea of Debby's past romantic history, but it sounded plausible.

Joanna looked surprised but thoughtful as they finished freshening up and Bobby could tell she had finally got through. When they returned to the table they were surprised to find quite a few people looking over towards them. Nick, Debby and Jim were missing.

"What happened?" Asked Joanna, worriedly.

"Debby and Nick had a huge fight," explained Terry. "She rushed out in tears, Nick is over by the bar getting drunk. Jim went after her to make sure she was all right. He said he'd try to talk her into coming back once he'd calmed her down."

Bobby gave Joanna a look that clearly said, I told you so! Joanna looked almost ready to burst into tears.

"Come on Bobby, it won't hurt you to dance with your own husband for a change." Simon practically dragged her on to the floor before she had a chance to comment further. He could see she was trying to wind Joanna up, and he had a pretty shrewd idea why.

"That was a bit cruel, even for you, wasn't it?" He asked angrily, gripping his wife's arm rather too firmly. They both smiled mechanically as they passed a couple they knew.

"I don't know what you mean; I was only trying to warn Joanna that Debby is after her husband. Do you mind loosening your grip - you are hurting me." Bobby replied indignantly.

"It would appear I don't keep a tight enough grip on you. I know why you are so keen to warn Joanna, it would be very convenient for you if Debby was warned off, wouldn't it? Well, let me give you a warning too. I may have turned a blind eye occasionally, but even I can be pushed too far. Joanna is a nice woman and she's going to be devastated if she ever finds out about Jim. You needn't think I'm going to let you make a fool of me over a prat like that! I suggest you go back to the tennis lessons - those young instructors are more your level!"

Darren whisked Joanna away onto the dance floor too, and made her laugh with his clowning around, and gradually things returned to normal, and everyone pretended nothing had happened.

Some time later Jim reappeared. He strode in trying to look concerned but everyone present formed their own conclusions.

"I couldn't persuade her to come back so I dropped her at home, she'll be fine in the morning. Too much wine I expect," he explained. Actually she had been pretty fine that night he thought but he kept up the solicitous friend act quite well.

"You were gone long enough weren't you?" hissed Bobby. "Did you stay to tuck her safely in bed?" She kept an eye on Simon as she spoke though, as his warning had shaken her complacency.

"You know Bobby, jealousy is a very ugly emotion" whispered Jim "Anyway you know I wouldn't take advantage of Debby, and you should know better than most how faithful I am to my wife!" She really was becoming quite a bore now, he thought, it seemed it was time for a change.

"I'm sorry it's just that I missed you." She whispered seductively "I had something special planned but I don't think we'll get a chance to be alone now."

Jim eyed her speculatively, she certainly was very imaginative and if she promised something special it was bound to be good, maybe he ought to keep the juggling act going just a bit longer.

Joanna witnessed the little exchange between Jim and Bobby. It's good of her to try and protect my marriage but if there is any real reason for concern I'll sort it out myself, she thought determinedly.

Nick wandered drunkenly back to the table. Knocking over a glass, he slumped in to a seat.

"Sorry about this," he slurred "women! Sometimes I think they are more trouble than they are worth. Who needs them? I reckon I would be better off without her. Slut that she is…One of these days she'll be sorry for the way she treats me," he muttered darkly as he reached for a bottle of beer.

Mel gently removed the bottle. "I think that one is empty. Oh what a shame! The bar is closed. Never mind we would only pay for it in the morning," she added cheerfully.

Darren tried to lighten everyone's mood. "Are you going to walk home with us Nick? Right everyone, before we go, what's the next event in our hectic social diaries?" He wasn't entirely sure what was going on but he didn't like it. He tried to end the evening on a promising note.

"Well I suppose it's the joint dinner party at Bobby and Simon's place on the third of December. Has everyone decided what they are bringing?" asked Mel. She joined in her husband's attempt to lift the mood. Their dinner parties were always a good evening. The venue changed around a bit between the various houses and everyone contributed towards the meal.

"Yes I think it's all in hand," said Bobby briskly, things had definitely gone too far this evening and she was desperate to back track as far as possible. "I do like the idea of everyone bringing one dish it certainly saves me a lot of hassle," she added brightly.

"Oh there's far too many of us for one person to cook for and this way no -one feels guilty! It's the perfect arrangement," answered Joanna, she was still feeling shaken but always ready to pour oil over troubled waters. "Besides you have got the most space - our dining room is far too small for all of us."

The evening broke up shortly afterwards, and despite Karen's light-hearted worry no one took home the wrong vicar.

As she arrived home with her husband she thought about the forthcoming dinner. She smiled as the idea formed in her mind. She was sure it would work. Everyone was right about the dinner party. It really was a perfect arrangement - a perfect arrangement for a perfect murder.

Chapter 6

"*That* bitch!" stormed Bobby. She and Mel were just discussing how Saturday night had gone. "Did you see how she hung all over Jim? It was pathetic! She was all over him like a rash! Talk about desperate! She has no class at all!"

They were on their adjoining stations of the Contours fitness class. An American version of circuit training that was increasingly popular in Britain. Mel had arrived first but had been swiftly joined by Bobby. The continuous class only took thirty minutes so timing was everything. They all tried to get along a few evenings a week.

"Hang on Bobby - if anyone should be angry it should be Joanna. You are married to Simon remember?" Mel said half jokingly.

"I'm hardly likely to forget, am I? He's driving me crazy at the moment. I think he's getting too old for me! Anyway, Jim is wasted on Joanna - she is such a wimp! She really doesn't see what is going on right under her nose!"

"Lucky for you!" pointed out Mel. "I like Joanna, you can't help liking her. Don't you feel even a little bit guilty?"

Bobby grinned. "I suppose so. Still, I wouldn't mind changing places with her. Honestly, Simon can be so infuriating!" She thought of her solid, dependable husband and groaned. Jim was so much more exciting. Simon was boring and predictable.

"You don't really mean that, do you?" Mel asked anxiously - she liked Simon, and would hate to think of him and Bobby splitting up. "I mean, you wouldn't really divorce him would you?"

Bobby sighed. "I guess not - I always swore I would never get divorced. My parents are divorced you know, split up when I was little. I was brought up hearing how terrible life was for an 'abandoned woman'. You know what my mother is like - makes a melodrama out of everything. I always said it would never happen to me. I wouldn't give my mother the satisfaction; she'd have a field day!" Bobby's mother was a very bitter woman. Since her husband had left her she had become something of a man-hater. She had warned her daughter about marriage and told her it was bound to fail.

"Between you and me though, I am getting very fond of Jim. I know it's stupid, but there is just something about him." It was true - Bobby was definitely getting hooked.

"You must be joking! Simon is a wonderful guy. You couldn't stand Jim for long. You'd never know what he was up to! I sometimes think Joanna has the right idea - what you don't know can't hurt you. Perhaps she deliberately turns a blind eye." Mel couldn't believe Bobby would give up so much for a womaniser like Jim.

"You may be right but I can't see it lasting for much longer. Sooner or later it will all fall apart. You mark my words. I do like Joanna, but she is so weak."

"Change stations now," the automated voice of the recorded instructor interrupted them. Bev the human counterpart tried to focus them on their workout. "Remember ladies we chat on the resting stations" she urged, "remember why we are here."

Mel smiled apologetically, Bobby grinned wickedly, she was not there for the exercise.

"Jim needs a strong woman - someone who will stand up to him." She continued. "Joanna would be better off with someone like Terry - or Simon! Hey! That's an idea! Maybe I can convince her to do a straight swop! What do you think?"

"In your dreams! She won't let go that easily - besides, what about Debby?" teased Mel.

Bobby scowled. "Oh I'll soon sort her out. She's no match for me. I was with Jim long before she appeared on the scene, and I will be long after she's gone as well!" She had never liked Debby much before, and now that she had taken a fancy to Jim she liked her even less.

Mel shook her head. No good was going to come of all this. The one innocent party in all of it was the one who was bound to lose out in the end. Joanna was heading for heartache, she was quite sure of it.

"Now move away from your station and find your heart rate." The beat music paused as everyone fell silent to check their pulse. Considering the lack of effort Bobby had made on the exercise her heart rate was surprisingly high.

In the momentary silence Karen arrived.

She smiled a silent greeting and took her position at the adjacent station as the music began again.

"What did you think of Saturday?" Karen asked. "There were some great costumes, weren't there?"

"Yes - pity about Nick and Debby though. They could show a bit of restraint in public!" Bobby said with lofty disdain.

"Oh, I think a lot of that was the drink talking - I don't think it was such a big deal really," Karen replied. She was not aware of all the various undercurrents.

"I wouldn't be so sure. I worry about them." Mel said, "I hope they will be all right"

"Change stations now," instructed the tape and as they all obligingly moved around Joanna arrived and suddenly everyone was dedicated to the workout.

Later that night she lay awake thinking. It really was about time poor, distraught Debby committed suicide. Everyone had commented on her problems. Debby simply could not cope with life. Oh, they would all be so shocked when Debby chose the ultimate solution, but really - was it so surprising? The public rows, the obvious marital break-up, and of course there was always the worry about Nick's financial situation. No - it would be sad - but not totally unexpected.

She thought through her plan carefully. It had to work. If she failed and Debby survived she would know that someone had tried to kill her. The only one who would know that it was not a genuine suicide attempt would be Debby herself. Would anyone believe her? She could not take that risk. No, she had to be sure and succeed first time. She could not afford to take any chances. Too much rather than too little. She would make absolutely certain that there was enough to kill her - and quickly! Even a small amount too little and Debby could linger for days, she would still die, the damage would be too severe, but if she lingered she would talk. That was dangerous. Everyone knew that would-be suicides sometimes changed their minds. Sometimes they denied trying it at all - but she could not risk Debby convincing anyone that she had not attempted suicide. When she poisoned Debby she had to be very, very efficient about it.

Chapter 7

*T*he day of the dinner party dawned cold but clear. The girls gathered at Bobby's house in the early afternoon to help prepare the dinner and bring along their own contributions to the evening's meal. They all went to great pains to keep the conversation light, and if there was some tension in the air, everyone ignored it. Gradually they all relaxed and sat down for a coffee before going home to get ready.

She was feeling very odd. Part of her wondered if she would actually go through with it, and part of her was almost eagerly anticipating the event. She wondered if she was going mad. People didn't calmly plan murder, not ordinary people like her. This was Linwood, not some bustling cosmopolitan city where crime was rife. Despite her discreet research on the Internet she wasn't even sure if it would work, or how it would work if it did. She hoped it would be quick, she did at least feel that much compassion for her intended victim.

Unusually they all arrived at about the same time. Jim and Joanna walked up the drive just as Nick, Debby, Darren and Mel, who had all come along in the same car, arrived. Karen and Terry turned up just as they were all exchanging greetings and hanging up coats. After the incident at Halloween, both Nick and Debby were determined not to argue, and a kind of strained cheerfulness existed between them. Everyone pretended not to notice and they all chatted animatedly as they took their seats in the spacious lounge. Simon had already laid out champagne glasses with a sugar cube in each one onto which he carefully added just two drops of bitters, he then added a measure of brandy and topped up the glasses with champagne. It was a ritual they always went through when they had dinner parties. Simon was famed for his champagne cocktails and they certainly were a great relaxer.

She felt like she was on the outside looking in on them all. She watched, in a kind of detached way, as Simon prepared the cocktails and everyone passed them around. In the general confusion it was so easy to drop a couple of high dosage soluble Paracetamol into Debby's glass. The tablets fizzed up, but since the dissolving sugar was fizzing away anyway, it was a simple matter to dip her finger into the top of the glass to prevent it frothing over. That was an old trick told to her years ago by her friend Lorraine who worked in first class on an airline, and it certainly worked. The sugar formed slight sediment in the glass, and if there were any traces of the tablet they were undetectable amongst the sugar.

Of course she knew a couple of Paracetamol tablets were not a lethal dose, but there were plenty more to come, and Debby had already unknowingly taken a couple in her coffee that afternoon. Indeed since the 'Saints and Sinners' night she had surreptitiously added them to Debby's drinks on every possible occasion.

They had another round of drinks, some of the men had a beer, but most of the ladies had another cocktail. Debby unwittingly had another dose. Everyone was really relaxed and happy. Debby was feeling a bit odd but she had been under a great deal of stress recently, so she put it down to that and the cocktails, which she always found strong. She had planned to appear a bit tipsy to give herself the excuse to flirt with Jim without anyone realising how serious she was being. She was determined to get a bit deeper into his affections this evening, but knew she would have to be subtle about it with so many present. Nick was trying harder and harder to reconcile with her and it was driving her crazy. She didn't want or need a failure - she wanted a success - and if she played her cards right she was going to get herself one.

"Would you rather have something else?" enquired Simon solicitously, noticing that Debby was hardly touching her second drink. She had always loved his cocktails but didn't seem to be enjoying this one. He was immensely proud of his skills as a bar tender, and was puzzled by her lack of enthusiasm.

"Oh no, they are lovely" assured Debby, as she took a large sip, "I'm just trying to pace myself, I don't want to be flat on my back too soon!" She winked slyly at Jim.

"Wouldn't be unusual," murmured Bobby, but catching a warning glance from Simon she said, "They are pretty strong, Debby perhaps you're right not to knock them back." She didn't care particularly if Debby made a complete prat of herself, in fact, it would really rather suit her plans if she did.

Debby promptly drank the cocktail down defiantly. "Oh I'm made of stronger stuff than that you know - oops!" She swayed as she sat down suddenly. What on earth was wrong with her? She felt slightly uncoordinated and unable to collect her thoughts. She had taken her anti depressants before they left the house and now she was feeling spaced out.

"How's dinner doing?" asked Nick quickly, alarmed at how drunk Debby appeared to be getting. He was determined they would not make exhibitions of themselves again, and if Debby was drunk, she was dangerous. The best option would be to get some food into her, and quickly. Perhaps if they all enjoyed a pleasant evening together she would mellow, and, who knows how the evening might end? He was ever optimistic.

"Well Mel made the first course, salmon mousse with cucumber sauce, garnished with a continental salad," announced Bobby. "It's a cold starter, so ready when we are - shall we go through now?" She had arranged the small ramekin dishes containing the salmon mousse while Simon had been laying out the champagne glasses, and although they had not been out of the refrigerator long, she was anxious that they were not served too soon.

They all went through to the dining room. The table looked lovely, the crystal sparkled, Joanna had made a beautiful flower arrangement for the centre. She was a keen amateur florist and often entered village competitions with her arrangements. During the summer months her garden was one of the finest in the village. Karen had folded the linen napkins to form a perfect lotus blossom shape. Everyone remarked on how perfect it all looked, and they sat down for the first course.

"How's that new contract from Maynards looking?" asked Terry to Jim across the table. "If we get much more business from up North we may have to consider opening a branch up there." Jim groaned "Oh God! Not already!" Bobby, seated beside him, noticed his brief expression of dismay, and before he had chance to answer she quickly interjected.

"Now come on - no shop talk tonight. Is that all you men think about? Now then, what are everyone's plans for Christmas?"

"Thanks!" whispered Jim and he smiled at her in gratitude. She was really on the ball there, he thought. Joanna would never have been so quick; she had saved him from a long boring conversation.

Everyone started discussing their various arrangements, and whose relations were visiting from where, and the evening progressed on a congenial note. Bobby was surprised how easily she was able to monopolise Jim's attention. Debby didn't seem as quick witted as usual, and Simon was being neatly distracted by Darren, who was discussing with him the merits of Mercedes cars over all other makes. Simon, ever keen to discuss his beloved car, paid little attention further down the table. Joanna and Mel were chatting about little Lucy's forthcoming role in the school Nativity play.

A rack of lamb and the usual accompaniments followed the fish course, accompanied by a delicious chilled white wine. Most of the party moved on to a classic red wine with the main course, and by the time they reached the dessert they had all consumed quite a large quantity of wine. The dessert was an attractive confection of individual lemon sorbets, served in hollowed-out lemons, attractively garnished with tiny paper umbrellas.

"Oh, I don't think I can face any dessert," groaned Darren, who had surreptitiously finished off the baby roast potatoes.

"I'm not surprised," laughed his wife. "I saw you gobble down those potatoes, you don't fool me you know! Anyway, it's only a light sorbet, and it's too late now to worry about the calories!"

"Well we all have to worry about the calories sometimes, don't we Joanna?" asked Debby with a small smile. "But it's just so hard when there are so many temptations." Debby was pencil thin and always had been, but she knew Joanna often worried about her weight, and it didn't hurt her campaign to have others compare the two of them. Joanna smiled back weakly.

"I'm afraid I'm not as good at calorie counting as I should be. Still, there is more to life than dieting, isn't there?" she tried valiantly.

"Of course there is!" Debby replied emphatically "And anyway, that just means there is more of you to love doesn't it Jim?"

"That's right - more bounce to the ounce, eh love?" agreed Jim affably. Blissfully unaware that that was the last thing Joanna needed to hear at that moment.

Debby smiled like a cat that had got the cream and Joanna squirmed in embarrassment. The men at the table may not have been totally aware of the jibe, but all the ladies definitely were.

"Well, my husband has certainly got more than his fair share of bounce, I can assure you." Mel swung the attention away to a less sensitive soul.

Darren laughed. "It's a fair cop. I suppose I deserved that, but can I help it if you ladies are such wonderful cooks?" He could see how Joanna felt, and was happy to come to the rescue. "I hope I get a meal like this for my birthday next month. I haven't forgotten you promised me a beef Wellington, Bobby."

"I know, and you shall have one. It's the middle of January, isn't it? That makes you a Capricorn."

"That's right - he's a randy old goat and he eats everything!" laughed Mel.

"He's right about the meal though," agreed Jim. "It has certainly been wonderful so far, and you are all to be congratulated." He reached for his spoon "Now, how do we tackle these little devils?" He had certainly enjoyed his meal; Bobby had been scintillating company and had been most entertaining. She had not applied any sort of pressure on him, and her charm - combined with the wine - was making him feel decidedly jovial. She's a great girl, he thought, brains and beauty!

The lemons had a delicious piquant flavour, which they all appreciated after their heavy meal.

"These are quite powerful you know I happen to know that there is a generous measure of vodka in them, to give the lemons an extra kick," Mel cautioned. They all exchanged recipes regularly, and Russian Lemons were a favourite with them all.

As she slipped into her detached alter ego, she smiled; there certainly was a powerful punch in Debby's lemon sorbet. It contained a highly concentrated mixture of Paracetamol. She had substituted the sugar with saccharin of course, to make room for so much Paracetamol, but the more concentrated sweetness hid the bitterness of the drug, which, along with the vodka and lemons, made for an unusual dessert. She had been very careful in making sure Debby got the right one, but the tiny coloured umbrellas made it quite easy. Green, she had decided, green for jealousy. She watched as Debby ate it. She saw how she frowned slightly at the first taste, but when she saw the others obviously enjoying theirs, she took another spoon of the unusual mixture and, to her murderer's great relief, she finished the whole thing. Debby had by then taken a lethal dose and, although it would be some time before it took effect, the damage was beginning.

After dinner they all went back into the lounge, and Bobby brought through a tray of coffee while Simon offered the liqueurs. They were congenial hosts, and kept an extensive array of after dinner drinks for their guests.

"Are you all right love?" enquired Nick quietly, as he looked at Debby. "Perhaps you've had enough, you'd better stick to coffee." Debby looked very pale, her face had an unnatural sheen and her eyes had a slightly glazed look about them. He hoped she wasn't going to be sick.

"I'm fine" she hissed. "For God's sake don't make a fuss. I just feel a bit rough, that's all. It must have been something I ate. I can hold my alcohol thank you!" She did feel unwell, but the last thing she wanted was Nick fussing over her - now if it was Jim - she wouldn't mind so much.

"Do you have any pain anywhere? Can I get you anything?" asked Bobby. She was not accustomed to her dinner guests turning green after their meals, and found it rather disconcerting.

"Don't take aspirin" advised Karen "I read somewhere it irritates the stomach if you are not feeling well." Travelling by train every day she got through several magazines and usually had advice on everything from holidays to health care.

"I always keep a couple of Paracetamol in my handbag if you'd like them," offered Mel. "With my kids you never know when they are going to give you a headache!" She laughed nervously, trying to ease the discomfort everyone was starting to feel.

"Thank you Mel, I'll give that a try." She didn't really want anything, but as least it would stop everyone offering their own remedies, and maybe they would get rid of the aching pain she was getting in her stomach. "I'm sure I'll feel fine soon - please - just ignore me and carry on."

Bobby got her a glass of water and she took two tablets. She tried to think what could have given her this stomach pain. Perhaps it was something she had eaten.

"I do hope it wasn't my salmon mousse?" Mel enquired anxiously, voicing Debby's exact thoughts. She did look poorly and everyone knew that fish could make you very ill if there was anything wrong with it. She had made one batch of the mousse, and poured it into individual ramekins, surely if there had been anything wrong with it, they would all have been feeling the effects? Still, she couldn't help feeling uneasy.

"Perhaps we had better go home?" suggested Nick. "It is getting quite late, will you be all right to walk, or shall I ring for a taxi?"

"No, I'll probably feel fine once I get into the fresh air and it's not far - perhaps we'd better be going. Thank you for a lovely evening, I am sorry about this, I do hope I haven't put a dampener on the evening." Suddenly Debby couldn't wait to get outside and away from the house; she had a horrible feeling she was going to vomit, and that was not at all the image she wanted to present this evening. If she had not felt so wretched she would have faced the evening out as she wanted so much for it to have been a success. She could tell Jim was losing interest. She had got so close to hooking him after their intimate moment at Halloween. Now she was leaving the coast clear for Bobby to get back in, but she couldn't help it, she felt really ill.

Simon got their coats, and with everyone's sympathy and advice still ringing in their ears they hurried out into the clear night. They had not got more than a hundred yards away when Debby thought she was going to pass out, the pain was getting worse and she was coming out in a cold sweat.

"Let me ring back and I'll get help." Nick was getting really worried now. He had never seen her like this and he was starting to panic.

"No!" Debby replied, through gritted teeth. "Just get me home. I just want to get to bed, I'll be fine soon. " But she didn't feel fine, far from it. Between them they managed to get home, Nick ended up half carrying Debby by the time they reached the house.

"Are you sure you haven't taken anything that could make you ill?" He asked, puzzled, she appeared to be drugged, and he knew she had been to the doctors recently with stress.

"Just a couple of mild happy pills, that's all, oh, and the couple of Paracetamol that Mel gave me," replied a very woozy Debby.

"Oh for God's sake! How could you be so stupid?" Nick felt relieved, but very angry. "You gave me such a scare, everyone knows you can't mix drink with that stuff. Go to bed and sleep it off. A couple won't kill you, but it won't do you any good. You made a right fool of yourself back there, you know. Why the hell didn't you stay off the booze if you were taking those things?"

Debby wanted to argue with him but she didn't seem to have any energy - her whole mind was filled with the pain and nausea, she just wanted to crawl away and sleep until the pain was gone.

An hour later she was only semi-conscious. Nick rang the local doctor, he explained she had taken a couple of anti depressants and she had been drinking. He asked what he should do. The doctor was puzzled by the apparent severity of the symptoms.

"Are you sure that's all she's taken? Did you actually see her take them?" It sounded like a classic case of overdose to him. Whether she was perhaps exaggerating in a bid for attention, he naturally couldn't tell over the telephone, but he advised Nick to send for an ambulance, just to be on the safe side.

The ambulance came, and the paramedics could tell instantly she was in a bad way.

"What's her name?" the driver snapped at Nick. What was wrong with people? Couldn't he see how serious this was? He should have rung ages ago.

"Debby, Debby Sherman," stammered Nick, frightened by the urgency in the man's voice.

"Debby? Debby can you hear us love? We're trying to help you." The driver asked more gently "What have you taken love? Come on, you've got to tell us. We want to help you - but you have to help us too." While his colleague worked on Debby he turned to Nick demanding quickly, "Right show me the packet."

"Packet?" Nick was confused, he had been drinking heavily himself, and he didn't know what was going on. Surely it can't be that serious? She said she'd only taken a couple of happy pills.

"Medicine packets! Where are the packets she took the drugs from?" Where was this idiot's brain? Was he on something too? Or didn't he care?

"Mr. Sherman, your wife is seriously ill. Now we need to know exactly what she has taken, how much and when," he explained rapidly.

"I...I don't know, I mean, well she said she'd only taken a couple of happy pills – anti depressants, you know the things, the doctor gave them to her, said she was stressed or something, I mean, well, she only told me that afterwards..." He was getting flustered. Could she have done something stupid? She wasn't that unhappy was she?

"She is going to be all right isn't she?"

"Please Mr Sherman, if you want to help us, and your wife, find the packet. You said 'afterwards', what do you mean, she told you after what?"

"Well, we have been drinking, and I didn't know she was taking them, I mean, I would have stopped her, I know you shouldn't... well, mix them, but I didn't know."

Nick raced upstairs and into the bedroom. In Debby's bedside drawer he found an assortment of bottles and packets, he stood staring at the odd collection, some of them had been in there for months. The medic had followed him up and stood looking over his shoulder at the array of half empty containers.

"Are there any elsewhere?" The medic sighed, he hated cases like this, it made his job so much harder, and there was a real danger they could lose that girl downstairs.

"No this is it. I am sure of it. This is her new prescription." Nick handed the medic the fairly full bottle of Prozac.

"What's all this?" The medic spotted several empty packets of generic Paracetamol.

"How long have you had these? Do you know if she could have taken some of these?" It was nearly empty. The drawer was littered with empty packets. Nick stared at the contents of the drawer. He never looked in there and he had no idea how many there had been in it earlier.

"I don't know!" he said miserably. He broke down "I just don't know, I mean we just keep them in, I mean, well, everyone does, don't they? We just buy more when we run out. I don't know."

The medic tried to calm him; he could see he wasn't going to get any more help there. Glancing through the drawer he tried to see if there were any more drugs, which Debby could have taken. There were a few half finished prescription drugs, and the usual home remedies for common ailments, but he couldn't see anything more sinister.

"Okay sir, now, let's go. I take it you want to come in the ambulance with us?" He could do with the chance to question the man further, but he couldn't afford to waste time there.

"Yes.... yes of course... she will be all right won't she....? I mean she won't you know.... you know, I mean...." his voice trailed away as they hurried out to the ambulance.

"Debby? Can you hear us? We're taking you to hospital now. I just want to know have you taken any painkillers. Any Paracetamol? "

"Paracetamol, yes, Paracetamol" murmured Debby, yes she had taken two, but it was so hard to tell them. She wanted to talk but she couldn't remember how. Someone had given her two tablets to take away the pain, but it hadn't worked. The pain was worse. "More" she mumbled.

It was no use, they couldn't make her understand. She had admitted she had taken them but they couldn't know how many she was talking about. 'More'? More than what? More than a dose? More than a packet?

While they worked on the now barely conscious Debby the medics carried on questioning Nick.

"How has your wife been recently? Is there any reason to suggest she may have taken an overdose of any sort? We are not here to judge' Mr Sherman. We just need to know so we can help her."

Nick tried desperately to gather his thoughts. Things had been bad, but not that bad surely? Debby would never deliberately try something like this would she? Or would she? She had been very quiet at dinner. Was that before, or after, she started feeling ill? Oh God! He just couldn't remember! This couldn't be happening to him.

"Well we've been uh... having a few problems recently, but well, I mean...I never thought...I mean she's never said...I mean, well, she's not the type."

"I'm afraid it's not always the ones who talk about it that try and do it Mr Sherman, but.... oh here we are. Stay close Mr Sherman the doctors will need to see you." The paramedic had a bad feeling about this case; it was usually the people who never talk about suicide who were the ones who succeeded. The ones who threatened all the time were usually just attention seekers.

As the ambulance pulled up outside the emergency department the doctors, alerted by radio, rushed out to meet it.

"Looks like an overdose. Some Prozac and unknown quantity of Paracetamol. Vital signs weak, some respiratory problems."

The efficient hospital team swung into well practised action. Blood samples were taken and Debby was put onto an artificial respirator. Nick stood dazed in the centre of the confusion until a nurse showed him to small office where she brought him a cup of sweet tea and talked to him, gently probing him for a few more details. It was evident he could not tell them any more of what she had taken but they would also need to know at some stage why she had taken anything. Nick tried to explain their situation to the nurse, she was kind and sympathetic but he could see that she thought Debby had tried to take her own life. Why can't they see? he thought. Debby's not like that! She wouldn't ever try to commit suicide. She's not that type of person at all. She's strong! She's tough - nothing hurts Debby. Or did it?

What's happening? Why are they taking so long? He wanted to be with her, she needed him, whatever else had gone wrong between them they could work it out.

The door opened, and the young emergency doctor entered, he looked tired, his face was lined with fatigue and sympathy for the distraught man to whom he had to break some terrible news.

"Mr Sherman" he began. "We've had the preliminary results of the blood tests, and we are now in process of conducting some liver function tests, but I'm afraid I have to tell you it is not looking good. Your wife has taken a massive dose of Paracetamol, which, it would appear from early results, has already entered her blood stream. I'm afraid there is severe damage to her liver, which would account for the pain she has been in and we are awaiting results to determine if the damage has spread to her kidneys. At present she is being kept alive on an artificial respirator. I am truly sorry. I thought you would want to be kept informed, we are doing everything we can but I am afraid there is very little hope."

"You don't understand doctor, there must be some mistake, Debby isn't like that! You see doctor, she wouldn't do this. You must be wrong." But he knew from the doctor's face that he was not wrong, and he broke down and sobbed.

An hour later they learned that the poison had entered Debby's kidneys and septicaemia had set in. The doctor explained as gently as he could that Debby's body had become toxic and there was no chance at all that she would recover. At 5.00 a.m. on Sunday morning Debby Sherman died.

Chapter 8

Steve Clarke hated this part of his job, he had been in the police force for ten years now, and had naturally dealt with many cases of sudden death, but the trip to the pathology lab still managed to make his stomach churn. Malcolm Young, the pathologist, was a jovial man, who obviously enjoyed his work, but his sense of humour left a lot to be desired. Still, he was a friendly chap, always ready for a chat, not surprising when you considered the company he usually had.

"Morning Malcolm. I'm here on the Debby Sherman case." He greeted Malcolm with a friendly smile; he liked the man, and had known him for a few years now.

"Morning Steve. Oh, yes. The overdose case, came in yesterday, hang on." He went over to his desk and picked up a large manila file. "I thought you would be attending this one, I see you got out of it again! Right there are the usual preliminaries, the coroner's officer was attending etc. etc. I take it you want a quick run down?"

"Just the usual, you can leave out the gory details!" Not that there was any chance of that, he thought, but it although it was quite usual to report on such details, he always enjoyed watching the young policemen turn green as he described the contents of the stomach - he always gave very lurid descriptions!

"You are a sick man," admonished Steve jokingly. "Have you ever thought of getting some therapy!" They always went through this bantering, Steve had, as a new recruit, once been violently ill after one of Malcolm's 'reports', and Malcolm hadn't let him forget it.

"Okay I'll let you off. I know you've got a weak stomach! Anyway nothing suspicious in the stomach contents. The food was all non-toxic. Death caused by liver and renal failure due to massive overdose of Paracetamol...."

"Any chance of accident?" interrupted Steve, making notes.

"Well, there is always the chance she didn't realise just how lethal Paracetamol is. If it had been aspirin they could probably have done something, but Paracetamol destroys the liver pretty quickly, and she'd had a skinful of booze, so she never really stood a chance. It wouldn't be the first one I've had done here who didn't really mean it." He sighed, despite his jocular demeanour he was not an unfeeling man and a death like this was such a waste of a young life.

"How about foul play?" asked Steve routinely.

"Well it would take some doing to slip 30 odd Paracetamol into her cocoa, wouldn't it? It would be easier to push her under a bus! Any reason to suspect it?" If there was any cause for suspicion he would double check his notes, but he couldn't think of how anyone could deliberately overdose someone with Paracetamol without them noticing it. It was not his fault of course; the lemon sorbet had melted before it had reached the stomach, leaving only traces of lemon and saccharin - nothing suspicious.

"No I don't think so, seems pretty straight forward to me. The husband is insisting that she's not the type to top herself, but then they always say that, don't they? He probably had a row with her and feels guilty."

"You're right there. Anything else I should pick up on? Save me ploughing through this lot. This one is on the boss's home ground so I've got to get it right."

"What, old Saunders? Oh he's not so bad. Did he know her? Where does he live then?" Malcolm knew Detective Inspector Saunders from work, but not really on a personal level.

"Linwood - it's only a small village, but I don't think he knew her personally. It is just that he doesn't like anything occurring on his patch!" Actually, one of his boss's favourite expressions was; 'If you live above the shop you get a discount!' And he considered a peaceful home life his 'discount'. Consequently he kept a close eye on the village. He valued his quiet home life and protected it fiercely.

"Well there is nothing special about this one, I'm glad to say - you're quite sure you're not interested in the last meal?" Malcolm chuckled.

"Do us all a favour Malcolm - get a life!"

"Get a life? Hey I'm the one just back from six months in Barbados remember?"

"Jammy bugger! How did you swing that by the way?"

"All part of the old 'building international relationships' directive." Grinned Malcolm loftily.

"Yeah right – more like favours for old pals I bet!" retorted Steve.

"Call it what you like I'm putting in for a stint in Europe next – thought maybe Spain, somewhere warm anyway."

"That'll go down well with Shelagh," commented Steve. He knew Malcolm was seeing one of his colleagues, Shelagh Veitch.

"You'd better make the most of her while you've got her, I was rather hoping to persuade her to come with me."

"That serious huh?"

"I'm working on it!"

"You old romantic! Well I'd better get back; the boss is going to be wanting this one sorted quickly."

Steve picked up his copy of the report and headed out of the building; grateful his visit had been so brief.

Driving back towards Linwood he contemplated his next move. He had spoken to Mr. Sherman at the hospital and it had been quite clear the man was totally distraught. He had kept insisting to Steve that his wife was not suicidal but Steve was unfortunately used to grieving relatives being unable to accept the death of a loved one. He decided to call in on one or two of Mrs. Sherman's friends to get a clearer picture.

Debby Sherman had attended a dinner party the night she died. He had a full guest list from her husband, so he planned to visit the other guests to try and determine her state of mind at the time.

Consulting his notes, he checked the addresses of all the dinner guests, fortunately they were all in the immediate area and he calculated that with luck, he would be able to see them all quickly and wrap the whole thing up. He decided to start with the hosts – Robyn and Simon Collins.

Bobby opened the door and showed the policeman into the lounge. She offered him tea, which he gratefully accepted, and they sat and discussed Debby Sherman and her possible motives for suicide.

"Would you say you were a close friend of Mrs Sherman?" he asked, as he tried to get a picture of the character of the rather attractive woman seated opposite him. She was obviously upset, but had still managed to put on full make-up and had clearly taken great care in her appearance generally.

"Oh yes. We were all great friends. Although I don't think she would have confided totally in me, as well... sometimes we held different opinions on things." She looked demurely down. She intended to hint that Debby had played around a bit but naturally, she herself would never dream of such a thing. Even in death she couldn't quite forget their rivalry. Naturally she was very distressed by Debby's death, but she was not a hypocrite, and she couldn't pretend she had ever really liked her. It was more a case of being sorry she was dead - but glad she was gone, she mused.

Steve instantly picked up the message, as he was supposed to. What was this woman playing at, he wondered?

"Had you had a disagreement about something recently?"

"Oh no, nothing like that at all, no, we were quite close really. I am shocked that she would do such a thing. I suppose it was suicide? I mean it couldn't have been an accident or anything?" she added hastily. Careful! she thought Don't overplay your hand; you don't want this man thinking you are a heartless bitch.

"I am not really at liberty to discuss our findings as yet, and anyway that will be up to the coroner to decide. Have you any reason to suspect Mrs. Sherman would take her own life?"

There was something she wasn't telling him he knew that, it was just a matter of getting it out of her.

"No, not really," she replied slowly, should she mention Debby's attempts to steal Jim specifically, or just hint at a failed romance, and let him find out with whom? "Well, that is to say... I don't want to speak ill of the dead and all that. After all Debby isn't here to defend herself, and I may be totally wrong in my er...suspicions. Debby was a nice girl, and I'm sure she wouldn't deliberately try and well...harm a relationship." She tried to look reluctant to speak further.

What a bitch! thought Steve, but he kept his expression bland as he said; "Mrs Collins, any information which may assist us in our enquiries should naturally be revealed to me in full."

"Well, I do know that her marriage was in trouble and that she was uh... shall we say...looking elsewhere," she said coyly. "Not that there was anything going on I'm sure! I mean ..." She stopped abruptly. "I mean, she wouldn't really cheat on her husband, but I could tell she was desperately unhappy." She would have liked to say she knew Debby was desperate, but that sounded a bit heartless - even for her. Still, if Joanna left Jim over all this, things could work out very nicely - thank you very much!

Steve was trying to assess the information he was getting. He could tell there was no love lost between the two women, that much was very evident. But why? There was a love rival; he was sure, but who? Was it in any way relevant to the case? He had the feeling he was being manipulated by this cunning woman, and he didn't like it at all. He was fairly sure she had been about to say 'my husband' when she stopped abruptly.

"Mrs Collins, forgive my asking a rather personal question, but are you familiar with the deceased's possible other interest?"

Was she screwing your husband? he wanted to say, but he exercised some tact.

"Well the thing is..." she hesitated, "can I talk to you in confidence?" She would be delighted if he went straight around to Joanna and told her point blank that her husband had cheated on her, but she didn't want it known where the information had come from.

"Mrs Collins. I cannot guarantee confidentiality if the matter has bearing on the case, however, if any disclosures are of a personal nature, I will endeavour to keep the details private as far as possible." It was a set piece he quoted frequently, intended to allay a witness's fears of retribution, should any information be traced back to them. If she was looking to set him up as a witness in her divorce settlement, she could think again!

"I am trying to avoid his wife finding out you see. It would destroy her if she thought he and Debby... well you know. And she is such a sweet girl; I would hate to see her hurt." She opened her eyes as wide as possible, and looked appealingly at him.

Steve was astonished! He had been convinced Debby Sherman had been caught with Mr Collins, and that was why his wife was being so bitchy. She was only trying to protect a friend. Perhaps he had totally misjudged her.

Bobby caught his momentary look of confusion and smiled inwardly, she was a better actress than she thought.

"Mrs Collins, naturally I cannot guarantee that certain facts may not be disclosed by the coroner. However, since you are uncertain if there was an affair, I feel I should know as much as possible to try and ascertain the truth of the matter. If Mrs Sherman was so depressed over an unhappy affair that she took her own life, then obviously the coroner should know. If on the other hand, there is no conclusive proof that such an affair existed, I see no reason to distress the gentleman's wife with any such suggestions." It was the only way he could play it, he didn't want to cause any trouble, but he had to find a reason for suicide if there was one.

"Yes, I do see that" Bobby replied with a sigh, appearing to look reluctant. "The gentleman in question is Jim Baines. He and his wife, Joanna, were at our house for dinner the night Debby died. Do you want his address?"

"That won't be necessary, thank you. I have already arranged to see Mr and Mrs Baines as part of my routine enquiry. Don't worry," he added with a sympathetic smile "I'll see them separately - and I'll be discreet."

As she leant against the closed door Bobby smiled. The initial shock of Debby's death was wearing off, and she was starting to fully realise the advantages. She was sorry that Debby had died of course, but as they say - it is an ill wind.

Chapter 9

Driving the short distance to the home of Jim and Joanna Baines, Steve contemplated the case so far. The evidence for suicide seemed to be mounting up, but he had to go through the formalities just the same.

Joanna answered the door. Steve was shocked at the contrast between the obviously distraught woman who faced him, and the poised woman he had just left.

"Come in officer, please excuse the mess. I'm afraid I've been a bit upset since poor Debby...." she broke off, and motioned for Steve to sit down. "I am sorry - how rude of me. Would you like a cup of tea?" Joanna tried to observe the niceties, but she was feeling very emotional, and found it hard to concentrate. She had dressed simply and tied her hair back with a ribbon to keep it off her face. She wore no make up, and her eyes were red from crying.

"No thank you Mrs Baines. I've just had one. In this job you tend to be awash with tea by the end of the day. " He tried to calm her with a small joke.

Joanna smiled weakly. "I suppose you do. I hadn't really thought of it. How can I help you?" She wasn't sure what she could tell him about Debby. She was sure he would hear anything unpleasant from Bobby, and she didn't want to criticise Debby herself - after all, she was gone now. Even if she had tried to seduce her husband, it was over now, and there was no point in maligning the poor girl after her death. It was simply not in her nature.

"As I explained on the telephone, I just want to get a bit of background information on Mrs Debby Sherman. I understand you knew her quite well, and that you had dinner with her on the night she died. I do hope you won't find this too distressing."

"No, no I'll be fine," she smiled briefly. "I am afraid I am a bit of wimp, my husband is always telling me I'm too soft, but I was so fond of Debby, and I feel so responsible for her death."

"Well we all get a bit emotional at a time like this Mrs Baines, even hardened policemen." Steve had liked Joanna instantly; she was clearly a caring, sensitive woman. "Tell me," he continued gently, "what makes you feel responsible for her death? I'm quite sure you shouldn't be blaming yourself."

"I can't help blaming myself; I knew you see, I knew she was unhappy. She and Nick were having such dreadful rows, and anyone could tell she was unhappy. Jim, my husband, said we shouldn't interfere, but I just wish I had told her I was here if she needed someone to talk to. Perhaps if she had confided in someone she wouldn't have done it." She broke down and cried softly.

Steve felt very sympathetic towards her. If Bobby Collins was right, it was not surprising Jim Baines didn't want his wife getting involved. He could see why Bobby Collins didn't want Joanna Baines to know about it.

Joanna looked at him through tear filled eyes. "I am sorry to carry on like this, are you sure I can't get you anything?"

"Quite sure, thank you. Now Mrs Baines, you say you knew Mrs Sherman - Debby - was unhappy. Have you any idea what the problem was?" He was treading carefully, as he didn't want to distress the woman any further, but he also had a duty to perform.

"She didn't confide in me much. I know things were tough for them financially - but I don't know if that was anything to do with it." Joanna looked thoughtful. "Have you spoken to Bobby? Bobby Collins? She seemed to think things were seriously wrong between Debby and Nick, but I don't know why. Perhaps she could help you more."

"Yes, I have spoken to Bobby Collins. She was most helpful. A thing like this shakes everyone though, doesn't it?" he added understandingly. "Is there anything else you think I should know?"

"I can't think of anything officer. I am sorry I can't be more help to you. I only wish I could have been of more help to Debby. I would never have thought her capable of such a thing." She shook her head sadly.

"We don't actually know that it was suicide yet, it may just have been a tragic accident. That will be up to the Coroner to decide. Anyway, as I said, you mustn't blame yourself. No one could have known what was going on in her mind. I am sure she appreciated your friendship immensely, and that you were as supportive of her as anyone could be. Sometimes there just isn't anything anyone can do."

He stayed for a while longer just to make sure his visit hadn't caused her any further grief, and surprisingly, they ended up chatting like old friends. Steve was impressed with how understanding Joanna was, she seemed to be genuinely interested in him, and he found himself warming to this immensely likeable lady.

Leaving the Baines' house he decided to drive into the local town and call in on Jim Baines at work. It was not far, and he could see the definite advantages of interviewing Jim alone.

Jim was in his office when his secretary showed the policeman in.

"Thanks Mary," he smiled at the young secretary, "could you bring us a tray of coffee please?"

Mary smiled back at him "Certainly J...Mr Baines. Coffee sir?" she enquired of Steve.

"Not for me thank you, I won't be long." Steve turned to Jim Baines. He was a bit of a ladies man - that much was certain. He caught the look he gave the secretary, and noted that it was reciprocated. He had a feeling he didn't like Mr James Baines much.

"Now sir, I understand that you knew the deceased, Mrs Debby Sherman, quite well," he started briskly.

"Well I knew her, of course. I don't know if I would describe it as 'knowing her well'. I mean, I certainly never suspected she would do anything like this." Jim felt a bit flustered. What exactly did this policeman know? He had been shocked at Debby's death; surely it wasn't because of him? It had only been a bit of fun after all - nothing serious.

"Mr Baines, if I may be frank, I have reason to believe you and Mrs Sherman may have been rather more than friends. I have no wish to cause you or Mrs Baines any embarrassment. However, it would help to ascertain Mrs Sherman's state of mind, if you could be completely honest with me." Steve sounded as stern as possible, he didn't really have much 'reason to believe' but he wanted to convince this man that he did - and force an admission out of him. He thought Jim Baines looked the type who could lie easily if the need arose.

"You haven't mentioned any of this to Joanna, have you?" he cried, alarmed at the mention of his wife's name. Joanna must never know of his brief involvement with Debby. What should he do? Admit he'd had a bit of a fling? Did policemen keep things like this confidential? He was a man after all.

"It's a bit awkward," he continued. "You see.... well... can I speak to you man to man? I mean, does this conversation have to go any further?" he asked desperately.

Steve gave the usual speech virtually as he had given Bobby, and sat back watching Jim, his face stern, as Jim floundered hopelessly in his own deceit.

"My wife doesn't know, must not know of my er...friendship with Debby. It was only a brief thing. I was just comforting her after an argument with her husband, and well... we just got a bit carried away. These things happen, don't they? But I told her quite firmly that it must never happen again," he stated resolutely.

"Not that I drove her to anything, you understand" he added suddenly, as he realised how it sounded. "I mean, she knew there was nothing in it as well as I did, I mean, she wasn't heartbroken or anything, I mean, she was a pretty tough lady, I mean she... er... well, she wasn't exactly shy herself, if you know what I mean.....". his voice trailed away as realised he was babbling.

"I think I get the picture sir," Steve replied coldly. What a bastard this chap was, he thought. Fool around - but drop her if it got too involved. Nice guy! "Is there anything else you can add which may assist me in my investigations sir?"

"No, I don't think so, officer," Jim replied miserably, he was aware how badly he had handled the whole interview, but the truth was - he was scared.

"I never thought she would do this - honestly! I am sure it couldn't be over... well...over me, I suppose. I am sure it would have to be something more than that. You won't have to bring this out in the open will you? I wouldn't want Joanna hurt." he added hopefully.

It's a bit late for that. thought Steve, but aloud he said "I cannot comment on what the Coroner will have to say in open court, but I can assure you, I will not mention any of this to your wife personally." For her sake, not yours, he added mentally.

"I understand sir that another of the dinner guests on that evening works here. Would it be possible for me to see Mr Terry Matherson while I am on the premises?" He had a pretty clear picture now, and if he could see all the witnesses today he could make out his report tomorrow.

"Yes, yes of course, officer." Jim jumped up "I'll have my secretary show you to his office immediately, and if there is anything else I can do, please let me know." Jim tried to smile warmly at the young policeman, but his smile died on his lips when he saw the man's unyielding expression.

Terry looked nervously at the police officer. He didn't really know Debby very well, and he certainly didn't want to be blamed for anyone finding out about her and Jim. Steve could see the situation he was in; Jim Baines was the man's boss, after all. He would probably get more out of him, (although he thought it probably unnecessary), if he interviewed him away from his office. He asked only a few routine questions, and told him that, should he have any further enquiries of either him, or his wife, he would arrange to call at their home. Leaving the unhappy accountant to repeat their conversation word for word to a waiting Jim, he left the building.

Next Steve called in on Mel and Darren Knight. They were both at home, having taken a few days off to try and help Nick with the arrangements. They both confirmed that Debby and Nick had argued violently on numerous occasions. They both knew the marriage was in trouble. They both hesitated when asked if they knew of Debby's involvement with another man, and although they replied truthfully that they had no proof of an affair, Steve was left in no doubt that it was a fairly open secret. When pressed further, both were adamant that Joanna did not suspect anything, and equally adamant that she should not discover any such involvement now.

"After all," Mel said sadly, "it's too late to help Debby, but I don't see any point in driving Joanna to the same thing."

"You don't think there is any danger of that, do you?" asked Steve alarmed. He was pretty sure that at least some of this would come out in court, and he didn't want to think of there being any tragic consequences. "I would suggest that you try to ensure Joanna Baines is not in court for the inquest. Although I am afraid, if it should be determined that Debby Sherman committed suicide over an unhappy affair, that is just the sort of story the local - and possibly even the national - press would have a field day over."

"Does it have to all come out?" asked Darren, out of concern for Joanna's feelings. "Couldn't they just say she was unhappy in her own marriage?"

"I don't know what the Coroner will decide, but I would suggest you keep a pretty close eye on Joanna Baines in the near future - I would hate to be here again in similar circumstances."

Chapter 10

She had done it! She had actually taken a life! Debby would never bother them again. It was obvious too, that she was going to get away with it completely. It was perhaps a shame that no one would ever know just how clever she had been, but that couldn't be helped. Perhaps one day she would tell Jim just how far she had gone for him. Perhaps he should know now, in case he was ever tempted again. But she knew better than to tell him yet. She couldn't be sure how he would react. How would she react if he killed someone for her? She toyed with the idea briefly. Of course that was silly; people don't go around killing their rivals. "But I did!" she thought triumphantly, then she sobered as she thought of Debby. It was a shame she had to die, but she just wouldn't give up. She just wouldn't leave him alone. If Debby and Nick had parted, as had seemed highly likely, she would have pursued him to the ends of the earth. Not now though, now she was safe - they were safe, and nothing or no one would ever spoil things for them again.

Simon was a troubled man. He had been interviewed at work by the investigating officer, and had virtually repeated what Mel and Darren had said. He knew that Debby was unhappy, and he suspected her marriage was in trouble, but he claimed he didn't know why. He had omitted to mention Jim's involvement, as he didn't want any stories getting back to Joanna, and so he decided quite deliberately not to mention it. He could not see what was to be gained by dragging the whole thing out.

At the time of his interview he had felt - as they all had - shocked and saddened by Debby's sudden death. Now, upon reflection, he also felt something else. He sat in his office thinking. Something was not right, but he couldn't quite put his finger on what was troubling him. He thought he knew Debby. He would have sworn that she was not the type to suddenly commit suicide. He thought back to the night she died. She had seemed fine when she arrived. Things had been a bit tense between her and Nick, but that was understandable. Of course, he hadn't known then about their financial situation. That had come out in various discussions they had all had since her death, but even so, she hadn't appeared suicidal. She had joked with them all, flirted with Jim as normal, and drunk her usual amount. That was it!! He suddenly realised what was bothering him. Mentally he pictured Debby taking a sip of her cocktail, he saw again her frown as she tasted it, she hadn't liked it! There had been something wrong with her drink! He went cold. Surely no one would have put anything in her drink? No, he was being ridiculous! The policeman had told him she had taken a large quantity of high dosage Paracetamol tablets. Debby had only had a few drinks, and by no stretch of the imagination could that many tablets have been slipped into them. Still a persistent voice nagged at him. There had been something wrong with her drink. He must be wrong; he had made the drink himself and given it to her...no! No, he had not given it to Debby. Someone else had passed it to her; someone who kept her back turned briefly and had looked intently at Debby's glass, someone who had commented lightly when she noticed him watching her that she was seeing if the sugar had dissolved. Someone who had cause to hate Debby. He hadn't thought any more of it at the time, but now.... no, it couldn't be possible. What was he thinking? That Debby had been murdered? It was crazy! Things like that didn't happen in real life, not in Linwood. This was a quiet village, not some den of iniquity. He told himself sternly to get a grip of his emotions. His imagination was running wild, but still that image persisted, Debby frowning as she tasted her drink, and her - her innocent expression as she handed Debby her drink. He had to face her. He didn't know what he was going to say, but he had to face her.

He reached for the telephone and dialled. As the telephone rang he tried to imagine what he would say. "Hello love, it's only me, by the way, did you murder Debby last Saturday night?" Hardly! The whole thing was ludicrous. The telephone was answered.

"Hello." She sounded quite normal, but what did he expect? Maniacal laughter? Again his resolve wavered. He decided to press on regardless.

"Hi, it's only me - Simon. Are you alone?" he tried to keep his tone normal. He was not given to melodrama. He didn't want anyone to overhear them, as he felt rather foolish even discussing his absurd notion.

"Oh hi, Simon. Yes, a policeman called in earlier, but he's gone now. There wasn't much I could tell him really. It's all very sad, isn't it?" she replied conversationally, her voice sounding calm and untroubled.

"Are you going to be home for a while?" he asked urgently, "I wanted to talk to you." The sooner he talked things over with her better he would feel.

"Yes" she replied, puzzled. "I was just going to make a sandwich for lunch. Would you like me to make you one?" Simon didn't usually call her during the day. She wondered what he wanted. After her talk with the policeman she felt very confident.

"No thanks, I just need to see you; I'll be there in ten minutes."

He rushed out of the office, calling to his secretary that he would contact her later. He didn't know how long he'd be. His secretary looked surprised. Simon was a methodical man. He made appointments in advance; he didn't just rush off without saying where he was going. She wondered if he had had a row with his wife or something. Perhaps he's going to dash home with a bunch of roses! she thought laughingly, I hope he rang home first - or she might surprise him!

On the short journey back to Linwood Simon's mind was racing. He still didn't know what he was going to say. He supposed he should have told the police of his thoughts, but they would never have believed him. Anyway, how would it look if they started some sort of murder investigation? No, his best bet was to face her with his fears and have her alleviate them. She only had to laugh them off and he would believe her. He always believed her.

As he drove up the familiar drive she opened the door and stood waiting. A puzzled frown on her face. What could he want so urgently? Surely he couldn't suspect anything? She had been so careful. He couldn't know - but what if he suspected? The police were pretty convinced it was suicide, she felt sure of that. If the police - who were trained for this, were convinced - surely everyone else would be. What else could be so important to bring him straight here like this? What else could he be coming to tell her?

They went into the lounge and sat down. He took her hands in his and sat looking at her. His expression was sombre. She smiled encouragingly at him.

"I know this is going to sound ridiculous, but... oh, this is crazy... I just don't know what to say!" He dropped her hands and ran his fingers through his hair. "I think I'm going mad!" He shouldn't have come, he told himself.

"What is it?" she asked gently, frightened by his manner. "I should think after all these years you could tell me just about anything! What's bothering you?" It was serious - she could tell that. She clenched her hands tightly together to keep them from shaking.

"Last Saturday, at dinner, do you remember giving Debby her drink?" He pictured himself handing her the cocktail glasses.

Again he saw her turning her back to him briefly and passing the drinks. Had she paused? What did he see that bothered him? If only he could remember!

"Yes I think so." She frowned "I passed around all the drinks didn't I? I can't really remember exactly." She paused and thought Oh God! What had he seen? Why hadn't she just stuck to the doses in the lemon sorbet? She probably hadn't needed the ones in the drinks. Why did

she have to do it? She thought fast. "I remember resting the glasses on the table briefly while I picked up a napkin because one of the glasses was wet, and I was worried I'd drop it. Then I turned back and handed one to Debby and one to someone else - Terry, I think, why?" Her nerves were taut and she struggled to maintain her casual air.

"Look, I know it sounds daft, but Debby didn't like her drink." Even to his own ears it sounded feeble. She obviously didn't understand what he was getting at.

"So?" She looked blankly at him. Was it just that Debby hadn't drunk her drink quickly, or had he actually seen her drop the tablets into the glass? No, he couldn't have, she had kept her back turned to him. She had been so careful.

"Debby loved those champagne cocktails, we used to tease her about knocking them back, remember?" If only he could make her understand. He watched her carefully. Was she acting? He couldn't tell. He didn't want to believe it was remotely possible, but he just couldn't be sure.

"What are you saying, Simon? Do you think there was something wrong with the drink you made? The policeman told us she'd taken dozens of tablets, it couldn't have had anything to do with one drink!" She reassured him, deliberately misinterpreting his words to imply he felt guilty about the drink he made. "Don't be silly love; you had nothing to do with it." She reached over and hugged him. "You mustn't blame yourself."

"What if someone had put something in her drink? While it was on the table, you noticed the sugar hadn't all dissolved," he persisted. The vague feeling of unease grew.

"That's true." She changed her tack quickly "But who would do such a thing? You don't think Nick? Oh! But this is ridiculous! She died of a massive overdose; no one could have spiked a drink with that many!" Would that pacify him? she wondered.

"I know, I know I am being silly - I just can't help thinking I am missing something. You know that feeling you get when you set off on holiday and wonder if you have forgotten something?" he tried to lighten the tone.

"Yes I know, and invariably you haven't, it's just that you are being over anxious!" she smiled." But if you are really that worried perhaps you should do something about it. Have you told the police about this?" She held her breath. Her mouth felt dry and her heart was pounding. She fought to keep her composure.

"No, I thought they would think I was cracking up. What do you think I should do?" he asked. "Do you think I'm cracking up?"

"I think we've all been under a lot of strain, and we're all looking for answers. I don't blame you for not believing Debby could take her own life - I don't either, but the sad fact is that she did, and that nothing we do or say is going to bring her back. Now," she added briskly "are you going to stay for that sandwich or not?" She breathed a sigh of relief - he hadn't gone to the police. At least not yet anyway.

"No thanks. You're right as usual; I'm letting my imagination run away with me. I'd better get back to work. You won't mention this to anyone will you? I'd feel pretty stupid if it ever came out!" Somehow he just did not feel as reassured as he thought he would.

"Don't be silly" she smiled "I won't tell a soul." As she waved goodbye from the door she added under her breath "I certainly won't be telling anyone - and I don't think you will be either."

Chapter 11

The inquest was a brief affair. If Joanna was surprised that so many people suggested she did not attend, she didn't show it. She hadn't wanted to go, as she felt sure she would only be upset again, a fact Jim kept reminding her of, but she felt it her duty to attend. Jim would be there to support her, and she had to know what the Coroner decided. Jim had been very attentive of late, more so than usual, which was saying something, but she knew he worried about her. He was obviously concerned at how deeply her friend's death had affected her.

Evidence was given by the pathologist about the cause of death ascertained by the post mortem. Debby's own doctor told the court that Debby had seen him recently; showing signs of stress, and said that he had prescribed anti depressants. He added that he had not been of the opinion that she was suicidal; however, it had only been a brief appointment. Steve Clarke gave his report, telling of the many public arguments, and testifying that the only fingerprints taken from the packets of paracetamol found at the scene were those of the deceased, her husband, and the ambulance driver. The ambulance driver testified that Debby had admitted that she had taken the tablets, but that she had not been able to confirm how many.

Nick broke down several times during his evidence, and the Coroner expressed the court's sympathy for his obvious grief. No mention was made publicly of Debby's affair, much to the great relief of those friends attending.

Debby's parents sat close together at the front of the small courtroom. They looked totally shocked by the evidence as it was presented. They had no idea their daughter had been so unhappy. She had seemed fine when they had spoken to her recently. It was true she had been very touchy on the subject of children. When they had hinted once at the prospect of becoming grandparents, she had reacted quite angrily, but they assumed that she wanted to build her career. Debby's father glanced at Nick. Poor lad, he thought, if only things had worked out for them. He looks absolutely devastated. He gave a small smile of encouragement.

Debby's mother was, however, not so generous in her thoughts. She was ambitious for her daughter, and had been delighted when she had married a wealthy estate agent, or property developer, as she referred to him. When the property market had slumped she blamed Nick personally for his failure. My Debby deserved better than that wimp! She thought angrily. He drove her to this! She felt sure it must have been Nick's fault that they didn't even have a grandchild with which to console themselves. She glared across the room at him.

Simon sat at the back of the small courtroom and listened intently to all the evidence. He still felt misgivings, but even he had to conclude at the end of the proceedings that suicide was the only possible verdict.

She sat quietly throughout. Listening as the evidence pointing towards suicide mounted up. She almost felt like jumping to her feet and shouting. "I did it! I did it, you morons! I did it, and no one could work out how I murdered my rival. I have committed the perfect murder and no one can ever prove it!" She forced herself to pay attention.

The Coroner was summing up. He gave a brief speech on the tragedy and waste of such a young life. The verdict was recorded as suicide and the Coroner released the body for the funeral, which was organised for a few days later.

The day before the funeral she made a very special mince pie. She used dried fruit, grated apple, suet, spices, sugar, a touch of brandy and just a very few chopped leaves from the yew tree in the church yard. Carefully, she spooned the mixture into the small pastry case. Then she baked it for twenty minutes in a very well aired kitchen. She sprinkled the top of the pie with castor sugar to make it look attractive, and left it to cool. She sterilised all the utensils and ran them through the dishwasher several times to make sure not a trace of the toxic pie would be found. She wrapped the pie in a napkin and hid it at the bottom of her handbag. Then she set about baking sausage rolls and vol-au-vents for the funeral tea the following day. It really wasn't fair to expect Nick to lay on food for the mourners. He was not coping too well, poor dear. Still, she thought optimistically, he was young and quite good-looking, and a young widower soon attracts female attention. Perhaps he'd have more luck with his second wife.

The next day the parish church was packed to capacity. The village rector gave a very moving address about Debby and how she would be so sadly missed and how everyone should rally around her poor husband in his hour of need. Everyone cried. They all agreed that the flowers were very pretty and the service had been beautiful. Debby's sudden and unusual death caused some public speculation. A few members of the congregation were, perhaps, not attending solely to mourn the young woman's passing as a certain amount of morbid curiosity had arisen from the tragedy.

It was a terribly cold day being mid December, and most of the congregation returned to the Sherman's house for a warming drink, and to express their condolences. Nick looked dazed, and answered mechanically to all the well-meaning comments. Bobby, Joanna, Mel and Karen all hugged him and cried with him and offered him their support, but he didn't really seem to understand what was going on. Their respective husbands shook hands awkwardly, and muttered condolences, but it was obvious that they didn't know what to say either.

Everyone stood around chatting quietly. She saw her moment.

"Well Simon, what did you think? Lovely service wasn't it?"

"Yes," sighed Simon. "I still can't believe it's happened though. It just wasn't like Debby at all. Do you suppose we will ever know why she did it? It's so strange she didn't even leave a note." Glancing over at Nick he said, "I feel so sorry for Nick - he looks absolutely punch drunk."

"I do hope he's eating well. In this cold weather, and after such a shock, anything could bring him down. He must keep his strength up or he could be really ill." Simon had confirmed her fears. He was still pondering Debby's death; sooner or later he would work it out.

"I don't suppose he's given much thought to eating," Simon replied glumly. Actually he hadn't eaten much for a few days himself. His thoughts kept troubling him, and he had lost his appetite. Maybe he should follow her advice himself.

"Well, you always feel better after you've eaten something. Here, have a mince pie and I'll take one over to him." She handed Simon a small, sugar sprinkled mince pie on a paper napkin, and turned quickly away to Nick.

Simon took the small pie and popped it into his mouth to wipe his sugar coated fingers. He chewed briefly and swallowed, looking up; he saw her watching him over her shoulder. Puzzled by her expression, he started to speak, when suddenly a terrible pain gripped him, and he fell to the ground. In the split second before he hit the carpet he realised what she had done. Everyone turned around at the commotion. Karen reached him first.

"Simon? Simon? What is it? Oh Simon - say something! Are you all right?"

Simon did not answer. He didn't intend to be rude of course; it was just that by the time she spoke to him he was, in fact, already dead.

Pandemonium broke out. Joanna tried to pump his chest, and Karen tried mouth-to-mouth resuscitation. Someone ran to call an ambulance. Bobby stood white faced - staring down at her prostrate husband in a state of total shock. Mel led her gently to a chair, and someone gave her a glass of brandy.

The paramedics arrived. They took over from Joanna and Karen and tried to revive Simon. They tried a portable defibrillator and shouted at everyone to clear the body, but it was to no avail, and they rushed him to the waiting ambulance where they carried on their resuscitation attempts. Bobby went with them in the ambulance.

"Does he have a history of heart problems?" asked the young medic, noting Simon's blue lips - a classic sign of heart failure.

"No, no he has always been very fit, is it his heart then?" Bobby asked anxiously.

"I'm afraid it looks like he's had a massive coronary. Has he been complaining of any tightness in the chest - or any pain?"

"I don't think so. He hasn't said anything to me, he's been a bit quiet but we have all had a lot on our minds. A friend of ours was buried today," she added quietly.

They arrived at the hospital and were rushed straight through to the emergency room. Despite all efforts they were unable to resuscitate Simon and at 3.20 p m he was declared officially dead.

Mel and Darren arrived at the hospital shortly after the ambulance, and sat with Bobby while the doctor broke the news to her. She sat numbly staring at him as he spoke.

At the funeral tea everyone waited to hear the news. Nick was trembling violently. He had been close to breaking point all day, and the turmoil of the ambulance arriving and the paramedics working so desperately proved too much for him. Joanna sat holding his hand, and someone sent for the village doctor. Dr Armstrong duly arrived and administered an injection of sedative. Joanna and Jim agreed to stay with him and see to his guests. No one knew quite what to do. Gradually most of the guests left, murmuring condolences, leaving only Karen, Terry, Joanna and Jim. They all set about collecting up plates and glasses and generally clearing up. The paper napkin, which had held the lethal pie, was collected up with the general debris, and tossed casually in the bin.

Steve Clarke arrived just as they were loading the dishwasher. He had been alerted by the hospital, and was quick to respond. His boss, Detective Inspector Saunders, who, upon hearing of two sudden deaths in as many weeks, decided to check out the facts personally, accompanied him.

"I would appreciate it if you would all leave the clearing up for a while, and give me a short statement," he announced. He was a tall man with an unmistakable air of authority that brooked no argument.

He went around the small group talking to everyone and making a few notes. It soon became apparent that no one could actually tell him exactly what had happened. He spoke to the woman who had found the victim, a Mrs Karen Matherson.

"I got to him first but he was just lying there. It was horrible - his eyes were open but he wasn't moving. I couldn't believe it! He had seemed fine a few minutes before. I tried mouth to mouth, but he just didn't respond - then the ambulance men took over and....." she broke off, crying.

"Thank you madam, I am sorry to cause you distress." He moved on, but got much the same story from everyone. Simon had seemed well and showed no signs of any illness, and had suddenly keeled over and died, apparently instantly.

"I am not happy about this," he said quietly to his junior colleague. "There is usually some sign, however brief, of an imminent heart attack - pains down the arm or in the chest. This man died too quickly." He stopped as a PC entered the room and spoke quietly. He listened intently for a few moments and then turned to Steve.

"Right Steve," he snapped, "the hospital is not happy with the cause of death. I want a full statement from everyone present, I want a complete list of everyone who was here earlier and I want you to get down to the morgue and attend the post mortem. I want the time of death, cause of death, full medical history - the works! This is Linwood for God's sake, a quiet village, we don't get strange murders in a place like this, and I do not intend for this one to spoil my reputation - or make notoriety. This is my patch and I intend to get to the bottom of this, and fast! The other PC's will start on the statements; you get down to that hospital. Oh, and Steve, I want to know what he had for his last meal!"

Steve nodded at his boss and headed for the door. Malcolm, he thought grimly, I've got some good news for you!

Chapter 12

*T*he following days were fraught in the village. Christmas was fast approaching, but no one was feeling very festive. The small group of friends clung to each other for mutual support. Nick appeared incapable of rational thought, wandering aimlessly around, invoking much sympathy and concern from everyone. His parents came to visit him and were greatly disturbed by the state of their son's mental health.

Bobby, for once, lost her usual glossy appearance, and dressed soberly, wearing little make-up. Jim and Joanna spent a lot of time with her, trying to help her through such a painful time. Everyone believed Simon had died of a sudden heart attack, possibly brought on by the shock of Debby's sudden death, or perhaps simply due to his stressful work.

The police had not as yet discussed the possibility of foul play with anyone involved in the case, as they were still awaiting the complete results of the post mortem. Inspector Saunders, although quietly organising statements and guest lists, was not going to tip off any possible suspect by revealing too much too soon. He was aware from the preliminary results that they were not dealing with a natural death, but for the moment he was biding his time and gathering information.

Steve Clarke sat in Detective Inspector George Saunders' office and went through the results of the second post mortem with him. In such cases there was a preliminary post mortem held, often irreverently referred to by the police as 'the knife and fork job' and when something unusual, which warranted further investigation, was found, a more detailed examination was carried out by the pathologist. Samples were then taken, recorded, and stored for future reference and possible evidence.

Reading from his notes, Steve explained the findings. He was not looking forward to his boss's reaction when he got to the rather unusual results of the samples analysis.

"The initial post mortem showed cause of death to be sudden cessation of the heart, indicated by darker colouring in the left ventricle, due to an unknown substance. Detailed investigation showed cause of death - heart failure brought on by a poisonous alkaloid known as taxine. Traces of hydro cyanic acid, ephedrine and a volatile oil also present. Death would have been almost instantaneous. Taxine is rapidly absorbed through the alimentary tract and causes instant cessation of the heart," he paused, trying to sound as professional as possible. "Source of lethal agent found to be Taxus Baccata, or the common yew. Stomach contained chopped yew leaves found in the remains of a mince pie consumed by the deceased within the last minutes prior to death." He kept his eyes fixed studiously on his notebook. It did sound rather absurd.

"WHAT! Are you seriously trying to tell me that someone put chopped yew leaves in a mince pie? For God's sake man - it sounds like a plot from a Hollywood melodrama!" George Saunders had been in the Force for some years and had seen some pretty odd cases, but this was just ludicrous. He glared at the hapless policeman. "Are you aware what the press are going to make of this? Is the lab absolutely sure that was the cause of death?" The village would be turned into a circus over this. He groaned, it was just the sort of case the media had a field day over. He had to get the whole thing sorted fast before anyone got wind of it. His whole professional life was at stake, not to mention his home life, when the story got around.

"I know how it sounds, but that is it. I couldn't believe it myself, but the facts remain. The common yew is one of the most highly toxic plants around and, unfortunately, very accessible. There's a large yew tree in the grounds of the village church for starters." When he had read up on the Taxus Baccata, he had found that animals had been discovered dead under yew trees, with the leaves still in their mouths. He wondered, briefly, whether to share that particular anecdote with DI Saunders, but glancing at the man's thunderous expression decided perhaps not.

"Right!" declared George Saunders. "We keep this aspect between ourselves for the time being. I do not want jokes about mince pies flying about the station. The victim was poisoned - enough said! Now. Who did the catering for the funeral tea?" At least it should be a fairly simple matter to determine where the pie had come from.

"Well, sir, we do have something of a problem there. It would appear that quite a number of people attended the funeral and that several friends and relations brought food to the house both before, and after, the service. Mr Sherman has no idea who brought what." He had a long list of people attending the funeral, but could not be sure it was entirely comprehensive as he was relying on individual memories at a time of stress.

"I want every person at that funeral to be interviewed. Find out who made what, and when they brought it to the house. There was only one person poisoned, so someone must have taken the trouble to make sure the right person got the right pie. The murderer must have been in the room at the time. We also have to establish a motive. Who stood to benefit by his death, and were they present at the time? What else have we got on him?"

"We have established that the victim was a senior partner in a firm of architects. The business is doing quite well, with no apparent financial difficulties. I have requested a copy of their last returns from Company House, but it's not expected to show anything unusual. The other partners would not benefit from his death as the business was largely built on his reputation..." he paused as he turned over the page in his notebook.

"Any major business deals at the moment? Rival company wanting him out of the picture?" interjected Saunders.

"Nothing special going on - just routine. It was a fairly small concern. One or two big projects, which made his name, but recently just run of the mill stuff. He has got a local government project, but it is half way through - no sense in taking it now."

"Insured?"

"Yes. He was well insured, although not in any particularly excessive amounts. His second wife, Robyn Collins, being the main beneficiary. His first wife was written out of his will when he married the second wife. She has since remarried, and has little or no contact with her ex-husband. I have had a brief informal interview with his bank manager, and there doesn't appear to be any financial problems. I actually met the victim myself last week, when I interviewed him over the suicide of a family friend. Seemed calm and rational. I also interviewed his wife, and again I didn't notice anything out of the ordinary."

"I want to run over the notes of the suicide case too. Two sudden deaths coming so close together seems a trifle excessive to me," he commented dryly. "Any apparent connection between the two?"

"They were both members of a group of friends. The suicide case attended a dinner at the home of Mr and Mrs Collins on the night she died. He said she appeared quite normal, and he seemed to be astonished to learn of her subsequent action. He had heard of her marital difficulties, but not in detail. It was a small gathering of ten people, apparently quite a regular event. I interviewed all the guests that evening. I have my notes if you want them."

"I'll read through them later. Was there any particular attachment between the two victims that you were aware of? Both members of the wife-swapping club, perhaps?" He gave a wry grin.

"Not that I am aware of, sir. Mrs Sherman, the suicide, was however, known to be having an extra-marital affair with another member of their circle of friends. Could be that she also had a fling with him, but I don't see how that would cause his death. Had he died first, I could see her motive for suicide, but not the other way around."

"Jealous wife perhaps? Maybe she only found out after the girlfriend died. To do him in at the girlfriend's funeral seems a bit like poetic justice."

"I don't think so sir. It was the victim's wife who informed me of the other affair. Her story was corroborated by others." Steve remembered how his first thoughts had been that Bobby Collins was the duped wife, but he had been completely wrong.

"How about the widower? Revenge for his wife's death maybe? This sort of poisoning does indicate a female perpetrator, but he could be cleverer than we think. We wouldn't want to be accused of being sexist. What's the husband like?"

"He was absolutely devastated by his wife's death. But surely he would kill the ex boyfriend? Anyway - I can't see him making mince pies on the day his wife is buried. He was surrounded by family most of the time, and sedated the rest of the time. No, I think he is well out of the picture." He remembered trying to interview Nick, the man was barely coherent.

"Which brings us back to the wife. What's she like? They live in that modern thing up at the top of the village, don't they?" Saunders tried to picture her. He had probably met her in the village, but he couldn't place her. It was only a small community, and most people knew each other, at least by sight, but he tended not to socialise much. He pictured the house quite well though. He disliked modern architecture. Perhaps the murderer was a traditionalist?

"Yes sir, he designed it himself. She's blonde, attractive, and quite a bit younger than her husband - glamorous type. She was quite scathing about Mrs Sherman carrying on with a married man as I recall. Seemed very concerned with the wronged wife." She certainly had not been overly fond of Debby Sherman.

"That doesn't always mean much. If she is that much younger than her husband maybe she plays the same game. Find out if there are any boyfriends in her life. Maybe she did him in for the insurance. Perhaps she wanted to fund a toy-boy. Might be a good idea to check out the first Mrs Collins too. Was it an amicable divorce? How recent? What grounds, etc?"

"The divorce was a few years ago now sir, and having met the lady I would imagine we could rule her out. She wasn't at the funeral, it seems she hasn't kept in contact with her ex-husband's friends, and anyway, she is quite happily remarried. When I informed her of his death she was very upset. I don't think she bore him any ill will. However, she wasn't overly concerned with the second Mrs Collins' feelings of loss."

"I suppose that is understandable. There isn't usually much love lost between first and second wives. If she wasn't at the funeral we could probably rule her out, but check first. Find out where she was that day, just in case. She could have slipped in with the crowd." It didn't sound very likely, but so far nothing sounded very likely.

"Yes sir. I'll get back to you on that one. I don't think we will get too far there though." He was as baffled as his boss.

"Well check it out anyway; we haven't got much else to go on. Someone wanted him dead." He frowned - they had a distinct lack of suspects at the moment.

"Yes sir. I will get right on to it. Are you going to conduct any of the interviews personally?" He was acutely aware of George Saunders' personal interest in this case.

"Yes. I want to be in on this one at every level. I will speak to the widow first, usually a good place to start. I want you to start with some of the friends and acquaintances. It would help if we could see them all separately, before the word gets around. They all think at the moment that Mr Collins died of a heart attack.

Try and spring the news of the poison on them and watch for their immediate gut reaction. Someone is not going to be as surprised as they should be."

"I'll start the interviews first thing in the morning. Anything else I should be checking for?" asked Steve.

"Yes. You could find out who was baking mince pies last week." As he spoke he realised it was probably quite a tall order. It would not be considered unusual to be baking mince pies two weeks before Christmas.

Chapter 13

*T*hree days after Simon's death, everyone except Nick gathered at Joanna and Jim's house to discuss the funeral arrangements, and make plans for the forthcoming holidays. Bobby arrived last, wearing a simple black dress. She looked pale and drawn. Her eyes were darkly ringed and her appearance generally was very reminiscent of how Nick had looked the last time they had all seen him.

Nick had gone to visit his parents for a couple of weeks, much to everyone's relief. They had all been wondering how he would cope with another funeral and it was best he was away from it all for a while. His parents, retired, lived in Kent, and were glad of his company for Christmas, albeit in such tragic circumstances.

"How are you feeling, Bobby?" asked Mel sympathetically. "Is there anything we can do to help?"

"No thank you Mel," Bobby spoke quietly, "there isn't anything anyone can do now. I am on my own and I have got to face up to that fact." She was still in a state of shock. She felt very guilty. She had not always treated her husband very well, and now he was gone. Suddenly she couldn't imagine her life without Simon. She had often contemplated life with another man, namely Jim, but, illogically, she had never really envisaged a life without Simon. You are being stupid! she told herself. You wanted your freedom and now you've got it! But she didn't feel free - she felt dreadfully alone.

Jim looked across the room towards Bobby. She looked really beautiful, she had a poignant look about her, and he wanted to rush over and comfort her. Simon's death had both shocked and saddened him. It also made him acutely aware of his own mortality. It just goes to show, you never know what's around the corner, he thought to himself. You have to live life to the full - and enjoy it while you've got it.

"I had better go and speak to Bobby" he told Joanna, "there may be something practical I can do, she might want stuff moving or something...." he trailed off lamely as he hurried away.

"Bobby?" Jim hesitated, searching for the right words. He felt awkward and unsure of himself. "I, er...I want you to know I am here if there is anything you need. I am really sorry about Simon. He was a great guy, and I'll miss him."

"Will you?" She asked looking him straight in the eye. "Will you really Jim? I think we both let him down rather badly - don't you?" She tried to transfer some of the enormous guilt she was carrying around onto him.

"Of course I am sorry! I never meant him any harm. I mean... well..." he lowered his voice "we just couldn't help ourselves, could we?" He was feeling decidedly guilty himself, and tried to justify himself as best he could.

"You are right," she whispered, glancing around to make sure they were not attracting attention, she continued. "What we have is special. It's not just a cheap, sordid affair - we are both better people than that. You can't help who you fall for, and at least this way Simon will never be hurt - we should take some comfort from that." She sighed and looked up at him tearfully.

"Er...yes" stammered Jim, not at all happy at the way the conversation was heading. Actually he thought it had been a cheap affair, but perhaps he was wrong. Perhaps he had higher moral standards than he gave himself credit for. Perhaps he had genuinely fallen in love with Bobby. What about all the others? a sarcastic conscience reminded him, but he ignored the inner voice and concentrated on the poor bereaved widow who stood before him. At least this way he didn't feel quite such a bastard.

"Look, we can't talk now, come around later. We can talk then. I need you Jim. I need someone to hold me, and love me, and tell me everything will be all right. I feel so terrible," Bobby pleaded. It was the truth. She did need someone to hold her. In her grief she was reaching out for comfort, and Jim was just the one to reach for.

Oh God! he thought desperately, What am I supposed to do? Simon is barely cold and I'm thinking of offering comfort to his grieving widow! How low can a man get? Still... he justified, he wouldn't want to see her unhappy, and after that business with Debby, who knows what a desperate woman might do?

Karen and Terry came over and started talking quietly to Bobby. They were both very upset, and wanted to offer their condolences.

"How is she doing?" Joanna asked quietly, as she approached Jim. She could see Bobby was distraught, and she was so worried about her. Echoing her husband's thoughts she continued, "After what Debby did, it frightens me to see her like this. Were you able to offer any help?"

"Well, she asked me to pop over soon and take down the big Christmas tree from their hall. She doesn't want to celebrate Christmas this year, and it's too big for her to shift by herself." He impressed himself with his fast thinking.

"Of course. Do you think we should invite her to us for Christmas? I would hate to think of her all alone." Joanna wondered anxiously.

"No! I mean... well - it might make it worse for her if she sees us together. You know - happy couple etc." He was extremely alarmed at the prospect of having Bobby and Joanna together under the same roof.

"Perhaps you are right, but I think I'll ask her all the same. I won't press her if she says no, but I'd feel better if I had made the offer." She walked over to Bobby and put her arm around her.

"How are you doing?" she enquired kindly "I was just saying to Jim that I was worried about you being all alone in that house, especially over the holidays. Would you like to come and stay with us?"

Bobby looked over Joanna's shoulder to Jim and saw him frown slightly. "I appreciate the offer Joanna. But if you don't mind, I would rather be alone. I want to just sit by myself and remember all the good times. Besides," she smiled "I don't think I would be very good company at the moment."

"Nonsense - we would be happy to have you. I don't think any of us are going to be doing any revelling this year so it will just be a quiet Christmas at home among friends. Still, I don't want to pressure you. You think it over, and if you change your mind, you know where we are. Jim tells me he is coming over to help you with your tree later. Would you like me to come too and help?"

"No thanks, Joanna. I do appreciate the offer, but I know how busy you are, and really there is nothing you can do. Perhaps later, if you wouldn't mind making something for the funeral?" She broke down crying as she contemplated the ordeal of the funeral.

"Do you know when it will be yet?" asked Joanna thinking, the sooner it was over, the better it would be for Bobby. The hiatus between a death and the funeral was always a trying time, and with the added pressure of Debby's recent demise, and with Christmas fast approaching, it was all rather overwhelming.

"No. There is some sort of hold up with the arrangements. As it was so sudden there has to be a post mortem, and presumably an inquest. It all takes time." She ran her fingers through her hair distractedly. "I suppose it will have to be after Christmas now. I don't even know where he is at the moment. It's all so horrible."

"Hey now, come on. Wherever he is physically, he is with you spiritually. You know that. He loved you and you loved him - you must always remember that. Simon was a good man and we will all miss him. I bet he's looking down on us all right now and willing us not to grieve. He wouldn't want us to be unhappy. He would want us to remember all the good times we had together, wouldn't he?" said Mel trying hard to bring some comfort to everyone.

The room fell silent as everyone considered Mel's words. They all looked around; each had their own thoughts about Simon being present spiritually. Some found the notion less comforting than others. One found it distinctly disconcerting.

Was Simon here? She wondered. Was Debby, for that matter? She offered up a silent prayer. Sorry Simon - you know I didn't want to do it. I hope you are at peace now. She felt strangely calm. Outwardly she showed all the signs of raging grief, but inwardly she felt cold and detached. She knew the police would discover the cause of death. She wondered why they hadn't done anything yet. Perhaps they would just put it down to heart failure. She didn't really think so though. According to her Internet research on poisonous plants there were several telltale signs that would show up in a post mortem. It was a shame there hadn't been time for her to think of something subtler, but she couldn't have risked a delay. Suddenly she felt incredibly powerful. She was the mistress of all their fates. She was invincible - no one could prove anything. There simply was no proof to find.

The police would probably question her, but there was not a thing they could actually do. There was no way they could charge her with either death. Sometimes, in her more rational moments, she was appalled by what she had done. She had never intended to kill Simon - he had been a good man, and very good to her. She had been very fond of him, but she loved Jim. Simon would have eventually discovered her secret; he was an observant and intelligent man. Once he realised what he had actually seen that night he wouldn't have rested until he had worked it all out. His conscience would not have allowed him to protect her, and she would have been caught. Jim was not the type to stand by her, she knew that. She would have lost everything. It wasn't her fault - she was only protecting herself. During her brief spells of rationality she wondered if she had lost her sanity. She didn't think she was insane - she felt quite in control.

The question was, what should she do now? Could she carry on normally? Would life ever be the same? Perhaps the answer was for her and Jim to go away together - leave Linwood and move to another place. Not immediately of course, that would be too obvious - perhaps in the spring? She loved the spring. The spring would be perfect for a fresh start. The only problem would be convincing Jim. She frowned; perhaps he should know what she had done for him?

Terry looked sourly over towards Jim. "He doesn't waste much time, does he?" he remarked to Darren. "Could at least wait until we've buried the guy!"

"I bet he feels awful. He's probably just trying to offer her some help. I should think he wants to make amends somehow." Darren had a generous nature, he could imagine how guilty Jim must be feeling and he felt sorry for him. It had obviously only been a game to him, and how could he have known that Simon would drop dead like that?

"Tell that to Nick! I tell you, that Jim is the most selfish bastard on this earth. I am sure part of Debby's problem was him. You saw him go after her at Halloween - it sure took him a long time to get back! She's gone - so he's back to Bobby. It's disgusting! And what about Joanna? She is a lovely lady, she deserves better than him. The sad thing is she doesn't even see it." he retorted bitterly. Terry was heartily sick of Jim – 'golden boy' of the firm – 'charmer with the ladies' - the guy was just a parasite as far as he was concerned.

"Hey! Steady on! Jim is not that bad. Okay so he's a bit weak where the ladies are concerned, but it takes two, you know. He doesn't exactly have to knock them over the head, does he? Besides, he was really cut up at Debby's funeral, and I am sure he genuinely liked Simon. There's no malice in him." Darren replied, surprised at the venom in Terry's voice. "Personally I hope Joanna never does find out. He'll grow out of it eventually, and she'd be lost without him - she worships him." Darren was ever the optimist; he felt sure things would settle down soon. After all, what else could happen?

Later that day Jim drove around to Bobby's house. She showed him through to the lounge and they sat down together.

"Oh Jim. I feel so awful. I feel so guilty about the way we treated Simon," she sighed.

"You must not blame yourself. It was my fault. I should never have started this thing, I just couldn't resist you." Jim always knew how to make a woman feel better.

"Where do we go from here? I just want to leave it all behind me. I wish I could wake up and find a year had passed. I don't think I can handle the next few weeks." She started to cry.

Jim put his arms around her. "Don't worry - you are not alone. I am here, and you have a lot of friends and family who care a great deal about you. What about your parents? Maybe you could go and visit them. After the funeral you could just slip away and totally relax for a while." She was starting to get a bit clingy, and that was the last thing he wanted. "When you get back, in a few months, we can talk again."

"I don't want to leave you for a few months. I want to go away with you. We could be so perfect together. Didn't you say you had business up North?" She brightened up as the idea grew. "We could both go up there together and start afresh. Not straight away of course, give it a bit of time. Just knowing we had a future together would get me through all this."

"What about Joanna? She is really devastated at losing two friends in such quick succession. You know how sensitive she is. We have got to give her time to get over this too. I couldn't face it if she.... well...took Debby's solution. For God's sake, we've got enough on our consciences now." He said rapidly, stalling for time. He didn't want to make any sort of commitment to Bobby. He still loved his wife.

"Oh yes! On the subject of Debby - just how close were you two?" Bobby's voice hardened. "Were you having an affair with her?"

"Of course not!" retorted Jim "I just felt sorry for her that was all. I knew she was unhappy, I just didn't realise how unhappy! I am only sorry we weren't able to help her. You know you are the only one I really love."

"And Joanna?" she asked quickly, seizing the moment.

"I am very fond of Joanna of course," he hedged "but I am not in love with her any more. I just don't know how to tell her so. She is not as strong as you. I don't know how she would take it."

"I'll tell Joanna. Not yet," she added hastily, seeing the look of horror on his face. "Later, I'll find a way of telling her gently. She would want you to be happy. No, leave it with me. I'll explain it all to her."

"Don't say anything without telling me first, will you." pleaded Jim. That was the last thing he wanted.

"Don't worry, we can tell her together if you like."

"I don't think that's a good idea." He didn't like the sound of that at all. "That would only hurt her more."

"Well I'll write to her then - I'll explain it all in a letter, and you can read it and choose the right moment to give it to her. How's that for a solution?"

"That would probably be best - but not for a while. Let us get the next few months over with, and then we can make proper plans." Joanna will never get that letter if I have anything to do with it, he decided quietly to himself

Chapter 14

*T*he next day, Detective Inspector Saunders arranged to call on Bobby to discuss a few aspects of her husband's tragic demise. He took with him Woman Police Constable Shelagh Veitch, in case Bobby Collins needed her. She was trained in dealing with distressed people.

Steve Clarke went through the list of Simon Collins' friends and acquaintances, and decided in which order to see them. He remembered how nervous Terry Matherson had seemed, there was a man who would reveal any secrets under pressure. He rang and requested an appointment. Terry, alarmed at being called, decided to come straight over to the police station. He didn't want to worry about it all day.

George Saunders sat opposite Bobby Collins and observed her carefully. She was pale, her eyes were red rimmed and she clutched a handkerchief in her hands. Every inch the grieving widow he assessed thoughtfully, but how much of it is genuine?

"Mrs Collins, thank you for taking the time to see me. I am sure you have a lot of arrangements to take care of," he smiled briefly, "I will try not to take up too much of your time."

"It's no trouble officer. I am afraid I really don't know what I am supposed to do at the moment. I understand I cannot make any funeral arrangements yet. With Christmas just around the corner, I tend to just stay at home. I certainly don't want to get involved with Yuletide celebrations." She spoke quietly.

"I do understand. Mrs Collins, it is my painful duty to inform you that your husband's death was not due to natural causes." He watched carefully for her reaction.

"I don't understand! He had a heart attack! They told me that at the hospital. What do you mean?" She looked shocked and confused. What is he talking about? she thought. What does he know?

"Your husband had heart failure brought on by a poisonous alkaloid in his food." He decided to withhold the mince pie aspect for the time being, "Mrs Collins, I....." he stopped abruptly and jumped to his feet, unfortunately he was not quite quick enough to catch Bobby, who had fallen to the floor in a dead faint.

Steve Clarke sat opposite Terry Matherson and observed him carefully. He was obviously nervous and somewhat distressed. The man would make an extremely poor liar if he did have anything to hide, he thought.

"Mr Matherson, thank you for taking the time to call. As I said on the 'phone, this is just an informal chat. I would like to get a bit more background information on Simon Collins, and I understand you know the family quite well."

"No trouble, no trouble at all," muttered Terry, "but I don't know what I can tell you. I mean, I don't know anything about his health or anything." He felt very uncomfortable. He had no idea what they wanted him for, but he disliked dealing with authority.

"Mr Matherson, how well did you know Simon Collins?" Steve started his questioning.

"Fairly well I suppose. We all went out together a bit. My wife is friendly with his wife." He didn't really know what else he could say.

"Would you say that he was a popular man?" Steve was trying to draw the man out.

"Yes I suppose so - everyone liked him. What has all this got to do with his heart attack?" he looked puzzled. The man's popularity was all rather academic now, wasn't it?

"Mr Matherson, I am afraid it is my unpleasant duty to inform you that Simon Collins did not die of natural causes." Steve watched for his reaction.

"What?? What do you mean? He had a heart attack. Bobby told us. I mean, well, the hospital said, and....." his voice trailed off as he tried to absorb what the policeman was telling him. Not natural causes - that must mean...no! It wasn't possible! Who would want to kill Simon?

"Simon Collins' heart attack was induced by person or persons unknown." Steve continued, "Mr Matherson, are you all right? Would you perhaps like a cup of tea?" Terry Matherson stared at him in total white-faced shock.

WPC Shelagh Veitch made Bobby a cup of sweet tea and gently calmed her. She sat close by as DI Saunders continued his line of questioning.

"Mrs Collins, do you feel well enough to continue?"

"Yes," she whispered, "Yes, I want to know. I am sorry about that. It was such a shock. Please tell me what happened to my husband." Her mind was reeling, who did he think had killed Simon?

"Your husband was poisoned at the funeral of Debby Sherman. We do not, as yet, know who administered the poison. We are hoping you will be able to help us with our enquiries."

"Me - help? What do you mean?" She looked alarmed. Was he accusing her? They always said 'A person is helping the police with their enquiries' when they had caught someone.

"Can you think of anyone who would benefit from your husband's death? Did he have any enemies that you know of?"

"No, everyone liked Simon. Why should anyone want to harm him? There must be some mistake."

"I am afraid not, Mrs Collins. Our laboratory is very thorough." He recalled his discussion with Steve Clarke the previous day. Here goes, he thought, "Mrs Collins, I am sorry to appear insensitive at a time like this, but I must ask - were there any problems in your marriage?"

"No! Certainly not! We were very much in love." She sobbed, and Shelagh put her arm protectively around her shoulder.

"I am sorry to press the point, but I have to rule out every possibility. Is there any chance of a third person perhaps being involved?" Did she suspect her husband had been seeing Debby Sherman perhaps? It was only a theory but he had little else to go on.

Bobby looked up abruptly, did he know about Jim? Oh God! Did he think she had murdered her husband to run off with Jim?

"I...I don't know what you mean," she stalled. How could he know? Was he just guessing?

George noted her immediate reaction. He had stumbled on something - he was sure of it! "Mrs Collins, was your husband involved with another woman?"

Bobby closed her eyes and breathed a sigh of relief. They thought Simon was cheating! Thank God!

"No, I am sure he would never cheat on me. As I said officer, we were very much in love."

Steve waited while Terry drank his tea. "Do you feel well enough to continue Mr Matherson?"

"Yes, I suppose so. I really cannot believe all this though. Are you sure there hasn't been some sort of mistake? A mix-up at the lab or something?" It all seemed so incredible to Terry.

"We are quite sure, Mr Matherson. Can you think of any person, or persons, who would wish to harm Mr Collins?"

"Certainly not! He was a nice guy. He and his wife were very popular, they er...." he stopped. Bobby! Had Bobby wanted to get rid of Simon? Everyone knew about her and Jim. Surely she would not go that far though? No, that was preposterous!

"Mr Matherson?" prompted Steve. "You were saying something about Mr and Mrs Collins?" He knows something, Steve thought.

"Oh yes. Sorry - I just can't seem to take it all in. Yes, I was saying, Simon and Bobby were a popular couple, always entertaining. We all had dinner there quite recently." He groaned, why did he say that? That was the night Debby died.

"Yes, I do recall that particular event. I understand that was the night Debby Sherman died. Mr Matherson, may I be frank with you? I have reason to believe Mrs Sherman was involved with a married friend of yours." He paused, noting Terry's discomfort. "Is there any possibility that a similar situation concerning Mr Collins was occurring."

"Debby and Simon?? Good lord no! Simon didn't fool around! He wasn't like that at all!" They were definitely barking up the wrong tree there!

George was rather perplexed. He had been sure that Bobby had suspected her husband of an affair. There had definitely been a change in her manner when he suggested it. She was very convincing in her denial though. He decided to pursue the point.

"Mrs Collins, are you aware of any possible connection between your husband and Mrs Debby Sherman? Your husband was murdered at her funeral. That would seem quite a coincidence wouldn't it?"

"Detective Inspector, my husband was not having an affair with Debby Sherman - or anyone else for that matter!" Bobby stated with icy firmness. "Believe me, I would have known. Debby Sherman was possibly involved with someone else, but not with my husband."

"Yes, we are aware of her affair with another party." George said dismissively, "I was just trying to ascertain a motive for a murder at a funeral. It is somewhat unusual." He was convinced he was drawing a blank there. So what was the story here?

So Jim was seeing Debby! she thought angrily The bastard! He swore to me he hadn't touched her!

George watched the emotions flicker across Bobby's face. She was clearly angry. Did she suspect her husband or not? Why was she angry if there was nothing in it? Was she just angry with him for suggesting it? There was something she was not telling him. Something to do with Debby Sherman perhaps?

"Mrs Collins, were you close to Mrs Sherman? I realise you were aware of her relationship with... another party." Should he name Jim Baines?

"Debby and I were not particularly close. I knew of her interests but she did not confide in me. I think she would have been aware of my opinion on the matter," she added primly.

"How well do you know Mr Sherman? Is it at all possible he could have mistaken his wife's affections and believed her to be involved with your husband?"

"And kill him you mean? Nick kill Simon? No way! I don't think he even knew she was carrying on at all. If he did he certainly wouldn't have suspected Simon! What's more, he would be totally incapable of murdering her lover - even if he did know who he was. Besides, she was already dead. What would he have to gain by it? No, Inspector, I am afraid you are completely wrong there!"

Steve Clarke looked at the man opposite him. He had looked distinctly uncomfortable when he suggested a possible affair, yet was adamant that Simon Collins was not involved. 'Oh, don't be so obtuse man! He mentally kicked himself. "Mr Matherson, are you aware of any relationship between Bobby Collins and a third party?" Jackpot! he thought triumphantly, as Terry squirmed in front of him.

"No! Well er...yes, well I mean, I don't know about a 'relationship' really. I mean, well..." his voice trailed miserably away. He was really on the spot. Should he drop Jim in it and risk losing his job? Suppose Jim and Bobby had conspired to kill Simon. If he didn't speak up that would make him an accessory or something, wouldn't it?

Steve watched him flounder for a while. Time to reel him in! he thought, pleased with finally getting something concrete to base an investigation on. "Mr Matherson" he said sternly "Are you involved in a sexual relationship with Mrs Robyn Collins?"

"WHAT!!! Me??? No way!! I am not knocking off Bobby!! What do you take me for" Terry practically exploded. "Jim Baines is carrying on with her. It is nothing to do with me. I only work for the guy!" He slumped back in his chair. At least I used to work for him! he thought glumly.

Steve was confounded. "I thought Jim Baines was involved with Debby Sherman?"

"That was only a brief fling I think. Jim and Bobby have been together for ages." Terry said wearily, no point hiding anything now. Sorry Jim - you are on your own! he thought.

Steve thought fast. Jim Baines has an affair with Debby Sherman - she dies, he goes back to the first mistress and then her husband dies too. Wow! Where was George Saunders? He ought to hear about this, and quick.

"Thank you Mr Matherson. You have been most helpful. I won't detain you any longer. Thank you for coming." He practically pushed the man out of the door and raced down to George Saunders' office. It was empty.

"Where's the boss?" he called urgently to the desk sergeant.

"Gone around to interview the widow in the Collins case. Do you want me to contact him?"

Bobby jumped up startled as George's mobile rang loudly shattering the silence.

George Saunders listened intently for a few moments. This certainly explained a lot. "Thank you. I'll be in shortly." He snapped the phone shut disconnecting the call and turned to Bobby.

"Robyn Collins, I am arresting you for the murder of your husband, Simon Philip Collins. I caution you that you do not have to say anything, but that anything you do say will be taken down and may be used in evidence against you. You may request the presence of a solicitor. If you cannot afford a solicitor, one will be appointed to you. Do you understand the charge?"

Bobby didn't answer - for the second time in one morning she had fainted.

Chapter 15

Melanie Knight was next for the shock treatment. Steve Clarke interviewed her at home. He tried to break the news to her a bit more gently, as he was fairly sure she was not involved, but never the less she found it equally upsetting.

"That can't be right!" she gasped. "Who would do such a thing? Simon was a pleasant and popular guy. No one would deliberately set out to harm him. Have you any idea who could possibly be involved?" She was visibly shaken. "Some sort of business deal or something?" It was the only thing she could think of to say. No one who knew him personally could ever harm him, far less actually murder him.

"I am sorry to have to inform you that we have, this morning, arrested his wife on suspicion of murder." He watched her face.

"Bobby? That is ridiculous! Why on earth would Bobby do such a thing?" She was genuinely astounded.

"I believe she is having a relationship with another man, it is our belief that she wanted to be free of her husband to pursue the relationship. Have you any knowledge of this?"

She had to be honest - it was too important to allow her to cover for them.

"Well I did suspect that something was going on - but I didn't think it was serious. I rather thought it was all just a game for them. I was always certain Bobby would never actually leave Simon."

"Well she won't have to now, will she?" commented Steve dryly.

"Mrs Knight," he began.

"Please call me Mel" she interrupted.

"Mel," he smiled. "When we spoke last time, following the death of Debby Sherman, I was under the impression that Jim Baines was having an affair with her. Am I right in this assumption?"

"Yes - well - that is, I think they were just starting something. I don't know how far it had gone, but I do know Debby was very interested in Jim. She told me as much herself. It was a sort of contest between her and Bobby I think, they were great rivals. Jim just enjoyed the attention - either way he won."

Mel remembered Halloween. Debby had won that round, but as it turned out hadn't been enough to prevent her desperate act.

"Of course, none of us knew what other problems Debby had. I suppose trying to get Jim was just a distraction to her. I guess it was just a way of taking her mind off her other worries. It is so sad really - there we all were wondering which one was going to get off with Jim, and all the time Debby was planning to kill herself. I would never have thought her capable of that."

"Jim seems to be quite a character." Steve murmured sarcastically. "Certainly a loyal chap, isn't he?"

"Jim is all right - just a big kid really. His trouble is he had never grown up. Joanna worships him, and he gets away with murder...." she gasped. "I didn't mean that exactly - oh you know what I mean - in Joanna's eyes he can do no wrong. What he needs is a woman who stands up to him. Deep down he is really quite a nice guy. He would do anything for you, you know."

Mel was genuinely very fond of Jim. She didn't approve of his lifestyle, but considered that was none of her business. She always hoped one day he would come to realise there was more to life than counting conquests.

"I take it you like the man?" Steve found that quite hard to comprehend.

"Oh yes. I know he is weak, but for all that, he isn't a bad person - there's no malice in him. I love him to bits but I'm glad he's not mine. He wouldn't deliberately hurt a soul. Actually he is a very likeable chap - he just needs to mature a bit!" She gave a wry smile.

"I'll take your word for that! However, to recap - Jim was involved in a fairly long term relationship with Bobby and merely had a brief fling with Debby?"

Steve was taking notes as they spoke.

"That's right - as far as I know." Mel was a very personable lady; most people found themselves confiding in her at one time or another. She was very discreet and did not divulge confidences. However, under the circumstances, she felt it her duty to reveal as much information as she could.

"Joanna knew nothing of either affair. He and Joanna appear to have quite a normal marriage to all intents and purposes." Steve didn't really find that too hard to believe. He used to be amazed at the sort of double life some people led, but after a few years in the job, he found himself quite blasé about it. He had once dealt with a bigamist who had two entire families - neither suspecting the other even existed.

"Right again, as far as I know." Joanna had certainly never voiced any suspicions to Mel about Jim.

He must be on Viagra! thought Steve, with a grin. Despite his disapproval - he had to admire the man's stamina!

Mel caught his look and despite everything found herself grinning back. "I bet I know what you are thinking! My husband always says whatever Jim is on - he wishes he had a bottle of it! Still I suppose they do say 'Variety is the spice of life!' Personally, I'd kill him if he were married to me! Oops - sorry - wrong thing to say!" she groaned "Oh God! I am sorry; I keep putting my foot in it today. Sorry - I'm afraid I'm just not used to this sort of thing."

Steve smiled. "Don't worry Mel; I would be most surprised if you were! You are absolutely sure that Joanna Baines did not know of her husband's behaviour? What about Simon Collins? Or Nick Sherman?"

"I don't know about Nick...." she frowned, "he was certainly very upset at Halloween. That was the night Jim went after Debby when she and Nick had a row and she stormed out," she explained quickly. "Nick was blind drunk, mind you, so I don't know how much he did realise - but it was pretty obvious to the rest of us what was going on! As for Simon hmm..." she paused for a moment and thought deeply. "I couldn't be sure. He was pretty sharp. I can't imagine much getting past him, but then again, I wouldn't swear to it. I think he indulged her quite a lot. Sort of turned a blind eye, if you know what I mean."

"So you don't think her husband discovering her affair would have been a problem for Bobby?"

"It may have been - but certainly not a great enough problem for her to commit murder! No, knowing Simon, he would probably have waited for it all to burn itself out. I can't imagine him making a public issue of it. He was a very conservative man who hated any sort of drama."

"I take it he would not have readily agreed to a divorce then?"

"Not unless it was handled very discreetly, but then Bobby would never have wanted one. As I said earlier, I am certain Bobby would never have left him. She was very bitter about divorce. Her parents are divorced, and her mother found life a bit of a struggle raising a family alone. She is quite hostile towards her father. She always said it would never happen to her. Bobby may give the appearance of being a tough lady, but underneath she is really quite vulnerable. I think that's why she has her little flings, boosts her confidence. I am quite sure none of it was that serious. The bottom line is that she loved her husband. I bet she is absolutely devastated by all this."

"What about Joanna? You say that, as far as you can tell, she never suspected anything was going on?" He had very mixed opinions of Bobby Collins, but he was convinced he had a fairly shrewd perception of Joanna Baines' character.

"Joanna? Never! - She can never see a fault in Jim. She…oh my God! I have just thought of something - does Joanna know about Bobby's arrest?" She panicked - this would destroy Joanna if Jim were implicated. "Is Jim under arrest too?"

"Not as far as I know. My superior officer is interviewing him at the station at this very moment. I'm going to see Joanna straight from here." He remembered from his last interview with this lady how concerned she was with Joanna's feelings, but unfortunately he had no choice now. The truth was bound to come out.

"I can assure you, Mel, I will be as tactful as possible - she is a nice lady" he added, surprising himself. He didn't usually make such personal observations. "Unfortunately, I am afraid in this case her husband's affair will undoubtedly become public knowledge."

"Can I come with you? She may need me." Mel was really worried how Joanna would react.

"I am afraid that will not be possible. I understand your concern, but my interview really should be conducted in private. I will however, be taking a female officer with me, should she need some assistance." He thanked Mel for her help, and left.

Mel wandered back into her kitchen and sat at the table for a long time, thinking. Would it have been possible for Bobby to murder Simon? She didn't think so, but then, who really knows what goes on behind closed doors? Darren arrived home for lunch. She told him the news and he was as concerned as she was.

"Well there is nothing we can do at the moment. Presumably she has got a solicitor and all that?" he asked.

"I don't know - I was so surprised, I didn't think to ask. Do you think we should ring the police station?" she wondered.

"I don't suppose they would tell us anything - we aren't family or anything. We could ring her mother?" He was as much at a loss as his wife. They stood looking at each other wondering what they should do.

"What if she hasn't heard? It would frighten her to death - oops sorry - poor choice of words," she replied. "I can't even email Bobby, apparently they have taken her computer looking for evidence."

"Well they're bound to find plenty of emails between her and Jim," commented Darren dryly.

"She hasn't been arrested for having an affair. I could send her a text. Do you think they would take her phone? Don't want to say anything they could twist about. I know - I will drop a note through her door asking her to ring me as soon as she gets in. That way at least she will know we are here for her. Do you think they will keep her long?"

"I have no idea. You don't think?" He hesitated to voice the doubt which was creeping in to his mind.

"No I do not! And neither should you! Bobby would never do such a thing! It is probably just that the police can't find anyone else, so they are going for her." She defended her friend stoutly.

"Well I can't think of anyone else either," thought Darren, but he was wise enough not to say so.

Mel was scribbling a quick note to Bobby.

"Right. I am going to drop this around to Bobby's house then carry on to work. I promised Mr Tanner I would pick up his stamps for him. We are going to carry on as normal until this whole mess is sorted out," she added defiantly.

News of Bobby's arrest spread like wildfire around the small village. Her friends treated it with total disbelief. One or two less charitable souls were more inclined to believe it.

"Well let's face it, she was much younger than him, wasn't she?" sniffed the village postmistress disapprovingly. "I think she is no better than she ought to be."

"She had the reputation of being a bit flighty, if you ask me." agreed her elderly customer, who was collecting her pension. "Of course I didn't actually know her myself, but I have seen her around. Always dressed very flashily, if you know what I mean. And she had a fancy car!" she added darkly.

"Fast car - fast morals I think," replied the postmistress, thoroughly enjoying the gossip.

"Actually, ladies..." interrupted Mel who was standing behind them in the queue. "Bobby Collins is a friend of mine, and I can assure you, you are both quite wrong. I hardly think dressing nicely, or being younger than your husband, is proof of murder. If everyone who drove a nice car murdered their husband the police wouldn't be able to keep up!" She turned and strode out. The village gallery where she worked was only next door, but by the time she got back she was shaking.

"Mel! Are you all right my dear? You look quite pale." The shop owner, Mr Tanner, came out from the back room. "Is anything wrong?" He was a kindly soul, and very fond of his assistant.

"Yes, I am all right, and no, nothing is wrong, thank you. I'm just a bit angry, that's all. Honestly, the way people gossip in this village - you would think they had nothing better to do!" She was fuming with indignation for her friend.

"Perhaps some of them haven't," suggested Mr Tanner. "And you must admit, my dear, we don't get such a scandal in the village every day!"

"The whole thing is ridiculous - of course Bobby didn't murder Simon. I've known them for years; she wouldn't do a thing like that. If she wanted to be rid of Simon she could have just divorced him. Divorce is certainly not unusual in this, or any other, village!" Bobby's views on divorce were not common knowledge, and she certainly didn't want to give the gossip mongers more ammunition.

"They do say he was rather well insured you know, and divorce is such an expensive business. Still, I am sure you know your friend far better than I do. If you think she is innocent, than I commend your loyalty. Now, did you get my stamps?"

"Sorry - I was so mad I left without them. I'll pop back later." Mel sighed. No one believed in Bobby. Was she being stupid to blindly defend her friend? No - she just couldn't see Bobby as a cold-blooded murderess. She just knew that Bobby was innocent.

She thought back to her own interview with Steve Clarke, had she made things worse for her friend? She didn't think so. She wondered how Joanna was getting on.

Chapter 16

When Joanna opened the door to Steve, he was again struck by her noticeable grief. She was obviously an emotional woman, who had cared deeply for her friends. WPC Shelagh Veitch, who accompanied him, had already been briefed on the situation. She gave her a reassuring smile and asked if she could perhaps make a cup of tea, while Steve and Joanna discussed a few things.

"Oh don't worry," smiled Joanna, "I can easily make some tea - it won't take a minute. You're not drowning in the stuff today then?" she added, remembering their last conversation.

"Haven't had time to drink one today." replied Steve, "it's been a bit hectic."

They went through to the bright and airy kitchen. Joanna loved this room; it had large windows overlooking her beloved garden. Along the windowsill she was growing herbs in little terracotta pots. The cupboards were in antique pine, and a large pine table was in the centre of the room.

"Why don't we sit in here?" suggested Shelagh. "It's such a pretty room." The kitchen had a welcoming feel to it and she hoped the soothing atmosphere would cushion the blow to Joanna when she learnt the news.

"Good idea - it's always nice and warm in here, and much cosier for a chat. Would you like some lunch? It must be getting on for lunchtime." She bustled around. "It wouldn't be any trouble."

"No thank you," replied Steve. "We had better get on with the interview first. It's just a formality, but we have to take statements from everyone who was connected with Mr Collins. I know you and he were good friends."

"Yes, we were very close," she sighed deeply, then straightened her shoulders; she must not let her emotions get the better of her again. This poor man had a job to do, and she wouldn't be helping him if she kept becoming hysterical. "Well I'll just put out some cake and biscuits then - in case you get peckish. I've got some mince pies around here somewhere..." her voice trailed off as she faced the larder and started rummaging around opening cake tins.

"No! I mean...don't bother on my account. I really should be watching my weight and I never can resist those things!" Steve replied quickly. He had lost his appetite for mince pies recently.

"Oh!" said Joanna, disappointed, she liked to be hospitable. "Are you quite sure? They're only shop bought I'm afraid. I haven't had time to bake this week. I took all my home baking to Debby's funeral last week. Her husband really couldn't cope - poor love. So we all took around a few bits and pieces. It was such a cold day too. You have to offer people something don't you? I mean, some of them had come quite a long way. A hot drink and a snack keeps the spirits up I always think." She chattered with a false brightness, trying to hide her sadness. She didn't want to embarrass the young policeman again.

"I'll have one, thank you," said Shelagh gratefully, "I haven't eaten all day and I'm starving. This close to Christmas I forget about the calories!" She had no qualms about eating mince pies. She knew the victim had been poisoned, but she did not know exactly how the poison had been administered, besides, she felt quite safe with Joanna Baines.

Joanna made the tea, and carried the tray over to the table. There was a pause while she poured the tea and laid out a couple of plates of biscuits and, of course, mince pies.

"Now, what can I do to help? I was very fond of Simon you know. I never even suspected he had heart trouble. He kept himself very fit." Her voice trembled as she added, "I did try to pump his chest to get his heart beating again when it happened, but it was no good. It was just so sudden."

"There was nothing you could have done. The paramedics couldn't revive him - even with all their equipment," Shelagh said gently. Those closest to a victim often felt a great sense of guilt that they had been unable to save them. She was used to dealing with emotions like that.

"I suppose it was the stress of the funeral. It was so sad - poor Debby - so very young." she wiped away a tear and sat looking thoughtful. First Debby - and now Simon, she thought sadly, what a waste of life.

Steve and Shelagh exchanged glances. Shelagh moved her chair discreetly closer to Joanna. She hadn't been able to catch Bobby when she fainted and she was determined not to fail again.

"Mrs Baines." Steve began gently. He hoped she would be able to handle the shocking truth.

"Oh call me Joanna. 'Mrs Baines' sounds like my mother-in -law! If you don't mind, of course," she added - were policemen supposed to remain on formal terms? She hadn't a clue.

"Joanna," smiled Steve. "I am afraid I have some rather distressing news for you. Simon Collins' heart attack was not brought on by natural causes. He was poisoned."

Joanna's reaction was painful to see. Her eyes opened very wide and she gave a little gasp. The news obviously hurt her.

"Oh! Oh, but that is not possible! Who would hurt Simon? He was a lovely man. Everyone liked Simon. No - no you are wrong! You must be! It was his heart! He just couldn't bear all that sorrow. Simon cared about everyone! He did! He was so upset at seeing Nick..." she burst into tears.

Shelagh comforted her. She looked over Joanna's shoulder at Steve. "Wait." she mouthed. She didn't want to hit Joanna with the news of Bobby's arrest straight away. She wanted to give her a chance to recover from the first shock.

"Joanna, I am so sorry to have to tell you, I know how hard it must be for you but at least he didn't suffer. It was very quick - he didn't know a thing about it. He never stood a chance. Really there was nothing anyone could have done." Steve tried to reassure the distraught woman.

"What was it then?" she looked up puzzled. "What could act so fast?"

"It was a deadly alkaloid. Very fast acting. There is no antidote for it." He was not at liberty to give away too much information - he was probably saying too much already, but he wanted to try and reassure her a little.

"Who could have got hold of such a thing? And why? I just don't understand. Was it some sort of business thing?" she looked bewildered. "Why would anyone want to kill Simon? It doesn't make any sense!"

"We have actually made an arrest...." began Steve.

"Thank God! Who - is it anybody I would know? What sort of a person would kill a man like Simon?" she spoke angrily.

"We have arrested Bobby Collins. She has not been charged - yet, but she is helping us with our enquiries."

"Bobby? Bobby Collins? No! No I'm afraid you are wrong there. Bobby would never hurt Simon. She loved him! They were a very close couple. No - no you must be wrong." She was stunned. Bobby kill Simon? Never. "What on earth makes you think she did it?"

"We have reason to believe she was seeing another man. It would appear that her marriage was not as happy as it seemed." He knew he ought to say who it was she was seeing, but he was avoiding it for as long as possible. Joanna was still trembling violently, and he was afraid of her reaction.

"Bobby? With another man? No, not really. Oh yes, she is a flirt. We've all seen her flirting, but I am sure there was never anything in it. What man? There isn't a man alive Bobby would leave Simon for! I remember her telling me once that she would never get divorced. She said divorce was a nasty, sordid, expensive business, and she was lucky she had Simon so she would never have to go through it. She told me that herself. So she must have been happy with Simon!" Suddenly she realised how her words could be interpreted, and she quickly added, "I mean, she said she was very happy with Simon and could never part from him. I don't mean that she wouldn't divorce him if she wanted to leave him. She didn't want to leave him. I mean...she disapproved of divorce but that doesn't mean...well, you know what I am trying to say," she finished lamely. She groaned inwardly, as she realised she had probably painted a very black picture of her friend.

"Oh no! I am saying all the wrong things. Don't listen to me! I am just trying to tell you that Bobby could not - and would not - have killed Simon! Honestly, she loved him! Truly she did!" she emphasised.

"Please don't upset yourself. We'll get to the bottom of all this. I'm sure Bobby appreciates your loyalty." It was very apparent that Joanna Baines had no idea of her husband's affair. Steve doubted that she would be able to assist him with his enquiries.

"Mrs Baines, Joanna, Simon ever talk to you about any worries he had? Perhaps mention any trouble he was having in his life - personal or professional?"

"No, he seemed quite content in every way. I know he and Bobby were very happy together." she added defiantly. "I saw him quite regularly, and he was always very cheerful, As a matter of fact, he was more concerned for me than for himself."

"In what way?"

"Oh, he was concerned that I was too soft-hearted, I think. He said he didn't want to see me hurt, and that he would always be there for me if I needed a friend."

"Was there anything specific which made him concerned for you?" Did Simon Collins know about his wife's affair? he wondered.

"Not really..." she hesitated; "he just had some silly ideas at times," she smiled. "You know how protective some men are!" The policeman seemed to be hinting at something. I wonder what he suspects? she thought warily.

"Was he perhaps concerned about you and Jim?" he asked casually.

"So that was it! Bobby and Simon must have discussed warning me about Debby. Bobby probably mentioned it to the police - but why should she mention that?" Joanna couldn't really see the connection; perhaps she just wanted to demonstrate what a nice guy Simon had been.

"He was a bit worried about Jim's flirting with Debby, Debby Sherman. I told him there was nothing in it, Jim flirts with everyone. It is just his way - it is all very innocent really." She decided she may as well tell the whole story. "Anyway," she continued, "Simon was worried I'd get the wrong idea and get all upset. It was very sweet of him, but there was no need. You see officer, I know my husband, he likes to play at being a Casanova type, but that is all it is - play! He would never be unfaithful to me."

"So you don't believe your husband was seeing Debby?" Steve asked. He found it hard to believe she could be that naive, especially since Jim had admitted to him that he had had an affair with Debby Sherman, but it was not his place to enlighten her.

"Good lord no! We were all just friends - that's all."

"And you have no reason to suspect your husband may be involved with... anyone else?" Steve persisted gently.

"Of course not! But why...? Oh I see! You don't think Jim is this mysterious other man in Bobby's life, do you?" Seeing the expression on the policeman's face she laughed. "So that's it! Poor Bobby gets arrested because my husband is such a terrible flirt! Well, I am afraid you are back to square one then. Jim and Bobby are definitely not having an affair!"

Chapter 17

"**Y**es! Bobby Collins and I are having an affair!" Jim admitted. It was obvious to him that the police knew all about it, so there was no point in lying. "That does not mean I would conspire with her to kill her husband though!" he added quickly. "It's really no big deal. Just a bit of fun. A bit of excitement. It's not serious."

George Saunders eyed the man suspiciously, he quickly formed the same opinion of him that Steve Clarke had - the man had the morals of an alley cat. Did that make him a murderer though? He didn't think so. It was quite apparent that Jim Baines was simply a philanderer. He really didn't think a man like that would get involved in anything as serious as this. It was far more likely that he was just after a casual affair.

"You won't tell my wife, will you?" begged Jim. "For her sake, I mean, I don't care about myself, but I would hate to see her hurt. She is a wonderful woman." He tried to look remorseful, but didn't quite succeed.

"Mr Baines, it is not my place to inform wives of their errant husbands. It is of no concern to me. I am however, deeply concerned at the moment, about the emotions of Mrs Collins. Would you say she was in love with you?" he asked sternly.

"I don't know. Well...I suppose so, she says she is, but I don't really know. You know what women are like. They tend to view things more seriously than they actually are." He remembered how clinging Bobby had been recently. Did she really love him? He hadn't given the matter that much thought.

"Seriously enough, shall we say, to kill their husbands?" George proposed, calmly.

"No! No I am sure she wouldn't do a thing like that." Jim replied nervously.

"Had she ever mentioned leaving her husband?" George kept his voice expressionless.

"No," Jim stated firmly.

"So you never discussed the possibility of a future together?"

Had they plotted together? Unlikely - but then Jim Baines seemed the type of man who would say anything to a woman to get her into bed.

"No," Jim was sure he was trying to suggest that they had planned something together, but he was not about to give him any grounds for his suspicions.

"I am not sure Mrs Collins is of the same opinion." George was not exactly lying. For all he knew, Bobby might not be of the same opinion - he was just trying to determine the truth in the relationship. Actually he had not as yet discussed this much with Bobby, who was, at that moment, downstairs being booked in.

Jim thought fast. What had she said? What had she told them? Sometimes in bed they had had silly conversations about setting up a love nest together, but it was only idle chat. It didn't mean anything. Jim just said whatever he thought Bobby wanted to hear.

"Well, she used to talk about what a good team we would make, but it was all just pillow talk. You know the sort of fantasies women weave," he said with a wry smile. He was trying to appeal to the chauvinistic side of the man facing him across the table. Trying to convince him that women pictured cosy little scenarios they had no intention of ever fulfilling.

"Therefore she never mentioned divorce." George Saunders was not impressed by his attempt at manly camaraderie.

"No, she didn't approve of divorce - said it was tacky," Jim said definitely. Bobby had actually said divorce was expensive and tacky, she had been quite bitter on the subject, but he left that bit out. He wanted to demonstrate that he and Bobby had never really imagined a future together.

"So, to recap - she talked of your future together, but said she would never divorce her husband?" George summarised.

"Yes!" replied Jim, firmly. "Well no! I mean... she didn't think we had a future together, because of Simon. I mean, well she wouldn't leave Simon. I mean...well she wouldn't want to leave Simon." Too late, he realised the trap he had walked into.

"Look, she never said anything about getting rid of Simon in any way," he stated categorically. This man was putting words into his mouth.

"So how did she think you would have a future together - a cosy little ménage a trois perhaps?" George asked sarcastically. "Of course - this is leaving aside the question of your wife too, but that is not my problem."

"We didn't really picture a future together," protested Jim.

"You said she did." He indicated the tape player on the desk. "Would you like me to rewind it and refresh your memory?"

"I mean she may have fantasised about us having a future together, but it was just a game - neither of us really believed it," he said wearily. What did he have to say to convince the man?

"Because of her husband?"

"Because it was not that serious a relationship."

"In your opinion."

"Yes"

"But not necessarily in hers. I see. Tell me Mr Baines, when you were having your cosy little chats, did she ever talk about her husband?" Seeming to end that particular line of questioning, he swiftly moved on to a new one.

"Sometimes," Jim replied cautiously, what was he getting at now? He wished he knew just what Bobby had told them.

"Would you say she loved her husband?" His voice betrayed nothing. He could have been asking if Jim thought it would rain today.

"Yes, I am sure she did," Jim affirmed. Bobby could not have killed Simon if she loved him.

"So much so that she slept with you?" George asked with a small smile.

"I told you, it was just a fling," Jim replied sulkily.

"Yes of course, so you said. Her husband was quite a bit older than her, wasn't he?" George changed his line of questioning yet again.

"A bit, I suppose. I never really thought about it."

"She never complained about that?"

"No, not really," he answered cagily.

"Perhaps she found him a bit boring occasionally?" George suggested, his tone light, as if he were just making a gentle observation.

"Well he was a bit meticulous, she used to find that a bit irritating I think." Jim replied in a similar tone, he had to say something. At least they were finally having more of a conversation. He wanted to build some sort of rapport with the man.

"Meticulous? Kept everything in order, did he?" His face suggested he would find this a bit irritating himself.

"Yes," Jim started to relax a bit, perhaps this man could sympathise with a young woman stuck with an older man.

"Kept the house all straight. Paperwork all up to date. That sort of thing?" George grinned at Jim. "Some people get a bit fussy about minor details."

"Yes, " agreed Jim, nodding vigorously. "A real stippler for paperwork was Simon."

"Well at least we don't need to check his car tax then!" George smiled benignly.

"Oh no! I don't think there are any worries there." Jim said expansively, "Tax, insurance - everything always well covered!" He stopped abruptly. "Car insurance I mean, I don't mean life insurance. I expect he had life insurance, but I don't know.... well...I wouldn't know, would I? None of my business. Bobby and I never discussed his insurance or anything, well it is not the sort of thing you discuss, is it? I mean, what would we want to discuss his insurance for?" He gave a nervous laugh. "That wouldn't interest us, would it? I mean, why should we care..." He gave up. He could see he was just digging himself a deeper and deeper hole.

"Quite." George replied crisply. "Thank you Mr Baines, you have been most helpful." He rose to his feet.

"Can I go now?" asked Jim eagerly. Thank God it is over! he thought, relieved at the prospect of getting away from all those awkward questions.

"Not just yet, if you wouldn't mind. I would appreciate you waiting here while I check a few details. Perhaps you would like a cup of tea, or a sandwich? It is getting on for lunchtime." He nodded to the police constable at the door.

Jim's heart sank - so it wasn't over yet.

George Saunders leaned over the desk and spoke directly into the tape player.

"Interview suspended, subject offered refreshments 1.20 p.m."

He switched off the tape player and walked out of the door.

Let him stew for a while, he thought with a smile. He walked down to the duty sergeant's desk.

"Arrange for some refreshments for our 'guest' in interview room 2, would you please?" He smiled at the desk sergeant. "I think he might need a cup of tea and a sandwich."

"Certainly sir, shall I bring you in one too?"

"No thanks, I think I'll let him eat alone - it might help his digestion. Where is Mrs. Collins?" He knew that Bobby must have been booked in by now.

"They have put her downstairs. She has sent for her brief, he said he'd be along a.s.a.p. I have arranged for some lunch for her. Don't want to give the brief any cause for a complaint."

"Good idea. Let me know when he arrives - I'll be in my office for about half an hour, then I am going back to finish off with Jim Baines. He should be quite anxious to speak to me by then."

It would be interesting to offer them both a mince pie, he thought, as he walked along the corridor, but decided that was probably not a good idea. I wouldn't mind watching their reactions though. The idea certainly had its merits.

Jim sat at the table and buried his head in his hands.

'Subject', he had called him 'Subject offered refreshments', that was him! He was pretty sure that 'subject' was just a euphemism for 'suspect'. They thought he had murdered Simon! He hadn't even known Simon had been murdered until he arrived here. Who would murder Simon? It seemed so far-fetched. No one would murder Simon - he was a nice guy. He racked his brains trying to make sense of it all. Bobby had been awfully clinging recently, he had thought that earlier. She said she wanted to run away with him. Was that because she had murdered Simon? Could she have murdered Simon? It seemed incredible - but who else could have done it. If she had, did that make him an accessory? He hadn't been involved, but would the police believe that? Would he be guilty just because he had given her a reason to kill her husband? No! That was ridiculous. It wasn't his fault. They hadn't conspired to kill Simon. If she had done it, she had done it alone - it was nothing to do with him. He didn't want to be implicated. If Bobby had read more in to their relationship than there was, that was not his fault.

Ten minutes passed, Jim began to sweat. "It's warm in here isn't it?" he said conversationally to the policeman at the door.

"Yes sir," replied the policeman, staring straight ahead.

There was a knock on the door and another policeman entered carrying a tray. On it were some sandwiches and a cup of tea.

"I'm not really hungry," Jim smiled desperately at the policeman, trying to invoke some response.

"I should have them if I were you sir, you never know how long these things could take." he replied grimly.

Jim chewed the sandwich miserably; he was having great difficulty swallowing.

"Look, uh... have you any idea how long that chap will be? I mean, my wife could be getting worried," Jim said nervously.

"We could contact your wife if you would like us to, sir. Inform her you are helping us with our enquiries. We wouldn't want the lady getting alarmed, sir."

"No, don't bother. I expect it won't take long now," Jim said, hopefully.

"As you wish, Sir. Let me know if you change your mind."

Jim blanched. 'Helping the police with their enquiries' that was what they said when they had caught someone. He heard it on the news all the time.

"Am I under arrest?" he asked, stunned by the expression the man had used.

"No sir, you are merely helping us with our enquiries."

"Oh" whispered Jim, not entirely sure what the difference was.

"Shouldn't I have a solicitor present?" he asked, remembering the various TV police programmes he had watched.

"If you feel it necessary, you are at liberty to request one. As you volunteered to come in and make a statement we did not know you wanted a solicitor present. Would you like me to make such arrangements?"

"No, no, not really. No reason for one, is there? No reason at all. As you say, I am just making a voluntary statement. No reason to bother with a solicitor and all that. I mean, that would be silly, wouldn't it? Why should I want a solicitor? No, no I was just wondering, that's all." He tried to look nonchalant - and failed dismally. He picked up another sandwich and started to chew slowly.

Chapter 18

Oliver Wilson, solicitor at law, felt very uncomfortable. He was trying to explain to Bobby Collins that this was not really his field. As the family solicitor, he dealt mainly with routine legal matters; contracts, wills, that sort of thing, but since he was the only solicitor she knew, he was the one she had called.

"You need a criminal solicitor for this. I wouldn't be a great deal of help to you," he stammered unhappily. She was a forceful woman, and he was rather nervous around her.

"It won't come to that. I am not a criminal for God's sake! Look, all I want is for you to be here with me today. Now - you say I have not been charged with anything?"

"That is correct, but you see..."

"But I have been arrested?" she interrupted. What the hell was the difference? she thought angrily.

"Yes - but they can only hold you for 24 hours. Actually, that is not quite correct, after 24 hours your case has to be reviewed by a Superintendent. He has to show reasonable cause to hold you for a further 12 hours. However, if they want to hold you for longer than 36 hours they have to go to court and get official permission - though this is rarely granted without strong evidence or previous history etc. If you were considered a danger to the public, for example. Unless of course, they come up with sufficient evidence to charge you, and then...." he began to warm to the subject.

"They will not come up with 'sufficient evidence', because there is not any evidence to come up with - sufficient or otherwise," Bobby interrupted coldly. "If you don't mind, Oliver, I would appreciate a little support here!" At first she had felt frightened and confused; she just wanted to grieve for Simon. She wanted to be left alone. Now she was beginning to feel a cold rage. How dare they arrest her! They had nothing on her. The police were obviously clutching at straws - they had no suspects, so they brought in the wife. As good a place to start as anywhere.

"I want you to keep me informed of my rights for now, that is all. I very much doubt that this stupid accusation will go any further. However, if, for some incredible reason it does go any further, then I will rely upon you to procure for me the best criminal solicitor or barrister - or whatever the damn person is called - that money can buy! Do I make myself clear? I am completely innocent. There is absolutely no way the police can prove anything against me. What I intend to avoid is this thing becoming any more public than it has to. If I start out by bringing in fancy lawyers, how will that look? I will never be able to show my face in public again. No - you are the family solicitor, and you will handle it, just as you would handle any other family crisis."

"I don't think you realise just how grave this situation is Bobby!" pleaded Oliver. He had known Bobby and Simon for several years, and knew full well how stubborn she could be. This matter was rather more serious than suing the local dry cleaners for ruining a dress. "The accusations against you are the most serious there are. Bobby, please - be reasonable. You need the proper help."

"Oliver - they have no case! How many times do I have to tell you? There is no way on this earth they can even accuse me of such a ridiculous charge. Why would I kill Simon? I was his wife, for God's sake! I loved him. I would never harm him. What possible reason would I have?" That was true, she did love Simon. She felt bereft without him. Oliver Wilson, however, did not know that she had indeed had reason to kill Simon, a very powerful reason to kill him. She still mourned him though - they had once been very happy together, and despite her relationship with Jim, she would always love Simon in her own way.

"Bobby..." Oliver hesitated, "you will have to be completely honest with me. You must have some idea what the police suspect you of. Was there anything wrong between you and Simon? Could you have been overheard arguing publicly perhaps?" There had to be some grounds for the arrest.

"Certainly not! What do you take me for? Can you honestly imagine Simon and me brawling in public? Don't be ridiculous!" she snapped at him. Simon hated any kind of public scene - Oliver knew them well enough to know that.

"I am only trying to think of a reason for the arrest. Did you have any financial problems?" Did the police think she had murdered him for his money? Simon had been a wealthy man - it was a fairly plausible reason.

"No - Simon gave me anything I wanted. You know that. Money was never a problem between us." She started to panic, Steady Bobby, she told herself, you can get through this. Remember how angry you are - don't think of the sorrow - don't be weak. She took a deep breath. "They will be coming for us any minute - what do I do? What am I supposed to say?"

Oliver sighed - this was not going to be easy. He was not going to know what the grounds were until the interviewing officer questioned her. How could he prepare for that? He felt sure there was something she was not telling him.

"Have it your way then Bobby. I suggest you are open and honest with them. You say you have nothing to hide..." he noticed her furious expression, "I mean, you have nothing to hide, so just answer their questions as fully as possible. Do not try and conceal anything from them. It will only make things worse in the long run. Naturally, I can intercede, and warn you against answering any questions which I fear may prejudice your case, but... since you are so sure they cannot ask you anything you don't want to discuss..." he shrugged, "I suppose you will just have to be totally honest. You don't have to answer them though. I should advise you of that. You can choose not to answer - but of course I cannot say how that would look."

Bobby started pacing up and down the interview room.

"Well, they are certainly taking their time. The sooner we get on with it the sooner I can be home and put this whole thing behind me." Suddenly she thought of Simon, and her eyes filled with tears. No! she forced herself not to cry, Come on Bobby - you can do this! Focus on the anger. She realised that by concentrating on her anger she was helping herself get through her grief. Anger was a powerful emotion, and it was driving her now. She hoped it would be enough.

The door opened and Detective Inspector George Saunders entered. He sat at the desk opposite Bobby and Oliver and switched on the tape recorder.

"Interview with Mrs Robyn Collins. 2.00 p.m. 17th December. Mrs Collins' solicitor is present." He gave the basic information and than sat back and looked at Bobby.

"Right Mrs Collins, you understand that you have been arrested in connection with the death of your husband, Simon Philip Collins?"

"Yes." Bobby spoke calmly and clearly. She was determined to get through this ordeal with dignity. They would not break her - she was tough. Despite her grief, she would not break down in front of this grim faced man.

"For the record, you have not as yet been charged with any offence. At present you are helping us with our enquiries."

"So I have been led to believe. However, I fail to understand how I can be expected to help you. I know nothing of the circumstances surrounding my husband's death," she stated distinctly.

He ignored her remark. She was certainly a cool customer; he had to admit that much. Was she that callous, or was it just a facade she was hiding behind? He could see she was struggling to keep her composure - but was it grief or guilt?

"Mrs Collins. Would you describe for me please, the relationship you had with your husband," he started with the basics.

Bobby looked puzzled, what did he mean? Their relationship was obvious.

"He was my husband - that was our relationship. We were a normal married couple." She forced herself not to think about the happy times they had had together. She had to remain calm - a lot depended on it.

"How long had you been married?"

"Five years."

"Would you say it was a happy marriage?"

"Yes," she swallowed, struggling to keep her emotions in check, "yes, we were very happy together."

"Mrs Collins, when we spoke this morning, you were adamant that your husband was not in any way involved with another woman."

"That is true. Simon would never cheat on me. I told you - we were very happy together." Surely he wasn't back on that line again. She had said it often enough. If he thought she had killed Simon out of jealousy - he was very much mistaken.

"Since our conversation this morning certain information has come to light. Information concerning you and another party. Would you perhaps care to comment?"

So that was it! Oliver was not really surprised though. He had often thought Bobby and Simon were ill matched. Still, that did not make her a murderess.

"My client has the right to know just what information you are alluding to," he interjected. Actually, he was quite proud of himself, it sounded very good. Maybe he ought to go back to this side of law - it was certainly more interesting than drawing up wills.

Bobby's face was crimson. So this is what it is all about, she thought. Shit - who told them?

"We are currently questioning a certain James Baines who is, I believe, well acquainted with your client," George said calmly, addressing Oliver Wilson.

"All right!" Bobby said defiantly, "I am having an affair with Jim Baines, but that doesn't mean I killed my husband. Simon knew nothing of my relationship with Jim."

"Would you say it was a serious relationship, or merely a brief affair?"

"I am not in the habit of indulging in casual affairs, if that is what you mean!" He made her sound like some sort of slut.

"So your relationship with Mr Baines is of some importance to you? You are, shall we say, extremely fond of him?"

"Yes, but that still doesn't mean I didn't love my husband."

"Surely it must be rather, er.... inconvenient for you, having two such great loves in your life?" George asked with mild sarcasm.

"I managed quite well. I do not believe I am unique in this."

"No, I am quite sure you are not. Mr Baines, it would appear, must be quite an expert in juggling er...partners. I understand he has a wife, and until recently was also quite involved with another friend of yours – Debby Sherman." He waited for her reaction.

Bobby's eyes narrowed. The bastard! she thought. What had he told them?

"I was not aware Jim was involved with Debby Sherman. I was under the impression that was just unsubstantiated rumour."

"You are, however, aware he has a wife?"

"Of course. I know them both well. I was not aware I was being held on a question of my moral standing."

"I am just trying to ascertain how serious the relationship is, and whether it would be just cause for you to conspire to murder your husband." George replied matter of factly.

"I can assure you I did not murder my husband. Jim and I were lovers, but we certainly did not conspire to kill Simon."

"Did you and Mr Baines ever discuss a future together?" George asked casually.

"Not really." Bobby replied warily, what had Jim told him?

"Mr Baines seems to be under the impression that you had."

"Well we may have idly discussed it, but not in any great seriousness." Thanks Jim! she thought, bitterly.

"I see. Tell me Mrs Collins - what are your views on divorce...?

Chapter 19

*B*obby was held for twenty-three hours and forty-five minutes. It was a deliberate ploy by George Saunders to break through her composure - but it failed. She was interviewed several times but she still stuck firmly to her story. She remained resolute throughout. She had no idea who would have wanted to kill her husband. She was not involved in any way. Reluctantly, Detective Inspector Saunders released her – 'pending further investigations'.

"What did you think?" George asked Steve wearily. Steve had been present at some of the interviews with Bobby Collins.

"I just don't know, sir" he sighed. "She is certainly a tough lady." He remembered the first time he had met her, and how he had ended up being impressed by her concern for her friend. Ironic now, when it turned out she too, was having an affair with the friend's husband.

"You can say that again! She didn't waver once. She certainly seemed upset at his death though," he looked thoughtful, "either she is a bloody good actress, or she genuinely cared for the man - which?"

"I think she did care for him. That doesn't mean she didn't kill him though. She certainly fooled me, when I first met her." Steve explained how Bobby had appeared so worried about Joanna, when all the time she was carrying on with Jim herself.

"Perhaps she wanted you to tell the wife so she would throw him out, leaving only her husband as an obstacle. How serious do you think this thing with Jim Baines is?" asked George.

"Personally, I can't imagine what she sees in him - the guy is an absolute creep. I certainly don't think he was serious about her. Seemed more concerned that his wife didn't find out. She seems quite besotted with him though. They do say there is no accounting for taste - or lack of." Steve had not been impressed the first time he had met Jim and he was even less so now.

"Yes, I got the impression it was a bit one-sided too. When I went back to him after I'd left him to stew for a while, I think he would have said anything to clear himself. He certainly was not about to stand by the girlfriend." He grinned as he recalled how panic-stricken Jim had become. He had been pathetically grateful when George sent him home.

"Still," George continued, "even if she had wanted the wife to throw him out, leaving him free - she could just have divorced the husband - she didn't need to kill him."

"Quite a few people have said that she didn't approve of divorce." Steve pointed out.

"Yes, she told me so herself, but it's one thing to disapprove of divorce. It is still quite a drastic step to kill your husband to avoid one."

"Money?" suggested Steve, running through the various possibilities. "Would she have got much of a settlement if they divorced? They had no kids remember. I would think she is a lady who likes her creature comforts. She doesn't strike me as the 'love in a garret' type."

"True. Jim Baines doesn't seem short of money though. He has a good job, doesn't he? I seem to recall reading somewhere in your notes that he was Matheson's boss. He must be quite high up in the company."

"Great job - in line for running the company when his boss retires. Unfortunately, his boss is also his father-in-law. I think his prospects might take a tumble if his wife threw him out."

"Ah! Yes - I can see that could pose quite a problem. That gives even more basis to suggest Bobby Collins, possibly with Jim Baines, but it is proving it that will be the problem. If that is the situation I would be rather concerned about the safety of Joanna Baines too," replied George.

"Surely they wouldn't risk another move now - not with us watching for it. I certainly can't imagine Jim Baines killing his wife. He was terrified of losing her - whether it was for his job's sake I wouldn't know, but even so - I just can't see him involved." Steve liked Joanna, and disliked the idea of her being in any danger.

"I would agree with you there. It is more likely to be Bobby Collins acting alone. I think if Jim Baines knew anything he would have told us. Trouble is -I don't know for sure - at the moment we have absolutely no proof. If we can't prove it there is not a lot we can do. I agree it would be foolhardy at the moment to kill again but..." he shook his head, "we simply don't know what we are dealing with here. The killer or killers may not be thinking rationally. We need to get some concrete evidence - and fast - I have a bad feeling about this."

"What about forensics? Have you heard anything from them yet, sir?" The forensic people were going through Bobby's house while she was being interviewed. They were extremely thorough.

"Not really - she had been baking recently. There were traces of flour on the kitchen counter, but that doesn't mean much. She admitted she made some things for the funeral. She volunteered the information that she had made..." he checked his notes, "sausage rolls, mince pies, sandwiches and a cake."

"They must have done well for food at that thing - Karen Matherson, Melanie Knight and Joanna Baines all made virtually the same. They didn't turn up anything else then?" Steve was disappointed - the forensic team were usually very good at turning up even the smallest clue. It was often the tiny things that broke the case.

"No - nothing. They took away a jar of mincemeat but it was fine. They even found a tin containing some mince pies - but they were all perfectly good."

"So where do we go from here?"

"We carry on interviewing. I am still not entirely happy about that suicide case though. I have checked through your notes of the interviews, and I have to agree with you, but I feel sure we are missing something. Who was the pathologist?"

"Malcolm Young," replied Steve.

"Oh he's back is he? I remember him going off to the Bahamas, or was it Barbados? Somewhere exotic anyway. He's pretty sharp - if there was anything suspect, he would have spotted it. Seems one hell of a coincidence though, doesn't it? It must strike you as odd."

"Well it does now. At the time of course, it all seemed quite straight forward."

"She admitted taking the stuff? She didn't leave a note though?"

"The paramedic asked her if she had taken them - she admitted it to him. She didn't leave a note - and everyone was very surprised. Still they usually are - aren't they?"

"They usually say they are - but there are usually one or two people who suspected it was likely. You didn't turn up anyone who thought she might top herself?"

"No - everyone agreed she was not the type."

"Okay we go back through all the notes of the case. Check back with Malcolm and see if there was any way it could have been foul play."

"I did ask him at the time - just a matter of routine. He said she had taken about thirty tablets. He couldn't see how anyone could slip her that many."

"What about the food? It was after a dinner party wasn't it? Could they have been in her food?"

"No. He checked the food. Nothing toxic. You know Malcolm and his stomach content analysis!" Malcolm was renowned for his macabre sense of humour.

"Oh yes - I was forgetting - enjoys his work doesn't he? Okay. So it wasn't in the food - how about the drinks?"

"Not that many tablets though, sir, it just doesn't make sense. There is simply no way to hide that many pills. Even if she was drinking like a fish - you couldn't put more than two in per drink, without her tasting them - and I can't see her getting through fifteen drinks in one evening."

"I know - maybe I am clutching at straws. I am just trying to see if it was possible. Who did pour the drinks - do we know?"

"Well the dinner was held at Simon and Bobby Collins' house - presumably one of them did. Of course he is dead now so we can't ask him. I'll check with Bobby Collins."

"That's a good idea anyway. Find out exactly what Debby Sherman ate and drank at that dinner. I want to keep the pressure up on Bobby Collins. She is the only one with a motive so far. There has got to be a connection somewhere. The murder occurred at the funeral. There must be a link. We have just got to find it. I am sure we are missing something. Concentrate on the group of friends. Have we seen them all?"

"Yes sir, I drove down to Kent yesterday and spoke to Nick Sherman. I think we can definitely rule him out. He is on the verge of a nervous breakdown. He did keep repeating that he couldn't believe his wife killed herself though. He couldn't tell me anything about Simon Collins. He was shocked by the murder, as they all were, but he couldn't think of any reason. He is just about to crack up completely though, so I don't think he'll be much use to us."

"I saw him at the funeral - I am inclined to agree with you there. Who else is there?" George remembered Nick from his wife's funeral. The man was obviously a nervous wreck.

"You saw my notes on the interview with Karen Matherson? She couldn't help either. She works up in town every day and commutes, so she is not quite as close as the others. Her husband works with Jim, so she does get a bit of inside info on him - but it is mainly just gossip. She knew about Jim being something of a ladies' man, but didn't consider it as being serious. Neither did she believe that Bobby Collins would be capable of murder."

"What about Joanna Baines?" asked George.

"Nice lady. Bit thick though. Believes every word her husband says. She is in the clear though, isn't she? I mean, she is hardly likely to kill the girlfriend's husband is she? That leaves the path clear for her husband and the girlfriend. Anyway, I have met her couple of times and she was very fond of Simon Collins. Quite upset by both the deaths. Soft hearted type."

"She would have a motive to kill Debby Sherman though." George said thoughtfully.

"Not really - she didn't know about it. Anyway, I thought we had established that death as suicide?"

"I guess so - I am just not entirely convinced that's all. Still I suppose you are right, Joanna Baines certainly had no motive to kill Simon Collins. Who does that leave?"

Steve checked his notes - "Well of the original group of ten, two are dead and we have spoken to the rest. Mel Knight was stunned by the news, she is adamant that Bobby Collins is innocent. She also knew of the affair, but again did not think it was serious. She did, however, confirm that Bobby Collins was totally opposed to divorce. Might have some bearing?"

"I don't think I talked to her. What about Darren Knight? I can't remember meeting him either."

"He was at the funeral - big chap, sandy hair. Remember him? Oh no - hang on, let me just check...." he flipped back through his notes, "no, you didn't meet him. He and his wife went to the hospital to help Bobby. They hadn't returned when we arrived. I saw him a few days before. I spoke to him again yesterday - after he had heard the news unfortunately, so I didn't get his immediate reaction. He was certainly shocked though. He was perhaps a little less convinced than his wife about Bobby's innocence. He said he was, but I thought I could spot a bit of indecision. He did say he couldn't think of anyone else who could have done it though. I think he has a few doubts about the lovely Bobby!"

"Don't we all? What is he like?" Not having met the man personally, George wanted to get a better picture of him.

"Decent enough chap. Very straight forward. He seemed genuinely concerned about Bobby, but I did not get the impression he was interested in her sexually. Happily married, two kids - usual kind of family life. He too was very worried about the effect of all this on Joanna Baines. He wasn't sure how she would cope with it all."

"He knew of the affair?"

"Oh yes - I think everyone apart from the wife knew about it."

"Often the way." George reflected.

"Yes - and she still doesn't believe it. At least she didn't when I spoke to her - she may have had her eyes opened by now."

Chapter 20

*"W*ell I don't care what anyone says - I know my own husband! If he tells me there is nothing in it - then I believe him. You know Jim, Mel. He even flirts with you, doesn't he? Jim flirts with everyone! You don't think there is anything in all this do you?" Joanna pleaded to Mel.

Taking advantage of the Christmas break both were at late morning Contours class.

"Jim certainly flirts with me!" Mel laughed "and I can assure you there is nothing in that. Just ignore them, Joanna - you know what gossips are like. This is a small village and everyone thinks they know everyone else's business. Don't let it get to you!" She got out of that quite neatly, she thought.

"Change stations now," the automated instruction neatly interrupted them.

"Is it true then?" asked another class member, Naomi. "I heard someone say Bobby's husband had died. I thought it was a heart attack."

"Well I heard Bobby had been arrested and practically confessed, " declared another.

"Ladies please remember we chat on the resting stations. " It was a wasted plea.

"I feel so sorry for Bobby. It is too ridiculous for words. Bobby would never kill her husband. It doesn't make any sense. The police just haven't got a clue if you ask me, and they are desperate to pin it on someone." Joanna stated firmly.

"Well if she did she can do mine next!" one of the regulars called over causing a burst of laughter.

"It could not have been Bobby – no way – come on we all know her and it's just not possible." Naomi was adamant in defending their regular classmate.

"I certainly agree with you there. The whole thing is crazy! The only thing I just cannot fathom is - who on earth did kill Simon? I still can't believe he was murdered! Why would anyone kill Simon?" Mel was sure Bobby was innocent too.

"God knows! Perhaps it was some sort of business thing. That is the only thing I can think of. Still, no doubt the police will find out eventually - once they get over the idea that Bobby did it. This is our last one isn't it?" Joanna checked the clock.

"Yes come on we'd better get back I promised Darren I'd come straight back so he could join the fellas in the pub."

Half an hour later two friends were sitting in Joanna's kitchen. It was a couple of days after Christmas. Darren had walked up to the local pub and the children were out playing in the garden.

"Is anyone else coming over?" She walked over to the window and checked on the children. Joanna and Jim had a large garden and the children were having a great time playing with their new toys outside.

"Yes, I invited Terry and Karen, and Bobby. I think it is very important that she knows we are all behind her in this."

She handed Mel a coffee. "Are the children all right?"

"Fine - they needed a bit of fresh air. It's a lovely day and they are wrapped up warmly. You are right about Bobby though, it must be awful for her." She thought of Bobby - all the talk in the village must be really getting to her.

"I hope she comes - I did invite her to spend Christmas with us, but she wouldn't. It must be very hard for her at the moment, especially being Christmas as well. I wonder how Nick is coping." Nick was still down in Kent with his family.

"I haven't heard. I was going to ring, but his parents rang me the other night. They were very nice, but they told me they didn't think it would be a good idea to have any contact from here at the moment, in case it upsets him further. He is pretty near the edge you know."

"How dreadful. I do feel so sorry for him. Mind you he's young - he'll get over it eventually. Let's hope, in time, he meets someone else and remarries." Joanna paused thoughtfully "I wonder if Bobby will remarry?"

The doorbell saved Mel from answering. It was Karen and Terry. The friends exchanged greetings. Terry hurried straight off to join the men at the pub - Karen sat down in the cosy kitchen with her friends.

"Did you have a good Christmas?" she asked, "I mean, well.... under the circumstances."

"We did - I feel a bit guilty saying it, but of course when you have children in the house, Christmas can't just be ignored." Mel replied.

"We popped over to Bobby's on Christmas day for a drink. We did try to talk her in to coming back with us for a meal, but she wouldn't. I was just telling Mel, I'm hoping she will join us today, she needs to get out more." Joanna looked concerned.

The doorbell rang again - to everyone's surprise it was Bobby. She came in bearing a large bottle of wine.

"Hello everyone - sorry I am late. I brought a bottle of Christmas cheer with me. Thought we might need it!" She had actually already had several drinks, which prompted her to join the gathering. "I have decided I have hidden myself away too long. I was going crazy rattling around in that big house all alone." She had an air of forced gaiety about her that was quite alarming.

The men arrived back - they too had consumed a fair amount of alcohol, and were slightly the worse for wear. They had all been discussing the sudden death of their friend and deciding on whether or not Bobby could have done it. When they staggered in to the kitchen and saw Bobby sitting there they all looked guilty.

"Bobby!" cried Darren, "how the devil are you? We were all just wondering how you were getting on, weren't we lads?" His speech was slightly slurred.

"That's right," they chorused.

"I can imagine." Bobby replied dryly. It was pretty obvious they had all been talking about her. Jim couldn't even look her in the eye. He hadn't been near her since she was arrested, and she was furious about it.

"No. It's true. We have all been really worried about you. Would you like a drink?" Jim asked anxiously. He hoped she wouldn't make a scene here; he had just about managed to convince Joanna that everyone was wrong in their suspicions.

"I think you've had quite enough already," Joanna remarked.

"Well why not? It is Christmas, and you should have a drink at Christmas. Celebrate while you can! That is what I say, after all you are a long time dea...umm I mean... you don't know how long you...well, that is to say..." Terry's voice faded away into an embarrassed silence.

Karen groaned. "Please excuse my husband - he never could hold his drink, and unfortunately he does tend to engage his mouth before his brain is fully in gear."

"Don't worry about it. Look, this is silly; we have all been friends for years. Please - there is no need to feel embarrassed around me. I can assure you I did not kill Simon, and I appreciate your support, but there is no need to feel uncomfortable around me. I'll go if you think it would be better. I do understand."

"Don't be silly. We all want you here. You're right - there is no need to feel embarrassed around you. It's just that we are all afraid of saying the wrong thing. So now we have got it out in the open, we can all forget it. We all know things are not the same without Simon - or Debby and Nick - but for today let's just try to relax and forget our troubles. Let's have a drink. We can drink to them all and then, just for today, we can pretend none of this has happened. We all need a break. What do you say?" Joanna turned to the group.

They all quickly agreed. Joanna went to get some glasses from the dining room - Jim went for a corkscrew. Everyone talked at once to cover the awkward moment.

"You might have 'phoned me!" hissed Bobby, as she held the glasses for Jim to pour the wine into. Joanna was handing around some snacks.

"I couldn't - everyone is watching me. Look, we can't discuss this now," whispered Jim, glancing around nervously.

"When then?"

"I don't know - look, the police may even be watching your house for all I know!"

"Don't be so melodramatic! I must see you Jim."

"I'll ring you - leave it for now." He walked quickly away.

Bobby was absolutely livid. The bastard! He is going to drop me like a rock! How dare he? She took a deep breath; she would not give him the satisfaction of knowing how much he had hurt her. She had her pride. It was about all she did have now. Suddenly an idea occurred to her.

"Looking forward to your birthday Darren?" she asked with a brittle smile.

"Don't remind me. Another year older. It's all right for you ladies - you never look any older, we men have to suffer the pains of aging!" he groaned.

"Rubbish! Everyone knows men only look more distinguished as they get older. It's women who have to suffer! When was the last time you had your legs waxed?" Bobby laughed.

"Ah! I know something about that!" he remembered "You have them done every six weeks, and you never have them done twice in a week!" he triumphantly announced, pleased with his memory - unfortunately he then remembered that was the excuse Bobby had used for meeting Jim. Oops! he thought, trust me to remember that!

"Well done Darren, I am impressed - thinking of going in to the beauty business are you?" asked Joanna, oblivious to his discomfort.

"I er... I saw it on the TV the other day! It is funny what sticks in your mind, isn't it?" He gave a sheepish grin. His wife shot him an exasperated look.

"You were all supposed to be coming to me for dinner that night." Bobby looked wistful.

"That's right. You promised me a beef Wellington!" Darren declared, trying to make amends for his earlier error.

"I don't suppose anyone will be eating at my house for a while, not that I blame them." Bobby said quietly.

"Well we wouldn't want to intrude...." began Terry.

"Oh shut up Terry!" Karen interrupted, "We would all love to come to dinner - if it won't be too much trouble, of course."

"Yes - I think that will be a wonderful idea!" Joanna enthused. "It is not for a couple of weeks - by that time we will all probably be glad of the chance of a break."

"We can all bring something - you won't want to be too tied to the kitchen, Bobby" Mel added.

"That's a good idea Mel; it will be like old times. We can all get together and decide what to make." Karen was really beginning to warm to the idea.

"It's not that we don't miss the others, but we have to put this dreadful business behind us and go on. Simon wouldn't want us to be miserable for ever. This will be a good opportunity to show the world that we are all behind you Bobby. To hell with the gossips!" Joanna declared.

"You don't think it might seem a bit.... well...disrespectful?" suggested Jim tentatively.

"That's true" said Darren quickly, "after all, we wouldn't want to start the gossip going again just when it started to ease a bit..."

"Don't worry, I understand if you wouldn't feel comfortable coming around for a meal. We can celebrate your birthday some other way Darren." Bobby smiled and looked sadly at her friends.

"Nonsense! We would all love to come around - wouldn't we everyone?" Joanna looked encouragingly around.

"Yes, yes of course we would," Mel said smiling

"Looking forward to it" said Karen, beaming around the group, she nudged Terry sharply.

"Wouldn't miss it," Terry agreed quickly, glancing at his wife.

"Great idea," chimed in Darren, although with a little less enthusiasm then usual.

"Sounds wonderful," muttered Jim.

"Well, if you are all sure? That's settled then. January 19th at my house. I'll cook everything though, it'll keep me busy and we will all have a nice quiet dinner together." She smiled at Jim; her expression reminded him of the smile Inspector Saunders had given him when he had accidentally mentioned insurance.

Chapter 21

*T*he inquest on the death of Simon Philip Collins was opened on the 4th January, the formalities were observed and the inquest was promptly adjourned. The body was, however, released for burial.

On the 10th January the funeral of Simon Collins took place. It was a bright and sunny day. The mourners filed into the church. William Owens, the village Rector, shook hands with everyone as they arrived. He was a gentle, friendly man. He had lived in the village for many years and was well loved and respected. He often called in on his various parishioners just for a friendly chat. He didn't put any pressure on them to attend church, and regardless of religious persuasion he was equally amiable to all. He was renowned for always having a smile and a quip for everyone. Today however, he was having great difficulty in finding the right words to say to his congregation as they arrived.

By now, everyone knew that Simon had been murdered. They also knew that the police had been unable to discover the identity of the murderer. Each person present had their own ideas. Quite a few cast disapproving looks towards Bobby as she walked down the main aisle of the church towards the front pew.

Bobby stood tall, her head held high. She would not give those malicious gossips the satisfaction of seeing how they hurt her. She had loved Simon. She knew it, and anything else that had occurred was none of their business anyway. She was dressed entirely in black - even down to wearing all concealing dark glasses. It was a bit over the top but she felt safe behind them. No one could see her eyes properly and she felt more comfortable that way.

Joanna and Mel walked either side of Bobby. Morally supporting her every step. They looked defiantly around the church, as if daring anyone to put into words what they were all obviously thinking.

Simon's parents were already seated in the front row. An elderly couple, they had had their only child late in life. They were totally overwhelmed by his sudden and tragic death, and were completely bewildered by the entire situation. They simply could not imagine why anyone would want to harm their beloved son. Now they sat, in mourning clothes, holding hands together tightly for support. Bobby hugged them both before taking her seat in the front pew alongside them. They smiled gratefully at her. They knew nothing of their daughter-in-law's possible involvement in their son's death. Living a distance away, although they kept in contact, they were not familiar with the couple's daily life.

The close friends sat in the second pew. Mel sat directly behind Bobby and squeezed her shoulder in a gesture of support. Bobby glanced back and smiled her gratitude. The congregation stood as the coffin was brought in.

William Owens walked up the steps into the ancient wooden pulpit to give his address. He was deeply troubled, knowing the circumstances of the death. He was also acutely aware that the murderer may well be in the church at that very moment. A kindly soul, he hated to think that anyone could deliberately do such a terrible thing. He was also worried that the gossip surrounding Bobby Collins would turn into some sort of witch-hunt.

"Friends," he began, looking across at the sea of sad faces, "we are here today to say goodbye to Simon Collins. I knew Simon quite well and he was a kind man. He always had time for a chat when I called in to see him and his lovely wife Bobby." He smiled down at Bobby. "Today is especially sad because Simon was such a young man. We do not know what terrible motive caused someone to take Simon's life. That is not for us to judge. There is only One who knows the secrets of every heart. God alone will be the One to whom that person answers. We must all pray for Simon's soul, and for the soul of the poor lost sinner who committed such a terrible act. Judge not ye lest ye yourself be judged. He paused and looked around the congregation. "Let us thank God for Simon's life, for the memories we have of him, and for the love and friendship which he brought into our lives. I am sure that all of us here will miss Simon. Whether we knew him from his home or from his business life, we shall all treasure our own memories. I am also sure that each of us will offer our full support and comfort to his family in their grief. Let us pray."

Later, as everyone left the church and made their way to the small cemetery he hugged Bobby briefly. "If you want to come and see me, or if you want me to come and talk to you, let me know. I am here for you."

"Thank you Bill, it was a lovely service. I do appreciate your kindness." She dabbed at her eyes with a lacy handkerchief. "I will be in touch." She gave a wan smile and moved on.

Back at the house the mourners stood around in awkward groups. Steve Clarke was there with WPC Shelagh Veitch; both were dressed in plain clothes. They hoped to merge in with the mourners and keep a watchful eye on those attending. Like William Owens, they too suspected that the murderer was among those present. The food went largely untouched. Everyone felt extremely uncomfortable.

"Why did you have to say that about us coming to dinner?" murmured Darren to Mel. "I don't want to spend my birthday worrying about what's in my food, thank you very much!"

"Don't be ridiculous! The only health problem you are likely to incur is indigestion - from eating too much. Who would want to murder you?" Mel replied quietly.

"I bet that's what Simon thought!" retorted Darren.

"You don't honestly believe Bobby had anything to do with it, do you?" Mel whispered urgently.

"I just don't know. Can you think of anyone else?"

"We don't know what went on in his business life - do we?"

"Oh come on - he was an architect - not the leader of MI5!"

"We don't really know what he did. He may have had an entirely different part of his life that we know nothing about. Poor Bobby, it must be dreadful for her - even her friends don't entirely trust her."

"I didn't say that," Darren said defensively, "I just don't think a dinner party is a very good idea at the moment. That's all."

"Well I do! It will show her once and for all that we all support her. She needs that reassurance at the moment. I don't want to hear another word on the subject," she stated with an air of finality. "Now - why don't you offer around those vol-au-vents."

"I wish we weren't coming to dinner next week." Terry muttered gloomily to Karen. "It's going to be a real barrel of laughs."

"Oh for God's sake, don't be so miserable! Bobby needs us at the moment. We have got to show her we all support her. Prove to her that we don't believe all that silly gossip."

"Don't we?"

"Of course not!" Karen looked shocked.

"No, I know! I can't really believe it. You must admit though - it does look bad for her."

"All the more reason for us to rally around her 'A friend in need' and all that. Now for heaven's sake lighten up a bit. Here - have a sausage roll." She thrust one in her husband's hand and he bit in to it gingerly.

"Thanks," he mumbled, sarcastically. Karen ignored him and turned away to offer her condolences to Simon's parents.

"Joanna, do you really think it's a good idea for us to come to dinner next week?" Jim asked anxiously. "I mean, you know what people are saying, it might look bad for Bobby."

"It is precisely because of what people are saying that we must come to dinner next week. We have to show them all that we don't believe the rumours and that we are all quite happy to eat here. Besides," she looked sharply at him, "since you are the cause of a lot of the gossip I think the least you can do is support her now. I warned you your acting around would give people the wrong idea!"

"I thought I had explained all that! You said you believed me." Jim protested. "You know there is nothing in it."

"I certainly hope not, Jim." Joanna answered him quietly.

Jim looked at her in alarm. That was the first time she had doubted his word. It was all Bobby's fault, he thought, unreasonably, she was becoming a major headache. Trouble was, he was in rather deep now, he wanted to be rid of her - and fast - but he was afraid of what she might do.

"Jim." Bobby's voice made him jump.

"Oh! Hello Bobby - you startled me. How are you? Joanna and I were just saying how much we are looking forward to the dinner next week, weren't we Joanna?" Jim pulled Joanna over to his side; she had just started to wander off in the direction of some other friends. He draped his arm casually around his wife's shoulder. "Yes," he continued quickly, "we always enjoy your dinner parties, you are a great cook. Isn't that right darling? Isn't that what we always say?" he babbled.

"Thank you Jim," Bobby replied coldly, "I am looking forward to it too. I'm hoping to make something really special for you." She smiled at him, but her eyes narrowed in a look of pure malice. "I do hope you are going to enjoy it. Well, if you will excuse me - I have got a lot of people to get around." She turned abruptly and walked quickly away.

"What do you suppose she meant by that?" Jim asked nervously. "She didn't seem very happy."

"Of course she didn't seem very happy. This is her husband's funeral. And what on earth were you babbling on like that for? Honestly, you sounded like you expected her to poison you!" Joanna replied, exasperated by his flustered tone. She walked over to help Bobby hand around the tea.

Jim stood staring miserably towards the two women and wondered if they were talking about him. He had never realised how vicious Bobby could be - had she killed Simon? Seeing her recently it didn't seem that remote a possibility any more. He gulped - if she had done it once would she do it again? He was painfully aware of what everyone said about a woman scorned.

As she walked around the room smiling softly and speaking gently to the grieving friends and relations, her mind was racing. Jim had never loved her at all! He couldn't have. He was just like a spoilt child, wanting everything and never being content once he had got it. She had killed two people for him. Two people! He wasn't worth it. She thought of all the times he had sworn undying devotion, no wonder he sounded so convincing - he was probably saying it to half the women in Linwood. This is it! she thought determinedly. He was history - she didn't need him. She was going to get her revenge though. Why should he be allowed to live when Simon had had to die? Poor Simon, her eyes filled with tears; how she wished she had never started on this. Debby could, just possibly, have deserved it. She hadn't loved Jim, not really - she just callously picked him as a replacement for Nick. Debby didn't deserve much sympathy. Simon was a different story, he had been a good man and she bitterly regretted her actions now. Of course it was too late for regrets - but it was not too late to make the person responsible for it pay.

Chapter 22

*T*he following week passed quickly. Bobby refused all offers of assistance with the dinner, she was determined to do it all herself this time. Fortunately Darren's birthday fell on a Saturday, which was always a better night for any sort of celebration, and even under the present circumstances Bobby was determined to lift the gloom.

"It is kind of you to offer to help Mel," she explained on the telephone, the morning of Darren's birthday, "but I want to be busy. At least that way I haven't got time to think. I am not going to be miserable tonight I promise. I know we all feel a bit guilty about having a party at the moment, but I am sure it is what Simon would have wanted. I need to lighten the atmosphere in this house, even if it is just for one night. Do you think I am being callous?" she added worriedly.

"Don't be silly - we all understand. It will do us all good - especially you. Now, if you are really quite sure there is nothing I can do to help, what time do you want us round?"

"How about eight o'clock? That should give you enough time to get the children settled. I expect they get excited on Daddy's birthday!" Bobby smiled as she imagined the happy children, they were good kids and she was very fond of them.

"They certainly do! They woke us up before six this morning. They don't realise that Darren is not as excited at being a year older as they are!"

"Poor old soul! He's not getting any younger, is he? Tell him I'll have a nice bottle of tonic wine chilled for him tonight! I suppose at his age he needs all the help he can get!" Bobby joked; it felt good to be laughing again.

"That will really cheer him up! I had better go - I promised I would help the children make a cake for him this afternoon, should be a lovely sticky mess." Mel groaned as she contemplated all the clearing up she would have to do.

"Have fun - don't let him eat too much cake though. I'm doing a big dinner. I just hope no one will feel too nervous about eating it. I am reputed to be a poisoner you know!"

"Don't be daft! I am certainly looking forward to my dinner. You needn't worry about Darren either - the children's cakes are not usually that appetizing. We'll both be ready for a good meal tonight."

"I wonder if Jim can say the same thing. He has been avoiding me like the plague recently. Nice to know how much faith he has in me, isn't it?" Bobby added dryly.

"I take it the great romance is off then?" Mel had never doubted that it would not last, but she never imagined it would have happened like this.

"Definitely! I don't know what I ever saw in him. He really is pathetic. I cringe when I remember how besotted I was. I must have needed my head examined!"

"Oh well, they do say that love is blind. Mind you - I must say - I am surprised you invited them around tonight."

"I had to really - didn't I? It was all arranged before I realised his feelings, then at Simon's funeral, when I saw how reluctant he was...I suppose I should admit to a bit of spite - I couldn't help enjoying watching him squirm! However I can assure you - after tonight, I do not expect to have much to do with Jim."

"That's a shame though - it is sad to think we won't all be friends together any more. You still get on with Joanna, don't you?"

"Oh yes. She actually believes him when he says there was nothing between us. Mind you," she added bitterly, "I suppose as far as he was concerned it was nothing. I will enjoy tonight though. He practically choked when I offered him a sausage roll at the funeral - I found it in a pot plant afterwards. It should be fun watching him try and hide an entire dinner!"

"You are wicked!" laughed Mel. "Still, it serves him right. The whole idea is so stupid. I can't see you as a mass murderer somehow. Anyway, I had better go. See you later, bye." Mel was still laughing as she hung up the telephone. Darren walked in.

"You sound happy - you didn't get us out of it did you?" he asked hopefully.

"Certainly not! You're as bad as Jim - an ungrateful wretch. Why don't you walk the dog up to the village florists and get Bobby some nice flowers for tonight, she is going to a lot of trouble for you. Besides, we want you out the way for a while. The children are making you a nice surprise."

"It's freezing out there!" Darren protested. "You are a cruel woman! All right, all right - I'm going." He saw the menacing look in her eyes, and set off, muttering to himself, dragging a reluctant dog behind him - it really was too cold for a walk - even the dog thought so.

Mel and the children started on the cake - as she had predicted, it turned out to be a lovely sticky mess.

That evening as Mel and Darren drove to Bobby's house, Darren was still grumbling.

"There's going to be a lovely atmosphere there tonight. I mean - well - it's obvious we are all going to be thinking about Simon isn't it? It is a bit soon - don't you think?"

"Whose fault is that? This party is for you! Besides, it was all planned long ago and Bobby needs this evening. It is up to us - tonight will be what we make it. If you go along determined not to enjoy yourself then you won't. Will you please cheer up and start to make a bit of an effort? Come on love," she added softly, "you are usually the one person who can brighten the most miserable event. Besides, it is your birthday."

"You are right. We owe it to Bobby - and Simon, to make this evening as successful as possible. Right! We are going to have a good evening. We will enjoy ourselves. We will not get all morbid," he stated firmly.

"That's the spirit! Let's just hope we can convince the others."

They were the first to arrive. Bobby met them at the door and greeted them warmly. She was dressed discreetly, but not solemnly, in a green silk blouse with a black skirt.

"Happy birthday Darren. Thank you for coming." She took their coats and showed them through to the lounge. The room was set out exactly as it had been the night of their fateful last dinner party. The three of them stopped in the doorway of the lounge as they all vividly remembered that dinner.

"Shall I pull that chair over closer to the fire?" Bobby said hastily, trying to change the appearance of the room. "It is cold tonight, and that chair is a bit far away." She wished she had thought of this sooner - in all the hectic preparations she had not given a thought to the room.

"Yes, that's a good idea. I'll move that ornament over to that little table by the door, make a bit more room on the bar, in case you need it." Darren added, helpfully.

"Careful Darren! You'll knock Bobby's big planter over." Darren looked surprised by his wife's warning; he was nowhere near the planter. "Here," she continued, "let me move it over to the other corner out of the way. Sorry Bobby - he is so clumsy!" She smiled apologetically at Bobby.

Within a few minutes the room had been rearranged. Each of them thought of a lame excuse to move an item of furniture. No one voiced their concerns, and they each pretended the others were unaware of their motives. They all hoped by changing the appearance of the lounge it would not remind the others so strongly of the last time they had all sat down together to dinner.

The doorbell startled them just as they finished. Bobby went to welcome the other guests. Mel and Darren stood by the fire waiting for her to return.

"That was a bit nasty for a minute," whispered Darren, "it was like stepping back in time."

"I know what you mean. Still, I think we have improved things a bit - sshh... here they come," warned Mel, smiling warmly at the others as they entered the room.

"Shall I do the honours, Bobby?" asked Darren, who had moved over to the bar.

"Thank you Darren that would be lovely, you know where everything is." Bobby was grateful for his presence; she fought back a feeling of melancholy as she remembered how Simon had always seen to the drinks.

"I've brought some bottled beer along," Jim said quickly, "I seem to have developed a taste for it recently. I am sort of trying to cut back on the hard stuff after Christmas." He handed Darren a box of bottled beer.

"Really? You do surprise me - I always thought you hated the stuff," Bobby remarked, she had a pretty shrewd idea why Jim had brought along his own drinks - it meant she didn't mix any for him. What a bastard! she thought, she felt incredibly angry when she remembered how much she had loved him once.

"Here, give them to me, I'll put them in the 'fridge, they are better cold. I've got some lager glasses in the kitchen - I'll pour you out one." She took the beer and left the room.

Jim gave a nervous grin. "A friend of mine brought them back from a trip to France," he explained, "you ought to try them - they're quite nice really." He smiled sheepishly around at his somewhat sceptical friends - Jim had never been known as a beer drinker.

Bobby returned bearing a glass full of beer. "Sorry it's a bit frothy - I had a bit of trouble pouring it. It must have got shaken up on the way." She smiled meaningfully at Jim as she handed him the glass.

Jim looked at the pale liquid. It certainly looked clear enough - if only she had poured it out in the lounge where he could see her - he didn't like the way she was looking at him.

Bobby found it difficult not to burst out laughing; there was nothing wrong with Jim's beer. She was enjoying playing cat and mouse with him though. It was obvious from his expression that he was terrified of her.

"Anything wrong Jim?" she asked innocently, "I can get you something else if you would prefer?"

"Oh no! No! This is lovely." He took a sip "Delicious! Would you like one Terry?" he asked desperately.

"No thanks. I'll stick with my usual." Terry was enjoying Jim's discomfort. Serves him right! he thought gleefully, It is about time he got what he is due.

"Will you behave!" hissed Joanna. "You are making a complete fool of yourself! You hate that French beer - I don't know why you brought it." She felt very embarrassed and shot a quick glance around the room - everyone was studiously looking the other way. Darren was pouring the drinks and Bobby was handing them around. Mel and Karen were chatting together; Terry was standing over by the fireplace, with a broad smile on his usually serious looking face.

"I told you - I don't want Bobby making my drinks," he whispered back.

"We have been through all this. Why on earth would Bobby want to do you any harm? You are being ridiculous! Unless of course there is something I don't know about." Joanna was rapidly losing all patience with him.

Terry wandered over. "Business has picked up nicely after the Christmas lull," he commented cheerfully to Jim. Jim groaned - it was going to be a long evening.

"Shall we go through?" Bobby suggested and led the way through to the dining room. "Joanna - if you would like to sit there," she indicated a chair, "Mel, there, Darren -I have put you at the head of the table, since you are the guest of honour. Karen, perhaps you would like to sit beside Darren - but watch him - he is getting to a dangerous age!" They all laughed. "Jim - I put you next to me, I haven't had a good chat with you for ages," she added brightly, exchanging a grin with Mel.

"Right Darren, consider yourself warned. If you start acting like a dirty old man - I'll give you... ooh," Karen paused, and they all turned to look at her as she pretended to think of a suitable punishment, "I'll give you plenty of time to stop!" Darren beamed, everyone laughed, and the tension in the air lifted slightly.

The first course was smoked salmon roulade stuffed with cream cheese and dill. It was served in individual portions on an attractive salad base. It was already on the table when they sat down, having been placed there by Bobby shortly before they arrived.

"These look lovely," Karen enthused. "You are clever Bobby, what herb have you used?" she asked casually, as she picked up her fork.

Jim, Darren and Terry leaned forward to listen carefully to her reply. Bobby shook her head in mock despair as she watched their anxious expressions. Karen glared at them - it was only a casual enquiry, she hadn't meant to imply anything sinister.

"Dill." Bobby said flatly and picking up her fork, she took a large mouthful and looked defiantly around the table.

The men meekly started to nibble at the appetizer.

"Delicious," mumbled Darren.

"Great," agreed Jim

"Super," chimed in Terry.

Their respective wives exchanged glances and tried to smother their laughter. The meal was developing into a farce.

Enough is enough, this cannot go on! I just cannot stand this a minute longer! thought Bobby determinedly. "Actually," she commented, in a casual tone, "I had to use dill because hemlock is out of season."

"Oh I know," agreed Karen sympathetically, joining in the joke, "it is so hard to get hold of at this time of year - did you try the delicatessens in the high street? I hear they usually do a nice line in poison."

"I think that is in very poor taste!" Terry said sternly, glaring at his wife. "You could exercise a bit more tact considering Bobby's recent loss. You are being extremely offensive."

"I'm being offensive - I like that! You men are all sitting there like a bunch of idiots! For goodness sake - let's just relax and enjoy our dinner." Karen raised her glass "Happy birthday Darren - here's to a great birthday party!"

"Thank you Karen. You are quite right. We need to relax - that was the object of the exercise. How can anyone be expected to relax while you men are pussyfooting around, playing with your food? For heaven's sake, we have all been friends for far too many years to behave like this together. Now, let us drink a toast to Darren on his birthday - and to...absent friends - and then get on with our evening." She couldn't quite bring herself to mention Simon's name for fear of breaking down completely, but she wanted to get her point across.

There was a moments stunned silence, then, one by one, the friends rose to their feet. They raised their glasses and looked solemnly around at each other.

"To absent friends!" they all declared in unison, and then turning to Darren, "happy birthday Darren." They all sat down and the ice was well and truly broken.

The evening progressed, and gradually everyone started to relax a bit. Darren kept up a stream of jokes, and as the wine flowed the party atmosphere developed.

"Do you think I am old enough to qualify to be a 'dirty old man' yet?" leered Darren at Karen.

"Keep practising! You are definitely getting there!" she laughed.

"Happy birthday Darren - here is your beef Wellington, as promised." announced Bobby, as she brought in the large serving dish.

"It looks great," Darren replied, starting to feel quite merry.

Bobby started to carve. It was cooked to perfection, the pastry was crisp, the mushroom and onions surrounding the meat smelt delicious, and the beef itself was nicely pink in the centre. She served it onto the plates and everyone helped themselves to the vegetables.

"Is anything wrong, Jim?" asked Bobby, noticing Jim staring in dismay at his plate.

"Perhaps your piece is a bit rare for you, here - swop with me. I had the end portion, it's always a bit more thoroughly cooked. I prefer my steak rare." Joanna hastily swopped plates with Jim. "There, now you can really enjoy your meal." She glared at her husband.

"Thank you," Jim replied weakly, he had no excuse now. Mel winked at Bobby as she passed her some vegetables. "This looks really delicious Bobby - you must teach me to make it."

"Certainly Mel, I hope you enjoy it. It is a rather special recipe." It was a speciality of hers and she was proud of it.

"Jim - you don't seem to have much pastry now, here have this nice piece at the end, I know how you like pastry."

Bobby placed the end of the beef Wellington on to Jim's plate; it certainly looked tasty, as it had become quite encrusted with the mushroom and onion sautéed mixture. Mel was handing around the vegetables and Darren was ladling the Madeira sauce onto his plate. There was a general hubbub of conversation while everyone served their vegetables and got their meal.

The conversation picked up again. They finished their main course and Joanna helped Bobby clear the plates. If anyone noticed that Jim had left most of his meal they didn't comment on it.

"Finally we have - individual brandied soufflés!" Bobby announced, as she brought in a tray of small ramekins. "Here Jim - you have this one, it's a bit bigger and you haven't eaten much this evening." She handed Jim a dessert.

"Thanks Bobby looks lovely, but I don't want to be greedy - would anyone else like the bigger one?"

"Don't be silly - you go ahead. Enjoy it - it will do you good." Bobby grinned maliciously at him as she handed around the desserts.

Jim peered suspiciously at his soufflé. It looked all right but he couldn't be sure. He wondered if anyone would notice if he left this too. He was rather hungry by now and it did look good - what could be wrong with a brandy soufflé? You are getting paranoid! he told himself and resolutely he picked up his spoon.

"These are great!" enthused Terry, noting Jim's discomfort, "one of your favourites aren't they, Jim?"

"Yes, I love puddings; trouble is I am still trying to lose the weight I put on over Christmas. I ought to resist really." He tried one final ploy.

"Nonsense!" declared Darren, "it's my birthday and no-one is going to worry about their weight today. Eat up and forget the diet."

"Thanks a lot" muttered Jim. Oh to hell with it. he thought, One pudding is not going to kill me!

After dinner they all went back through to the lounge. It was getting quite late, the fire had burned down quite low, and a small note of sadness seemed to be creeping in. The enforced jolliness was beginning to crack a little, and no one was surprised when Jim and Joanna made their excuses and left.

"Wasn't that fun?" remarked Bobby wryly. "Oh well, we can relax now - coffee anyone?" she smiled round at her remaining guests.

As they drove away Joanna unknowingly echoed Bobby's words.

"Wasn't that fun?" she said angrily, "you really made an idiot of yourself back there. What on earth possessed you? I thought you said there was never anything between you two?"

"I did! There wasn't! I can't help it - she makes me nervous. Anyway I'm starving! I hardly ate a thing," complained Jim.

"Whose fault was that? The meal was delicious. I ate all mine. You will just have to settle for a sandwich or something." She paused, seeing her husband's look of distaste.

"Oh go on love, couldn't you just knock me up a quick omelette or something?"

"I'm sorry but I don't really feel inclined to cook for you tonight, not when you let a perfectly good meal go to waste. You can just make yourself an omelette."

They drove home in stony silence. Jim racked his brains trying to think of something to say to break the silence, but he knew he had pushed his luck too far, and so decided it was probably best to keep quiet.

Chapter 23

The next morning Jim woke early. It was just beginning to get light. The bedroom curtains were letting in the first rays of the weak winter sun and it looked as if it would be a pleasant day. He glanced around the room as it grew lighter. It was a pretty room, Joanna had chosen the decor. The walls were painted a warm cream colour with a frieze of peach flowers all around the room half way up the walls. The curtains and soft furnishings matched the frieze and were trimmed with heavy cream lace. The bedroom furniture was in antique pine - again Joanna's choice, and the overall effect was very pleasing. It was a calming room, cosy and comforting - rather like Joanna herself, he thought. It was ironic really, he considered, as he lay in the warm bed, he had always thought he craved a more exciting life yet when it really came down to it, stability had its rewards. Bobby he mused is satin sheets and excitement, Joanna is frilly cotton and security. He lay in bed contemplating the previous evening. He pictured Bobby smiling at him maliciously as she handed him his dessert. He had actually felt afraid of her.

Well, at least I survived the night! he thought grimly, Why on earth did I ever get involved with that evil woman? He glanced across at Joanna sleeping beside him. I must have been crazy! He vowed never to cheat on his wife again. It was a vow he had made to himself several times before, but this time, he could not have known, it was a vow he would keep to the grave.

Remembering how angry Joanna had been with him the previous night, he crept silently out of bed and went down to bring her a cup of tea. Reaching the kitchen he decided he would really impress her and take her breakfast in bed. He was extremely confident he could soon woo himself back into her favour - Joanna was very susceptible to his charms.

Humming softly to himself, Jim had just started preparing the breakfast when he suddenly felt a cramp in his stomach. He sat down abruptly; alarmed at the discomfort he was feeling.

"What's up?" mumbled Joanna, walking into the kitchen. She was wearing her nightdress and rubbing her eyes. "You're not usually an early bird."

"I was just going to bring you up a cup of tea. I've got an awful cramp in my stomach. How do you feel?" Jim was quick to ask. He wasn't being particularly solicitous, he was just anxious to know if she had the same pain.

"Fine. Don't start all that again. It's probably nervous indigestion." Joanna yawned. "I should think your stomach is tied up in knots with all that panicking you have been doing!"

"Oh well the cramp has gone now, anyway." The pain had passed. Jim felt rather foolish and he was anxious not to upset his wife again.

They sat at the kitchen table and drank their tea. Joanna idly stirred the sugar around in the bowl, tracing out patterns in a contemplative manner. Jim sat staring out of the window, watching a bird pecking at the bird feeder that was hanging from a nearby tree. It was a typically sleepy, Sunday morning.

"What do you fancy doing today?" Jim asked. They had no plans made for the day.

"Not a lot, actually," replied Joanna. "I could do with a quiet day. How about you? Do you want to go out?"

"No - not really. My stomach feels a bit odd." Catching his wife's expression, he quickly added, "I am not starting anything - I just said my stomach feels a bit odd, that's all."

"Perhaps you're hungry - you didn't eat much last night. Fancy a cooked breakfast?"

Jim groaned. "No thanks." He conveniently forgot his good intention of making his wife a nice breakfast. "I'll just settle for some toast. You are probably right about the nervous indigestion. Let's walk up to the village newsagent for the Sunday papers, I'll probably feel fine after some fresh air."

Jim did not feel better for the fresh air, his discomfort grew slowly and they decided to skip lunch. His anxiety did not help the situation, and by late afternoon he was suffering from intermittent bouts of abdominal pain and cramps in the calves of his legs. Although it was not too bad, Jim didn't feel able to get out of bed, so at his insistence, Joanna called in the village doctor. Working at the surgery herself she knew the workload the doctor had, and always felt very guilty on the rare occasions when she needed to call upon his services. Dr Armstrong was in fact aware of Joanna's reluctance to call him out, and appreciated her thoughtfulness. He called in at the surgery and picked up Jim's notes on his way to their house.

Joanna let him in and showed him up to the bedroom. He examined Jim and noted his symptoms. Joanna spoke to him as he came out of the bedroom where Jim was resting.

"Sorry to have to bring you out. What do you think it is doctor?" she asked anxiously. "He has been under a lot of stress recently, do you think it is due to that?"

"No. I think it is definitely something more physical than mental. I would suspect mild food poisoning. Has he had any shellfish recently?" It seemed a likely place to start.

"We were out to dinner with friends last night. Jim didn't eat much though." Joanna recalled the menu. "No. We didn't have any shellfish. We had smoked salmon to start, with cream cheese, could it be that?"

"Could be," he shrugged, "Cream cheese and fish don't always combine very well. Did you have the same?"

"Yes - we all ate identical meals, actually it was rather nice," she smiled.

"And you are feeling no ill effects?"

"I am fine," Joanna replied, puzzled.

"Was anyone else affected?" Perhaps Joanna had a stronger stomach than her husband. Some people were more susceptible than others to certain foods, but if there had been anything actually wrong with it, he would expect more than one guest to be ill.

"I haven't heard of anyone else being ill. I should think the others would have rung me if they were ill too."

"Well he isn't too bad at the moment. Starve him for today; he can have boiled water to drink. If he gets any worse call me again, I expect it will calm down quite soon. He must just be having a bad reaction to something, it happens sometimes. If it were more serious, I would expect you both to be ill."

"Thank you doctor. I am sorry to trouble you, but you see Jim has been a bit hypersensitive about his food since his friend died. I think he imagines he has been poisoned!" She laughed briefly to alleviate her embarrassment at her husband's vivid imagination.

"You, of all people, should be able to understand that!" Dr Armstrong laughed. "You know how many people have been coming to me with stomach pains - real and imaginary - since that case became so famous. In a village this size everyone knows about it. I sometimes think some of them are only coming to try and get a bit of inside information out of me to fuel the gossip." The doctor smiled at Joanna. "Don't worry - he'll probably be fine in the morning!" He started to head towards the door when a commotion from the bedroom made them both turn back. They rushed into the room and Joanna gasped in shock at the sight that confronted them. Jim was in a state of great distress. He had vomited a large quantity of blood over the bed, the cream quilt cover was stained a dark red, and the fear showed in Jim's eyes as he struggled to speak.

"Help me.... help me, Joanna.... she did it! I knew she would! Oh Joanna, I'm so sorry - help me!" he gasped for breath, fighting to control the dreadful retching.

The doctor was already reaching for the telephone to call for an ambulance as Joanna tried to comfort her distraught husband.

"You are going to be fine love, try and keep calm. It probably looks worse than it is. I am here - everything will be all right. You'll see - everything will be all right."

The ambulance arrived quickly. The doctor handed Jim over to the paramedics with a quick run down of his condition. He handed them Jim's notes. Joanna went with Jim to the hospital, holding his hand and murmuring comforting words. She looked ashen faced and the paramedics wondered briefly if they might have an extra patient by the time they arrived at the hospital. The ambulance sped off.

As he walked slowly back to his car, Dr Armstrong mentally ran through Jim's symptoms. He knew the man was desperately afraid - he had heard quite clearly what he had said. Could his fears be well founded? It seemed ridiculous really. The man was probably just succumbing to the hysteria that was sweeping the village following the dramatic death of Simon Collins. At that moment his pager went off, and he received a message that a child in his practice needed him urgently. He set off on his next call vowing to call the hospital at the first opportunity.

At the hospital Jim was taken straight to Intensive Care. Joanna stayed close by him until a young nurse came and showed her into a small waiting room.

"It would be better if you waited here for a while. We will come and get you as soon as possible. I'll bring you a nice cup of tea." She smiled reassuringly, "There's a telephone over by the door if you want to contact anyone."

"Thank you," Joanna murmured, obviously in a state of shock. She wondered whom she should call. Jim's parents were abroad. They had gone to Canada to visit relatives for Christmas and had stayed for a prolonged holiday. She could not ring them from the hospital, it would alarm them, and there was nothing they could do from there. She thought of calling her own parents, but decided against it. Her mother would panic and her father would have his hands full calming his wife, without being a comfort to his daughter. Friends...? Bobby! Should she ring Bobby? No, of course not. It would only remind her of Simon. Mel and Darren or Karen and Terry? The more she thought about it the more she decided she didn't want anyone with her. They would all be thinking of Simon. No one would know what to say. Joanna felt she could not cope with embarrassed friends at the moment. She looked up as the door opened and the nurse appeared carrying a cup of tea. Joanna took the tea with a word of thanks and sat, perched on the edge of the seat, watching the clock on the wall. The hands of the clock seemed to move so slowly, the room was silent. Surely someone would come soon and tell her how Jim was doing.

"How is he doing?" The Senior Registrar, Mr Andre Lemasurier, asked the young intern as he walked briskly into the cubicle where Jim was lying. The two doctors moved over out of earshot of their patient.

"Intermittent bouts of severe abdominal pain, vomiting blood, blood in faeces, cramps in calves of legs. Symptoms becoming more severe, abdomen tender to touch, stomach muscles in spasm." The hospital intern quickly ran through a synopsis of the patient's symptoms.

"What are you doing about it?" asked the older man as he glanced at Jim's medical chart.

"We have got him on a glucose drip and have taken samples of blood and fluids. His vital signs are being monitored. We are waiting on preliminary results before we decide on the next course of action. He is not very coherent, rambling a bit, but his wife has given us all the relevant information."

"When did he last eat?"

"Apart from a slice of toast this morning, last meal was at approximately eight o'clock last night." He glanced at his watch, "twenty two hours ago."

"Any history of a stomach ulcer?" It seemed the most likely answer. Toast for breakfast! he thought disapprovingly as he glanced over at the patient. Probably one of those who ate erratically lived too fast and wondered why they developed ulcers. He had seen it all before.

"None that we are aware of. His GP called us in and sent his notes along in the ambulance. They don't show any mention of suspected ulcer, and he has never complained of persistent stomach pain."

"On any medication?"

"No. According to his notes his GP hardly ever sees him."

"Does he have a history of alcohol abuse?"

"Not that anyone is aware of. Social drinker - doesn't smoke - no family history of stomach problems."

"Could he have taken any unprescribed drugs?" It was possible he had been trying to cure himself, and taken non-prescription drugs. Of course - there was always the possibility he had taken some sort of illegal substance.

"No - he swears he hasn't taken a thing. The man is terrified - I am pretty sure he would tell us if he had taken anything."

"Sounds like an ulcer to me - or severe food poisoning. Did we get a stomach pump?"

"He had already vomited before admission. We have a list of everything he ate last night. Several other people ate the same thing - no one else has been affected."

"More likely to be an ulcer then. How is his blood pressure?"

"70 over 50 and falling - too low to operate," The intern was aware of the dangers of operating on a patient in such a dangerous condition.

"I certainly would not be happy operating at the moment; we would probably lose him to a cardiac arrest as soon as we got him under. No, our best bet would be to get him stable. Try for a barium meal tomorrow. Set up a plasma drip as well. Make sure we keep his body fluids up. He should start to respond and as soon as his vital signs improve we can start to investigate. You say you are quite sure he definitely hasn't taken any drugs of any kind..." he broke off as the nurse interrupted them.

"Doctor!" she called their attention back to the patient. "His vital signs are weakening."

Both men hurried over to Jim. His face had taken on a yellow tinge, his skin look clammy, his breathing was shallow it was very apparent that he was failing fast.

"Developing jaundice. Signs of cyanosis. Increase fluids. Keep crash equipment ready." The Registrar snapped out his instructions as he examined Jim. "He is going into a coma. Where are those lab reports?"

"Sir. The police have arrived. They want to speak to you."

"What?? Not now nurse! I am rather busy at the moment." Mr Lemasurier pointed out, with heavy sarcasm. "What the hell do they want anyway?"

George Saunders had walked in to the cubicle behind the nurse, accompanied by Steve Clarke. The village doctor who, in the light of recent events, was erring on the side of caution had notified them.

"Sorry to interrupt doctor, but is there any possibility that the patient could have been poisoned?" He asked calmly.

"Is that likely?" Mr Lemasurier replied, thinking fast, poison would account for the bleeding. "Yes - there is every possibility. We would need to know what kind of poison though - and quickly if we are going to save him."

"Could it be yew leaves?" He felt faintly embarrassed even asking. It did sound pretty ridiculous.

"What? Oh never mind - we haven't got time for explanations" he racked his brains to remember what he had learnt about yew poisoning. "No, that is not likely. Yew leaves are an alkaloid poison. They are much faster than this. There would not have been time to do this much damage - any other suggestions?"

"Paracetamol?" queried George, playing a hunch. Steve turned to him in surprise - the boss obviously still had doubts about the Debby Sherman case.

"No - again too much damage of the wrong sort. What else?" he snapped.

"I am afraid that is all I have got to offer. Surely the lab reports could isolate a specific poison?" Wasn't modern medicine supposed to be wonderful? Did they expect the police to do the doctor's job too?

"They will - in time, but we don't know how much time we have got. Do you have a suspect? Could you find out what it was? I take it this is not entirely unexpected? Are you in the habit of allowing people you suspect of poisoning to roam the streets?" Wasn't the police force supposed to be more efficient than this? Surely they did not expect the doctor to do their job too!

"We have a suspect - but no proof. We cannot hold a person just because we suspect they may attempt a crime, not without a shred of evidence. The public would soon cry 'Police brutality!'" George turned to Steve Clarke, "Get around there fast and try and get something out of her."

"Yes sir, I'll radio as soon as I get any information." He turned and hurried out.

"He's a good man. He'll get what you need." George stated, with more assurance than he felt. He had every confidence in Steve Clarke, but he could not imagine Bobby Collins volunteering any information at all - and certainly not in time to save Jim. He realised he was assuming that Bobby Collins was the poisoner, but at the moment she seemed the most likely, if not the only, candidate.

"Let's just hope he gets it quickly!" Mr Lemasurier replied grimly. "If this man has been poisoned, we may not have time for confessions."

Mr Andre Lemasurier misgivings were well founded. While Joanna sat, sipping her cold tea and staring at the clock, Jim died of internal haemorrhaging resulting in complete cardiac arrest. Steve Clarke had not even had time to leave the hospital car park.

Chapter 24

"**M**ushrooms!" declared Malcolm as he handed Steve Clarke the post mortem report. "Or - to be more precise - Amanita phalloides, commonly known as Death Cap mushrooms. Very common in the woods around here. Victim ate some approximately fifteen hours before symptoms became apparent. Not a pleasant way to go. Very painful - lots of internal haemorrhaging - blood everywhere...." he warmed to his subject and began to elaborate.

"Mushrooms?" interrupted Steve; this case was becoming more and more bizarre. "First yew leaves, and now mushrooms, we had better get to this person before she - supposing it is a 'she', we haven't proved it yet - does any more cooking."

"Bound to be - only a woman could be this devious. You want to hope she doesn't publish a cook book - we could be swamped!" Malcolm couldn't resist the joke, this case was the strangest he had ever dealt with - and he had dealt with quite a few. "By the way - I don't appreciate being called in on these rush jobs. I was on a date when I got called in."

"I'm sure the lovely Shelagh would forgive you – you two are getting pretty close aren't you?"

"That was the general idea. I wasn't planning on working half the night to get this ready for this morning!"

"You know you love it! Anyway, we had to get something fast, we are holding a suspect and so far we have got nothing to keep her. What else can you tell me? Try and keep it professional!" Steve pleaded in mock despair.

"Well, we didn't get much from the stomach..."

"How very disappointing for you!" interrupted Steve with a grin.

"But, what we managed to scrape off the duvet..." Malcolm continued with great relish, enjoying Steve's look of disgust. "and subsequent samples from the hospital, we can tell that the victim had eaten a quantity of some sort of egg dish, some beef, fish, various vegetables, and quite an amount of red wine."

"I have got a list of what he was served that evening..." Steve paused while he checked his notes. He had gone straight to Bobby from the hospital. Bobby had, once again, been arrested. Although they were holding off from a detailed interview until the results of the post mortem were available, he had made a note of the entire contents of the menu for the dinner the previous night.

"Right here we go - smoked salmon stuffed with cream cheese and dill, beef Wellington with roast potatoes, roast parsnips, green beans, carrots, mange tout and Madeira gravy, followed by brandy soufflé. How does that sound?"

"Sounds pretty good to me. I wouldn't mind joining his dining club - though I would appreciate a change of cook! No mention of mushrooms though. The brandy soufflé accounts for all the egg, but we still need to find out where he got the mushrooms."

"What about the beef Wellington?"

"Oh yes that has got mushrooms around it hasn't it? Or is it pate? I'm not sure - I'm a pathologist, not a chef! Anyway, isn't that a whole fillet? How come no one else got the Death Cap mushrooms? You are going to have to do a bit more investigating there, my son!"

"I'll check it out. I must admit I am more a shepherd's pie man myself. After all this I think I'll stick with it too - I knew fancy food was bad for you!" He took the report from Malcolm and headed back to the station.

Once again, Steve sat opposite his boss and went through a post mortem report.

"Post mortem reveals ulceration and inflammation of stomach and bowels, fatty degeneration of liver, kidneys and heart, with congestion and haemorrhages in most of the viscera. Death occurred due to cardiac arrest following massive internal haemorrhaging" he read, again he found himself cringing as he got to the next part of his report.

"Okay. What caused it?" asked George Saunders wearily. "A poison tipped tooth-pick? Or maybe cyanide in his ice cubes, which slowly melted and killed him later? Let's face it, this whole thing is getting more and more warped. I am half expecting a white haired old lady to come in and tell us she has solved the case!"

"Mushrooms."

"Mushrooms?"

"Mushrooms sir. Amanita Phalloides, usually known as Death Cap mushrooms. Apparently the symptoms take about fifteen hours to develop, and the effect by that time is irreversible. He never stood a chance once he had eaten them."

"Fifteen hours - that ties in with the dinner party. Did he eat mushrooms there?"

"Well, that is where we have a problem, apparently there are mushrooms around the beef dish he ate, but everyone else ate the same."

"Terrific! So how come he was the only one poisoned? Is it a poison which only affects people vulnerable to it?"

"No. I checked that with Malcolm. They are fatal to everyone."

"I just can't see what we are dealing with here - a maniac I suppose."

"Well actually sir...." Steve hesitated.

"Yes? If you have any ideas I want to hear them."

"I was just thinking - suppose an ordinary housewife wants to kill someone. Look at her options - shoot them? Where would an ordinary housewife get a gun? Not many people around here have easy access to a gun, plus the fact, your average person wouldn't know how to use one, not with that degree of accuracy. Besides it takes a lot of nerve to shoot someone in cold blood. She would have to face them - and I don't think this person could do that. Knife? Both victims were quite strong men; she would be overpowered, same for strangulation. We know poison is more usually a female crime but Mrs Average is not going to have an exotic range of poisons available - is she? So she just has to use what she can get hold of. Both cases have involved very common poisons."

"True - good point. Okay, accepting that she - if it is a 'she' that is yet to be proved - however, for arguments sake, we will assume it for now, how does she ensure her intended victim gets the poison? How do we account for only one person being affected this time? The mince pie was individual - it might have taken a bit of juggling, to make sure the victim got the right one, but still, it is quite possible. The mushrooms take a bit more explaining. Are we sure the victim ate the poison at that dinner?"

"We only have his wife's word for it. He could have eaten something when he got home. I will go over it with her again later. I didn't get much out of her at the hospital - she was in a pretty bad way."

"Assuming for the moment it was in the beef Wellington - how does the murderer make sure he gets the poison? It would have had to be at one of the ends, it would be too difficult to judge slices in the middle - but she wouldn't serve a man first - she would serve the ladies first." George paused and stared thoughtfully out of the window. "Who do we know is a good cook? We need a bit of help here. I don't remember my wife ever making a beef Wellington - she is a bit anti red meats, always worrying about my heart. How about you?"

"We don't go in much for fancy stuff, I am afraid. Hang on a minute - what about WPC Shelagh Veitch? She does a lot of that sort of thing, I think. I remember her talking about her cookery when we were on surveillance together."

George Saunders picked up the 'phone. "Is Shelagh Veitch on duty at the moment? Great. Send her up to me would you?"

"She's not going to be a happy bunny. She and Malcolm were out to dinner last night when we called him in," grinned Steve.

"Really? I didn't know they were an item?"

"Looks like it's getting quite serious."

"Glad to hear it they've both been on their own too long – make a good couple."

A few minutes later there was a knock at the door, and Shelagh Veitch entered.

"You sent for me sir?"

"Yes Shelagh, come on in - take a seat, we need a bit of advice here. What can you tell me about beef Wellington?"

"Beef Wellington, Sir?" asked Shelagh in surprise.

"Yes - you know - fillet of beef and whatever. Have you ever made one?"

"Yes sir. What do you want - a recipe?"

"I want to know what is in it, how you make it, and how you serve it."

"Am I right in thinking this is the case that ruined my dinner last night then sir? " she smiled. "Okay first of all how many people was it to serve?"

George consulted the notes.

"Seven."

"Do you know how they like their beef?"

"Pardon?" It was George's turn to look puzzled.

"Well sir - if you know that some of them like their meat rare, for example, you calculate the cooking time accordingly. If you know that someone prefers their meat well done, you can always give them the end bits."

"Great! So you would serve the meat according to preference not according to any sort of 'ladies first' rule?" George smiled, finally they were getting somewhere.

"Usually sir. Do you want the quantities of the ingredients? I would have to go and check the recipe."

"No, that won't be necessary - I just need to know basically what goes in to it and how."

"Recipes do vary - but I usually sauté together mushrooms, onions and garlic with a few herbs. Then I leave that to cool. Prepare the beef..." she paused and looked questioningly at the Inspector. He nodded; he didn't need the details on preparing beef. Shelagh continued.

"Pre-cook the beef for ten minutes in a very hot oven, chill for a couple of hours. Roll out the puff pastry and spread a thick layer of the mushroom mix, put the beef on top, fold the pastry over and decorate."

"What do you mean by 'decorate'" interrupted George.

"Personal choice really. I usually put a ribbon of pastry along the top with a tassel or something at one end, and a few leaves dotted along. Depends on how much time I have got, and how artistic I am feeling. Some people really go to town on the decoration, but personally I prefer something simple. Anything else, sir?"

"So it would be fairly simple to ensure the intended victim got the right portion?" asked George.

"Pretty much though I would have thought you'd be better using either end to ensure whatever the poison was it didn't contaminate the portion either side"

"Good point. I want you in on this case. Your culinary skills are going to solve this one for us! Well this is going to surprise you – the cause of death was a Death Cap mushroom."

"Really sir? I usually use the regular type. I'd better warn Malcolm to watch his step – you don't mess with a lady who cooks!"

"Too right! Okay so if our murderer wanted to make sure Jim Baines got the poison, she could put it at one end of the meat, and make sure he got that end by decorating the pastry. You have got to admit - it is clever! Now we can try and pin her down. We have got the means - what about the motive?"

"The lovely Bobby certainly wasn't very happy with the victim the last time I spoke to her," commented Steve.

"True - but would that be enough for her to kill him?"

"If she had killed her husband for him and then he dumped her, I should think she would be a bit peeved. You know what they say about a woman scorned!" smiled Shelagh.

"Yes I suppose so, but it doesn't seem right somehow. She must have known she would be our prime suspect. Why kill him after dinner at her house? It makes it too obvious."

"Opportunity? If he was avoiding her she probably would not have had many chances to do it. A Death Cap mushroom is not the sort of thing you can casually drop into his coffee. I don't suppose he was exactly popping in to lunch very often."

"Okay. So we have got motive, means, and opportunity - how about some evidence?"

"Nothing so far. Forensics have got the remains of the beef Wellington, but presumably he ate the only poisoned bit, certainly what they have got is fine."

"It would be handy if we could find the peeled remains of the mushrooms in the bin, but I suppose that would be too convenient. I take it the kitchen has been checked?"

"Very thoroughly! No trace of anything out of the ordinary. I am afraid we have got no solid evidence at all."

"Back to basics then. We interview everyone until someone gives us what we need. I can't see your 'Mrs Average' coping with police pressure for long - can you?"

Chapter 25

*B*obby sat on the edge of the small bed in the police cell. The pressure was really beginning to get to her. What did they expect her to do? Break down and confess all? It was all crazy - they had nothing on her. There was nothing to incriminate her. The policeman who had arrested her had given nothing away when he spoke to her, he had merely informed her of her rights and told her she was under arrest for the murder of James Baines. Jim dead! She still couldn't fully believe it. She jumped up, startled, as the door opened.

"Your solicitor is here madam. If you would accompany me to an interview room." A policeman led Bobby through the police station and into a small interview room. It was the same room she had been interviewed in before. She remembered how angry she had felt then, she wondered if she had the strength to summon up that anger again - it had got her through the last ordeal.

Oliver Wilson walked in; he turned to the policeman who had escorted him to the room.

"Thank you officer that will be all. I will call when I am ready."

"Right you are sir, I'll be just outside if you need me."

They waited until he left, and then sat down at the table in the centre of the room.

"Oh God Oliver - this is a nightmare - what on earth is happening to me?"

"I was rather expecting you to tell me. I understand you have now been arrested for a second murder. I really do feel now that we are going to have to bring in a more qualified brief." Oliver prepared himself for an argument.

"Yes, I suppose you are right. What do I have to do?" Bobby said resignedly.

"Oh! Well...um. Leave it to me. I will make all the arrangements. Do you want to run through the facts with me first? Or shall I just get someone else straight away?"

"I don't know, I can't think any more. What do you think I should do?" The fight seemed to have gone out of her.

"Well, we could hold off for now until you are actually charged. If you are actually charged, of course," he added hastily, remembering her previous anger.

"Oh I expect I will be - I am the only person who could have done it, I think. I don't know why they haven't just locked me up and thrown away the key already!"

"Are you saying you did do it?" asked an astonished Oliver; she had changed completely since last they spoke.

"No of course not! I am just saying I can't prove I didn't," replied Bobby, with a trace of her old fire.

"Well, of course, it is not up to you to prove you didn't - it is up to them to prove that you did. Now..." Oliver adopted a business-like tone; opening his briefcase he took out a large yellow pad of paper. "Let us go over the facts..."

Several hours later a weary Bobby sat opposite George Saunders, Oliver Wilson flanked her. Shelagh and Steve sat silently observing.

"I have told you, I did not kill my husband, and I did not kill Jim Baines. I cannot tell you anything else because I do not know anything else."

"Mrs Collins, let us go over the facts. James Baines was your lover, correct?"

"Yes - he was."

"You had not been seeing him recently though?"

"No."

"Why was that?"

Bobby shrugged, "I don't know really, I suppose we had decided to cool things for a while. As a mark of respect to my husband." Bobby said quietly.

"It is rather a pity you did not show him that much respect when he was alive!" retorted George, trying to provoke her and break through her reserve.

"My client is not here on a question of morality, Detective Inspector," interjected Oliver.

George ignored him. "Whose idea was it to 'cool things for a while' Mrs Collins?"

"It was a mutual decision."

"Are you quite sure about that?"

Bobby looked at him warily, what did he know? Could he have known Jim dumped her? Her senses suddenly alert, she found some of her old spirit returning.

"What do you mean?"

"Well Mrs Collins, when I interviewed James Baines over your husband's death I rather got the impression that he was...shall we say...losing interest in your affair?"

"That was mutual - I found myself most unimpressed with his behaviour over my husband's death. He could probably tell I was tiring of him. I suppose male pride made him imply he was backing off - no man likes to think he is not irresistible."

"So I take it the affair was over?"

"I suppose so."

"How did that make you feel?"

"I didn't really think about it much, I was - I am still - mourning my husband. I regret ever getting involved with Jim." Bobby tried to keep her voice bland, but even she could hear the bitterness of her tone.

"You were angry with him?"

"I was angry with myself. I realise now what I have lost. I didn't appreciate my husband enough."

"Surely you must have blamed Jim Baines for that?"

"It was as much my fault. I am not a child, Inspector - I knew what I was doing."

"Did you know what you were doing when you killed him?"

"I did not kill him!" insisted Bobby.

George was getting extremely frustrated. They had made no progress at all. Bobby had stuck resolutely to her story throughout all their interviews. He tried again.

"Let us go back to the dinner. You made all the food yourself?"

"Yes."

"Isn't that unusual - I mean, you are barely out of mourning, didn't your friends offer to help you?"

"They did offer - I declined their help."

"Why?"

"I didn't want their help. I wanted to be busy. I have already told you all this."

"It could not be that you didn't want anyone else to see what you put in the food?"

Bobby sighed. "I did not put anything in the food - besides, we all ate the same thing!"

"Mrs Collins - did you decide on the menu yourself?"

"More or less. I had promised Darren Knight I'd make him a beef Wellington for his birthday. It is a speciality of mine and he loves it. I selected the other courses as I thought they would go well with the main course."

"I see. I understand that the first course was already on the table when the guests came through to the dining room, is this usual?"

"I thought it would be easier, hosting the dinner alone I did not want to have to be dashing in and out of the kitchen all night. The room is not too warm, and they were only served a short time before we sat down to eat - it was perfectly safe." She winced as she said the word 'safe'. It was obvious the Inspector would not think her cooking 'safe' at all!

George merely raised an eyebrow and gave a wry smile.

"The second course was the aforementioned beef Wellington - I take it you made that yourself?"

"Of course - I have told you - it is a speciality of mine."

"Quite," observed George, crisply, then continued "Mrs Collins who served the beef Wellington?"

"I did." Bobby frowned. He knew she had served all the food.

"And you handed everyone the portion you wanted them to have?"

"I just handed around the plates - I didn't specify portions."

"Do you remember what part of the meat Jim Baines got?"

"What do you mean – 'what part'? It was a whole fillet - we all got a slice of it."

"You did not ask if anyone wanted their meat more thoroughly cooked, for example?"

"I have made this dish several times. I know that they all like their meat about the same." Bobby was growing more wary - what was all this leading to?

"You did not remember which particular slice Mr Baines was served?"

"Of course not - I know he liked my beef Wellington, I even gave him extra pastry as I know he likes it so much. Why would I do that if I didn't want him to enjoy it?"

"Why indeed? Surely if you gave him extra pastry you must have given someone else a piece without pastry, so you did take special notice of how he was served?"

"No I didn't - there is always extra pastry at the end of the fillet, look this is getting ridiculous, if you want cookery lesson - buy a cook book!"

George ignored her outburst.

"Now let us discuss the dessert. They were in individual dishes I believe. Why was that?"

"They rise better in individual dishes. Besides, I always think they look more attractive, and it makes the serving easier. I always make brandy soufflés in individual ramekin dishes - any good cook would!" she added defiantly, starting to regain her former fighting spirit. It was obvious they could not prove anything - the man was merely fishing for information.

"The dishes are all identical?"

Bobby hesitated, remembering the point she had made about giving Jim the largest one. She thought fast - if she mentioned it she may arouse further suspicion - if she didn't, and someone else did... she sighed.

"Actually the dishes are identical, but sometimes one pudding may rise a bit more than another and look larger. I remember that as I brought in the tray of desserts I gave Jim the largest one - I made some joke about it at the time." She stared straight at the Inspector. "Make something of that!" she thought angrily.

George's expression did not change at all.

"Really?" he commented mildly. "Was Mr Baines particularly fond of desserts?"

"Not that I know of - it was just that he hadn't eaten much that evening, and I thought he might still be hungry." She shrugged "It was just a passing comment, I just thought I had better mention it - after all..." she added with a tight smile, "I want to be as cooperative as possible."

"Of course," replied George smoothly, then carried on in a conversational tone, "Mrs Collins, can you think of anyone else who would want to see Mr Baines dead?"

It was a question she had asked herself many times over the previous hours. If she wanted to be cleared of this, there had to be someone else responsible. The trouble was she just couldn't think of anyone.

"No - I wish I could really, but there is simply no one I can think of who would wish to harm Jim."

"Apart from you yourself, of course."

Bobby didn't even bother to reply.

Chapter 26

The following morning, Joanna sat facing George Saunders across the table in the interview room. WPC Shelagh Veitch was again supporting her. Clearly in a state of shock, she stared unseeingly at the wall behind Steve. He and Shelagh exchanged glances. They were not sure how much information they could hope to glean from Joanna considering her mental state. Dr Armstrong had sedated her the previous evening when she had virtually collapsed after leaving the hospital. The sedative should have worn off by now, although it was hard to tell by looking at her. She appeared to have shrunk somehow, her shoulders were hunched over and she looked small and quite grey. Her face was lined and she seemed much older than when last they had met.

"Mrs Baines." George began quietly, then realising she hadn't even heard him, he continued in a slightly louder tone. "Mrs Baines? Mrs Baines? I am sorry to trouble you at a time like this, but I am afraid there are one or two things I need to go over with you."

Joanna slowly turned her head and stared at him. She tried to concentrate on what he was saying. They had to talk to her - she knew that. It was just so hard to understand him though. Where was that nice young policeman? She had liked him.

"I understand, please go ahead," she whispered. "What do you want to know?"

"How did your husband seem last Saturday, before the dinner?" George watched her carefully. Despite her obvious grief, she was still a suspect in the case. Experience had shown that it was often the grieving widow, or widower, who was responsible for the death of a spouse. He had to concede Steve's point about her having no motive to kill the previous victim, but even so, he had been at this game too long to let any sort of sentiment cloud his judgement.

"Fine." She didn't know what else she could say - Jim had been perfectly healthy that day.

"Was he looking forward to the evening?" George kept his tone casual; he was treading very carefully to avoid provoking any hysteria.

"No," her voice trembled "No, he didn't want to go - I made him go. He didn't want to go at all. It was all my fault - I killed him - I made him go!" She broke down sobbing. Shelagh put a comforting arm around her shoulder, gradually Joanna calmed down.

"Mrs Baines - I am afraid I must get to the bottom of this. Why do you think your husband was reluctant to attend the dinner?"

"He...he was afraid." It had to be said; other people must have noticed how nervous he had been. If she didn't tell them they would think she had something to hide.

"Of Mrs Collins?"

"Yes. I told him he was being silly. I told him he had to go...."

"Yes, yes, quite," interrupted George, hearing her voice rise and realising she was about to become hysterical again.

"Did he say why he was afraid?"

"No. I asked him. I said, "Why would Bobby hurt you?" I remember asking him. He wouldn't answer."

"Mrs Baines, were you aware of the relationship between your husband and Bobby Collins?" He had read Steve Clarke's notes thoroughly but this was the first time he had actually spoken to Joanna personally.

185

Shelagh winced. This woman was already on the brink - a question like that could send her over. Mentally she braced herself for a fresh onslaught of tears. To her great surprise Joanna gave a small, but bitter, laugh.

"There was no relationship!" she declared, showing the most spirit she had all day. "Oh I know what everyone thought - but it simply was not true. My husband was a flirt, always had been, but he swore to me there was nothing in it."

"And you believed him?" Despite his training he found it hard to keep the surprise out of his voice. It seemed incredible to him, but, he had to admit, she was very convincing.

"Of course!" Joanna said staunchly. "Whatever else he may have been - he was not a liar!"

George decided not to pursue that line for the time being. He found that switching subjects often caused the suspect to lose their composure and they were more likely to answer spontaneously.

"Mrs Baines, I would like you to think back to the actual dinner. Where were you seated?"

Joanna paused and thought carefully. It was an oval table and Darren had sat at one end. Bobby had sat at the other. Bobby had said something about Darren being the guest of honour, or words to that effect. She pictured the scene.

"I was between Darren and Terry."

"Where was your husband?"

"He was next to Bobby, diagonally opposite me. It was a bit awkward really being seven of us. I remember thinking it made the seating arrangements all wrong."

"I suppose it would. Did you choose where to sit?"

"No, Bobby had it all worked out."

"Do you remember anything unusual about the meal?"

"Well... it was a bit tense. Jim was behaving very badly - I was rather embarrassed." She felt guilty criticising her husband, but she had to be honest.

"In what way was he behaving badly?" Again George watched her closely, had she noticed her husband flirting with Bobby Collins?

"Well he hardly ate anything, and he looked so nervous the whole time." Joanna remembered how Jim had merely toyed with his food.

"Was there something unpleasant about the meal?" Had the mushrooms tasted bitter? Mixed with the onions and garlic they should have been fairly undetectable.

"No, it was delicious."

"Do you remember Mrs Collins - Bobby, serving the first course?"

"It was already on the table when we came in. It all looked very attractive," Joanna added.

"Mrs Collins showed you to your seats and you all sat where she directed, with the starter already on the table," George recapped.

"That's right."

"Did you notice how much your husband ate?"

"Not much, I mean, I noticed that he did not eat much, he just sort of pushed his food around his plate."

"Then Mrs Collins cleared that course away and brought in a beef Wellington?" George asked.

"Yes - it looked really lovely. She had obviously gone to a great deal of trouble. Then Jim didn't want it."

"He didn't want his meat?"

"No. I was so embarrassed that I pretended his piece was too rare and swopped plates with him. I had been served the end piece you see, it's always cooked more."

"So you had the end piece. I see, and then you changed plates with your husband. Did he eat it then?"

"Well he had to, didn't he? After I had swopped plates especially so that he had what he wanted. Why?" She grew alarmed, "Was there something wrong with the meat? Is that what killed him? My God! I did kill him! I gave him that piece of meat!!"

"Mrs Collins, we do not know for sure what killed your husband. It may have been something he ate after the dinner. I am just trying to get some details straight."

George thought quickly. This was a new angle. Suppose the poison had not been intended for Jim Baines at all? He decided to continue the questioning.

"After the main course, I understand you were all served with individual desserts?"

Joanna hesitated, remembering how Bobby had insisted on Jim having the largest pudding. Should she mention that? It seemed spiteful somehow. She didn't want the policeman to think she was trying to accuse Bobby - if he thought she was capable of such spite at a time like this he might think her capable of anything.

"Yes, that's right. The dessert was in small ramekin dishes."

George noticed her hesitation. Was she hiding something? Surely if she suspected someone had killed her husband she would be eager to tell the whole truth. He looked at her warily.

"Did you notice anything unusual about the dessert?"

"No. No, not a thing. It was very nice."

"Did your husband appreciate it as much?"

"Actually he did. He ate the whole thing, everyone did." She paused, "Could that have been what killed him? I'm sorry; I still can't seem to accept Bobby would kill Jim. Bobby is my friend - was our friend - why would she do such a terrible thing?"

George ignored the question.

"No one has yet been charged with your husband's murder Mrs Baines; we are still conducting our enquiries."

"I thought you had arrested Bobby?" Joanna asked, puzzled. She vaguely remembered someone saying at the hospital that the younger policeman had been sent out to bring Bobby in, whatever that meant, she had assumed at the time it meant that Bobby was being arrested.

"Mrs Collins is merely helping us with our enquiries - she has not been formally charged with any crime."

"Oh! I am not sure I understand all this. Do you think the same person killed Simon? Could it be some madman? Perhaps Jim had something else to eat during Saturday. I wasn't with him all the time. I had my hair done Saturday; maybe someone called around while I was at the hairdressers? Or he may have gone out for a while - I mean - I don't know, he didn't say, I didn't ask...." Joanna began to babble, but even as she spoke she realised how desperate she sounded. She had to admit it - the evidence seemed to weigh heavily against Bobby.

George watched her calmly; who was she trying to convince - herself or him? Perhaps if she admitted, even to herself, that Bobby Collins was the most likely suspect, she would also have to face the fact that her husband had been unfaithful to her. Maybe she wanted to carry her rosy image of her marriage to her husband's grave? Or was she, perhaps, trying to cover her own tracks?

"We are investigating all possible scenarios Mrs Baines. Naturally the pathologist will be able to show the approximate time the poison was administered, in the meantime we have to try and determine exactly what your husband ate, and when. For example, did your husband have anything to eat when he got home that evening?"

"I don't really know," she looked embarrassed. "We had a bit of a row on the way home about his behaviour. I went straight to bed. Jim came up a few minutes later - he may have had a sandwich or something. I don't think so - he was quite quick following me, but I suppose he may have done." She sounded dubious about the possibility.

"We will send a forensic team to check your kitchen."

Joanna looked alarmed. What did that mean? Did they suspect her? Would they arrest her just because she was his wife? Didn't they always suspect the wife? Ironically her knowledge of police procedure was of a similar type to her late husband's - namely what was shown on fictional television programmes.

"Do you think there could be something at my house?"

"It is just a precaution. Please don't be alarmed, we always check every location the victim has been in a case like this." George smiled reassuringly, inwardly he thought not that we have ever had a case quite like this.

"I see. Do you want me to help? I could show them where everything is." Joanna asked anxiously, she didn't like the idea of strangers going through her home. She was also very keen to show that she had nothing to hide.

"That won't be necessary. They are pretty good at this sort of thing. Don't worry - they won't make a mess!" he smiled encouragingly at Joanna.

Several hours later Joanna surveyed her lovely kitchen in dismay. All the surfaces, including the door to the refrigerator were covered in a fine grey dust. It could most certainly be described as a complete mess. Still, they had told her she could clean it up now, and at least that part was over. She knew they wouldn't have found anything. At least there was something constructive she could do. She had always found housework strangely therapeutic. Carefully avoiding the clinging grey powder, she opened the cupboard under the sink and took out her rubber gloves. As she took out a cloth and some spray cleaner she wondered if Bobby had been charged yet.

Chapter 27

S teve and Shelagh drove around to the home of Darren and Mel Knight on the Monday following the fateful dinner. Darren had gone into work to deal with any essential business, but was due to return shortly. Mel opened the door; she looked exhausted, the strain showed clearly on her face. She smiled briefly at them, but it was very apparent she was deeply distressed. Showing them through to the lounge they sat down.

"I am sure you know why I am here Mrs Knight," began Steve.

"Yes, yes of course." Mel spoke softly, "Although I still can't believe all this has happened. Have you found out what actually killed him - I suppose there's no chance of it having been due to natural causes?"

"I'm afraid there is no possibility of that, Mel. We have established the cause of death, although I am not at liberty to give too many details, I can confirm that Jim died of poisoning."

"Was it the same thing that killed Simon?" She had assumed it was another case of poisoning, but it still seemed so incredible.

Shelagh hesitated; she was not sure how much they should divulge. They exchanged glances and Steve gave a small shrug.

"No. It was an entirely different substance." He was not sure whether he should have even said that much, but decided he could afford to give a little information out - in the hope of getting a bit more back.

"I just cannot understand it. First Simon and now Jim - it just doesn't make sense. It is like something you read about in the papers. That sort of thing just doesn't go on here -this is Linwood. We live in a quiet village, nothing like this has ever happened before..." her voice trailed off and she sat staring into space, totally bewildered by the turn of events.

"I am afraid it has happened though," Steve stated firmly, trying to bring her back to reality. "It's my job to try and prevent it happening again and, of course, to determine just who is responsible."

"You don't think it will happen again do you!" cried Mel, a look of absolute horror on her face. "My God! It couldn't happen again!"

"That rather depends on who is doing it - and why. Have you any ideas on the subject?" asked Shelagh quietly.

"No. I cannot think of any reason for all this."

"Are you aware of the fact that we are holding Bobby Collins?" Steve interjected.

"I assumed as much. You took her in last time, and it did happen after dinner at her house, but I still find it impossible to believe."

"Did she confide in you at all recently?" Shelagh resumed the questioning.

"Yes. We spoke at length on the subject of Simon's death. She couldn't think of anyone who would wish to harm him."

"What did she have to say about Jim Baines?"

"Not a lot. I think - well I know - that the affair was over."

"Do you know who ended it?"

"I am not sure really." Mel hedged, she was fairly sure that Jim had ended the affair. She knew that he refused to contact Bobby after she had been accused of Simon's murder. Still, she felt a certain amount of loyalty to Bobby, she knew how bad things looked for her, but she couldn't believe Bobby would be so vindictive.

"You must have a fairly good idea though," prompted Steve. "Look, I know this is difficult for you - Bobby Collins is your friend - but you must see how urgent it is for us to stop whoever is doing this. If you know anything - or even suspect anything, no matter how trivial it may seem to you - you must tell me."

"You're right, I know it." Mel sighed, "I am not trying to hide anything, I promise, it's just that I realise how black things look for Bobby, and honestly, I just cannot believe she would do such a thing. I mean, let's face it; it is rather obvious, isn't it? Jim dies after dinner at her house - surely she would not be so blatant. Quite apart from the fact that I just don't think she is capable of murder."

"I know what you are saying, but I can assure you that murderers do not walk around with wild staring eyes, swinging an axe! Sometimes the most ordinary of people carry the darkest secrets. I do agree with you about the 'obvious' aspect though. However, we do not know what motivated her - or even if it was Bobby Collins - I am not saying that it was - we have not charged her as yet. Now, can you tell me how she felt about Jim Baines - to the best of your knowledge?"

"She was not happy with him, I can say that much." Mel replied reluctantly.

"Why did she invite him to dinner then?" That was the puzzling aspect as far Shelagh was concerned. Not the behaviour for a scorned mistress, unless of course she was planning revenge.

"I asked her the same thing. Unfortunately the whole thing had been arranged for some time and she couldn't get out of it easily. She did say that she did not expect to be seeing so much of Jim and Joanna in the future - I don't mean that as it sounds - she didn't say it in an evil way, just that she was fed up with him and she didn't want to have anything to do with him in future."

Steve let it pass, he knew what Mel was trying to say, and that she was not trying to incriminate her friend.

"Moving on to the dinner itself - where were you sitting?"

Mel thought back to the evening, frowning as she tried to concentrate on the details.

"I was sitting opposite Jim, between Bobby at one end of the table and Terry in the middle. There was an odd number so the seating arrangements did not work out too well."

"Did you notice how things were between Jim and Bobby?"

"Decidedly frosty I would say. Jim was hardly touching his meal and Bobby was quite annoyed with his attitude."

"Did you see Bobby serving the food?"

"Oh yes - actually she made quite a joke about it, I mean, it is not funny now, not in the light of what happened, but at the time it was almost comical the way Jim avoided his food."

"I believe the main course was a beef Wellington?" Steve asked, in a carefully casual tone.

"Yes, it was lovely - but we all had a slice of that, there couldn't have been anything wrong with it."

"Do you remember who was served first?"

Mel shook her head; she had consumed quite a lot of wine by that stage of the evening, and hadn't really taken much notice of the order of serving.

"I am sorry - I can't really remember, does it matter?"

Steve shrugged; he didn't want to put particular emphasis on any aspect of the meal. Although he certainly didn't want to put words into Mel's mouth, he did want to know if she had noticed the plate swopping incident.

"Did you notice if Jim appeared to enjoy his meat?"

"Well he looked a bit reluctant at first, but then he had looked reluctant at everything, then Joanna swopped plates with him and gave him her portion. It was cooked more thoroughly - I don't think he really cared how it was cooked - I think Joanna was just looking for an excuse."

"To swop plates?" asked Shelagh.

"No - an excuse for Jim's behaviour. She made out that Jim's meat was a bit too rare for him to excuse his lack of appetite, then she swopped plates; I suppose she thought it would allay his doubts. It wasn't the beef Wellington was it? No, it couldn't have been - no one else was ill. Could it have been?" she asked anxiously.

"We don't know yet. Do you think there is a possibility that Jim and Bobby were just pretending to have parted - to allay suspicions?" Steve was trying to ascertain if the poison had been intended for Joanna, to free Bobby and Jim to continue their relationship.

"If they were, they were damn good actors! No, I am sure there was definitely nothing left between them."

The sound of the front door closing brought their conversation to a temporary halt. Darren walked in, looking tired and strained. It was unusual for him to be so sombre.

"'Morning," he nodded at the officers, "I had a feeling you'd be here. How's it going?" He smiled at his wife, and sat down on an armchair near to the policeman.

"I was just running through the events of last Saturday evening with your wife. I would appreciate a moment of your time too." Steve paused, and looked significantly at Mel. He wanted to speak to them separately, but he didn't want to make it too formal.

Mel immediately realised what the policeman wanted, and rising to her feet, she walked towards the lounge door.

"I expect you're hungry, love, I'll go and start the lunch. Would you both like a cup of tea or coffee?"

"Thank you Mel, I'd love a cup of tea - white please, no sugar."

"Thanks love, I'm gasping for a cup." Darren smiled gratefully at his wife.

"I'll give you a hand," offered Shelagh, leaving the two men to talk while she could chat more informally with Mel and possibly gain more of a confidence.

"Would you like to stay for lunch, officer? It won't be very fancy, but you're welcome to stay," offered Mel.

"No thank you, we must be getting back, I do appreciate the offer though - perhaps another time."

The men paused while Mel and Shelagh left the room and shut the door behind them.

"Was he poisoned too?" asked Darren. "I bet it was in the soufflé!" He had noted at the time Bobby's eagerness to give Jim a particular pudding.

"What makes you think that?" asked Steve, surprised at Darren's suggestion.

"Was it though?" persisted Darren.

"No, at least not as far as we know at the moment. Why should you think it would be?"

"Oh!" said Darren disappointed, he thought he had solved the case. "It's just that Bobby made quite a thing about giving Jim the biggest pudding, I just thought... well... nothing really." Darren's voice trailed off, he was starting to feel a bit foolish.

"I take it you believe Bobby Collins did it then?"

"That's obvious isn't it? I mean...well, who else could have done it?" Darren looked confused. He had thought it was a forgone conclusion.

"We don't know who did it yet. What makes you think it is so obvious?"

"Look, I'm sorry, I shouldn't have said that. I just thought that - well - I didn't really know what to think. Bobby was so odd at the dinner and everything. Then when Jim was poisoned I just assumed... You're right - it may not have been Bobby."

"In what way do you think her behaviour was 'odd' at dinner? Did she make any threats against Jim?"

"Good Lord no! It's just the way that she sort of looked at him as she served him. Mel said she was teasing him, but it didn't look very funny to me."

"How did she look at him?"

"Well, sort of...I don't really know how to describe it; I suppose she could have been teasing him. She looked as though she wanted to put the fear of God into him - and she succeeded!"

"Did you see her serve all the courses?"

"Yes...actually, come to think of it, no I didn't. The first course was already on the table when we came in."

Steve consulted his notebook. He knew the menu off by heart after all this questioning, but it looked more official.

"That would be the smoked salmon with cream cheese; it was already on the table when you came through from the lounge?"

"Yes, that's right. I remember because Karen asked what herb Bobby had used and she got a bit annoyed."

"She didn't like to share her recipes?"

"It wasn't that." Darren looked a bit shame-faced. "Actually we were all a bit nervous, you know, what with Simon having been poisoned and all that, and when Karen asked what was in it, well, I think Bobby got the impression we were concerned about it."

"I see. Then you went on to the next course...." he paused and once again checked his notes "beef Wellington - I believe that was a favourite of yours?"

"That's right. It was great too. Well at least we all know that was all right - we all ate that."

"Even Jim Baines?"

"Eventually - Joanna swopped plates with him, something about his being too rare - I think she was just trying to make him eat it. He hadn't eaten much up to then - and I think he was becoming a bit too obvious, Joanna was embarrassed." Darren added, by way of explanation.

"You saw them swop plates - did they do that immediately?"

"What do you mean?"

"Well, did Joanna have her plate in front of her for a while, and then change over?"

"I think she was served first - but it would only have been a few minutes before Bobby got around to everyone, then Joanna saw Jim looking at his food, sort of...well...reluctantly I suppose. Anyway, after the episode with the starter, Joanna jumped in and changed plates."

"Thank you." Steve made a few notes. "Were you aware of the relationship between Jim and Bobby?"

"I think we all were - except Joanna, I bet she still doesn't believe it! Still it was obviously all over by last Saturday."

"Why 'obviously'? Surely they would have been discreet in front of his wife?"

"Not always!" Darren gave a wry smile, "Anyway there was a definite frost between them. Jim looked really uncomfortable all evening and Bobby seemed to be enjoying tormenting him. I think he was panicking that she would either tell Joanna or...well I know this sounds daft but...well, none of us men wanted to eat there. The girls all reckoned we were being silly, but that didn't save Jim did it?"

"Do you think there is any possibility that Jim and Bobby were just pretending to have ended their affair? Did he ever confide in you about it - man to man?"

"He never actually told me that he was having an affair with her - although it was fairly obvious. I suppose they could have been pretending to hate each other - but it was a pretty good pretence!"

"Get anything else from her?" Steve asked as they left the house.

"Not really but I am pretty sure the affair was definitely over. I really think the plate swapping bit is a red herring. My bet is the extra pastry at the end. I don't think Joanna was ever the intended victim it just doesn't add up."

"Okay let's see what the others can add – Matherson's next?"

"Suits me. I'll keep back and watch for reactions."

Chapter 28

*L*eaving the Knight household they drove to interview Terry Matherson at work. As they drove towards the local town, they assessed the interviews with Mel and Darren Knight. It was obvious they were both beginning, albeit reluctantly, to suspect Bobby. Darren Knight seemed quite sure about it, especially after the strange incident with the puddings. Surely if Bobby was planning to poison Jim she would not have made such an obvious point when serving him? Unless of course, she wanted to make him really suffer!

As he pulled into the company car park, Steve recalled the last time he had been there. Remembering how Jim Baines had panicked about Debby's death, he gave a wry smile - who would have thought things would turn out as they had. He had to admit he hadn't liked the man, but he was still sorry he had died - he hadn't deserved that.

The receptionist looked up at him as he entered the front door. She was pale and had clearly been crying. Jim Baines must have been a popular boss. Steve thought, as he approached the desk.

"Good morning madam. We would like to see Mr Terry Matherson if he is available please."

"Yes sir, I'll just ring through and let him know you are coming. Will you be wanting to see anyone else?"

"I don't think so for today, thank you. I believe a colleague will be taking statements from members of Mr Baines' immediate staff."

George Saunders had arranged for a couple of Police Constables to take statements from the rest of the staff as a matter of routine, but they did not expect them to reveal anything new.

"Would you like me to show you to Mr Matherson's office?"

"No, don't worry - I think we can remember the way." Steve smiled at the girl, who gave a weak smile back and dabbed carefully at her eyes.

As they walked through the building the air of sadness, which seemed to surround them, struck them both. Voices were hushed and several people were clearly distressed. They reached Terry's office - the door was open and they could hear Terry's voice as he approached.

"...well I mean - it's bloody obvious really isn't it? Everyone knew about him and Bobby Collins - and she was not the type of woman to be messed with. A tough lady - I can tell you! I was there you know, when she did it - of course none of us really realised at the time, but looking back..." he paused dramatically "...well, let us just say the signs were there. Actually I am surprised the police have been so slow - what do they need - a signed confession? You'd have thought after she bumped her husband off they would have been a bit quick off the mark to prevent her striking again. I could have told them..." he broke off abruptly as he noticed Steve at the door.

"Oh er...Good morning officer. That will be all, Susan, thank you. You may go," he added pompously to his secretary, trying to regain his composure.

"Yes sir" she replied quickly and left, closing the door behind her.

"Please take a seat, officers. How can I help you?"

"Thank you. I am sure you know why I am here Mr Matherson. I would like to discuss your version of the events of last Saturday evening's dinner party."

Shelagh silently took a seat and watched Terry closely. He glanced nervously at her.

"Yes well...what exactly do you want to know?"

Steve took out his notebook and prepared to take notes.

"When did you arrive at the house that evening?"

"About eight o'clock I think, or just after. We met Jim and Joanna at the door; they arrived at the same time."

"How did they seem?"

"Fine - well I think Jim was a bit nervous, perhaps"

"What makes you say that?"

"Well, Joanna was sort of whispering to him to behave himself, I think they'd had a bit of a row."

"Have you any idea why there could be tension between them?"

"No." Terry paused and looked uncomfortable "Well I suppose Jim had been making a bit of fuss about going to dinner. Joanna and Bobby were friends, and Joanna didn't want to let her down."

"Mr Baines didn't want to go though?"

"None of us did really. I mean...well... would you want to go to dinner with a woman whose husband had just been poisoned?"

"Mrs Collins has not been charged with poisoning her husband though, and I understood she and Mr Baines were...shall we say... close?"

"They were - but I think Jim had been avoiding her a bit. He certainly hadn't been nipping out from work like he used to - during the day, that is. He used to be forever popping out on some pretext or the other. That all stopped just after Simon died. Whatever was happening, Bobby certainly wasn't very happy with him."

"And you think she may have killed him?"

"I didn't say that!" Terry replied quickly, and then paused before adding, "mind you - it is pretty obvious isn't it? I mean... well...who else would have done it?"

"Unfortunately we - the police that is - have not got a 'signed confession' and there is such a thing as evidence," Steve said dryly.

Terry blushed bright red.

"Look I didn't mean...that is to say...I wasn't implying that you weren't doing a good job or anything, I was just.... well...I just thought..." Terry sat back miserably; the police had a habit of making him look an idiot.

"I quite understand sir. Now if we could just go over the dinner itself..."

They learnt nothing new from Terry Matherson's version of the dinner. Terry had recalled the incident with the puddings. He too, had thought Jim had died as a result of eating the brandy soufflé. Like Darren, he had been most surprised when Steve had hinted that the poison had not been in the dessert at all. He had not noticed which part of the beef Wellington he had been served, nor did he mention the plate swopping incident.

They drove directly to Karen Matherson's house, Terry had told him she was at home, apparently she had been too upset to go in to work that day.

As they drove up the now familiar driveway, Karen opened the front door and watched as he parked the car. Dressed soberly in dark colours with her bright hair tied back off her face, she looked a totally different person to the bright bubbly character she usually was.

"Hello officers - Terry rang me and told me you were on your way. Come on in - would you like a coffee?"

"Thanks, I think we need one." He sat down in the lounge and checked through his notes while Karen went out for the coffee.

She returned shortly afterwards bearing a tray of coffee and biscuits. Setting it down on the coffee table in the centre of the room she turned to them both.

"Right, well, I suppose we had better get this over with," she sighed deeply, "I still find the whole thing totally incredible. What do you want to know?"

"I am sorry to have to go through all this again with you. I am sure you realise the gravity of the situation."

"Yes of course. Can I ask...?" she paused, uncertain if she should ask the question, "how is Bobby? I know she had been arrested but...she is still my friend and I will never believe she has done this."

"Mrs Collins, Bobby, is coping remarkably well I can assure you. Naturally she is under a great deal of stress, but actually she is surprisingly calm considering the circumstances." It was true, Bobby was managing quite well. She had now been interviewed at great length and had not once wavered from her steadfast position.

"And Joanna? I tried to see her, but she was at the station, and then later she told me she wanted to clean her kitchen up before she saw anyone. It worried me to death to see her like that, but she was adamant she had to get it done by herself."

"I think perhaps she needs something like that to occupy her at the moment. I am afraid the forensic boys probably made quite a mess - they usually do," smiled Shelagh.

"Forensics? At Joanna's? Why - for Heaven's sake? Surely you don't suspect her? The woman is devastated! Her life revolved around Jim."

"I know, I know" Steve said trying to calm her. "It is just a formality - after all, we don't know where Jim was poisoned, or by whom."

"And you think Joanna capable of it?" Her tone indicated her incredulity.

"My personal opinion is not an issue here, the fact remains, and as a wronged wife -and the last person to be alone with the victim - she does fall into the category of suspect," Steve explained.

Karen shrugged "I suppose so, but then again we were all at that dinner, you could just as easily accuse me or Mel - or even one of the men. Any one of us could have slipped something into his food."

Either you are a very clever actress..." thought Shelagh, watching her carefully as she spoke or, more likely, you have no idea how the poison was administered. If Karen thought something had been 'slipped into his food' it was obvious she did not know it was a Death Cap mushroom.

"You would need some sort of motive presumably," pointed out Steve.

"What motive has Joanna got? Even if she had found out about Jim and Bobby, why would she kill Simon? That would leave the way open for them! Or do you think each killed their own husbands?"

"I take your point - but until we know all the facts we cannot rule anyone out," Steve stated firmly.

"Was it the same poison? I suppose it couldn't have been really," she mused "Simon died very suddenly..." she shuddered as she remembered how she had tried to save him. "Unless of course Jim got less of it...was it the same?"

"No. As far as we are aware from the initial lab reports it was not the same substance." Steve replied.

"What I don't understand is how anyone could get hold of poisons. I mean - you can't just pop in to the local chemist and pick up a pound of arsenic can you?"

"There are many types of poison, some more readily available than others. Now, if we can get back to the subject of last Saturday." Shelagh took the lead and Steve reverted to the 'casual bystander' role.

"Yes of course, I'm sorry. It's just that I find the whole thing such a puzzle. Where do I start?"

"I understand from your husband that you arrived at the same time as Jim and Joanna?"

"That's right, just after eight, Darren and Mel were already there."

"Were you aware of any tension?"

"A bit I suppose - at the beginning we were all a bit tense, at least the men were. Joanna, Mel and I know Bobby too well to believe this of her."

"Moving on to the dinner - I understand Bobby was a little ...distressed, about remarks made to her about the first course?"

"Oh yes, that's right! I am afraid I made a bit of joke about it too - how awful. But surely that proves her innocence! She wouldn't make jokes about poisoning the starters if she actually had, would she?" Karen pointed out triumphantly.

"Not unless she wanted to build the pressure on her victim - make him squirm a bit perhaps? How did he take the joke?"

"I don't think he found it terribly amusing," admitted Karen, reluctantly.

They went on to discuss the following courses - Karen showed no change of expression when the beef Wellington was mentioned. She did remember the plate swopping incident and was of the same opinion as the others - that it had merely been a ploy to cover Jim's reluctance to eat.

"What do your remember of the dessert course?"

Karen groaned inwardly - she had been dreading that question.

"It was very nice - everyone ate it."

"Including Jim?"

"I suppose so - I didn't take much notice at the time."

"The puddings were in individual dishes weren't they?"

"Yes, that's right. Identical ramekin dishes."

"They didn't quite look identical though, did they? Wasn't one a little larger than the others?"

Karen sighed, so she did know about that - she thought she probably would.

"Who told you that?"

"Bobby did. She told us she gave Jim the largest pudding." Shelagh sat back and waited for her reaction.

"Oh! Bobby told you herself? Oh well, it must be all right then, you know all about it. What else can I tell you?"

"How do you think Jim felt about being given the largest pudding - or any pudding different from the others, for that matter?"

"I am sure you know how he felt. He wasn't too happy, but when we all teased him about it, he went ahead and ate it. Was it the pudding then?" she asked softly. "Oh God I hope not - we all joked about him eating it, please tell me it wasn't in the pudding."

"Actually no. It wasn't in the pudding. I probably shouldn't have told you that, but I can't see the harm in it. You can rest assured that you all badgering him into eating it did not contribute in any way."

"Thank God. I couldn't bear the thought of it!"

They discussed a few minor points and then they thanked her and left. As they walked back to his car they reflected that, sadly, they were still none the wiser for their day's work.

Chapter 29

early the next morning, Steve and Shelagh once again sat opposite George Saunders as they reviewed the case. They were all growing exceedingly frustrated by the continuing lack of tangible evidence. Despite all the painstaking work carried out by the team of forensic scientists who had scoured the houses of both victims, nothing had been turned up which could shine any light on the bizarre investigation.

"Right!" declared George, "Let's take this thing step by step, from the very beginning."

"Which beginning? The suicide or the first murder?" Steve queried. "Even where to start isn't clear with this one!"

"Okay we go with the suicide. Let's face it - it's just too much of a coincidence. The first victim...." George paused and checked back through the notes "Debby Sherman - what do we know?"

Steve too consulted his notes and read a brief summary of the life and premature death of Debby Sherman; "Debby Sherman, married to Nick Sherman, having an affair with Jim Baines, consults her doctor with symptoms of mild depression, attends a dinner party at the home of Bobby and Simon Collins, is taken ill at the party, and later admits to having overdosed on Paracetamol. Subsequently dies in emergency room. Post mortem reveals massive dose of Paracetamol. No suspicious circumstances."

"Taken ill at a dinner party. I still can't reconcile that. Why attend a party if you are going to top yourself? It just doesn't add up."

"Maybe she intended to make a big deathbed scene with the boyfriend, in front of his wife? Perhaps he'd ditched her?"

"Possible - but then why didn't she? Make a big scene that is. She left early with her husband before telling anyone what she had done."

"She admitted she had taken them herself," pointed out Steve.

"Who to? Any witnesses?" George remained sceptical.

Steve checked back.

"Medic attending found half empty packet of tablets and asked her is she had taken them - she admitted she had."

"Did she say how many? For God's sake - she could have taken two for a headache for all we know!"

"Apparently she was barely coherent by that time, and they were unable to ascertain how many she had taken," Steve admitted. He was starting to feel rather foolish, he should have checked more thoroughly.

"Sorry sir, it just seemed right at the time. The coroner recorded it as suicide - all the evidence at the time pointed to it. She had been to the doctor recently with mild depression," Steve added defensively.

"Did the doctor think she was suicidal?"

"Actually no. He stated in court that although it had only been a brief appointment, he was not of the opinion that she was suicidal."

"Lots of people consult their doctor with mild depression, granted a few of them probably do commit suicide - but if this man was her usual doctor..." he paused for confirmation of that fact, Steve nodded. "In that case I would have thought he would know if she were suicidal. What about the husband?"

"Husband went to pieces immediately. Devastated. Been away staying with his parents ever since. I must admit he was adamant she wouldn't do it - but then ...well, nearest and dearest usually are, aren't they?"

"True, I am not blaming you - if everything else hadn't happened I would never have picked up on it myself. Let's face it - we are clutching at straws here. Besides, it may still be suicide, let's carry on. So that is the victim's admitting the overdose covered - we don't actually know if she was admitting to an overdose at all. Let's get back to the dinner; she fell ill immediately after it. Could she have been deliberately dosed with tablets at the dinner?" George's mind was whirling with the possibilities.

"Sorry sir, we did check that one, remember? Malcolm Young did the post mortem and checked the food. He specifically said there is no way you can put that many tablets in food or drink without it being spotted - either by the victim or by the post mortem. I am afraid we have drawn a blank there."

George sat back thinking deeply, he was growing more and more convinced that Debby Sherman had not taken her own life - there had to be a way to deliberately overdose someone, but how?

"What did they have?" he asked suddenly, "At the dinner - what was on the menu? We can check every item against the stomach contents in the post mortem - I'm sure we are missing something. See if Malcolm can join us, we are missing something."

Stomach contents. Wonderful! thought Steve while they waited for Malcolm to join them. Malcolm's going to love this!

Malcolm joined them as Steve pulled out the notes.

"I got that menu from Mrs Collins, as you requested, hang on a minute..." he thumbed through his notes for a moment and then said "Oh yes! Here it is - salmon mousse with cucumber sauce..."

George checked through the pathologists report.

"That more or less checks out, remains of fish mousse were found, anything to add? Malcolm? Shelagh?"

"I've made it many a time but not with paracetamol. Can't see how it wouldn't show up though you could disguise the taste

I suppose. Fish has quite a strong flavour." Shelagh pondered aloud.

"No couldn't be done, the paracetamol would mingle with the mousse and show up in the post mortem," George stated firmly.

"Fair enough, okay what's next?" asked George.

"Rack of lamb with vegetables, all self served from serving platters in the middle of the table. Do you want me to run through each individual type of vegetable?"

"No, I don't think so, not if they helped themselves no way that would work. Anyway stomach contents showed partly digested meat and vegetables, no trace of drugs in them. Next?"

"That's about it - individual lemon sorbets for dessert, that wouldn't show up in the report. It's really just glorified ice."

"Big girl's ice lollies!" declared Shelagh, "Easy to distinguish one with some sort of garnish. Clever trick!"

"She's right. That's it!" agreed Malcolm triumphantly. "The ice would melt - just leaving the paracetamol!"

"Could it be done?" asked Steve, dubiously, "I know I'm no chef - but wouldn't it taste bitter?"

"I am sure it could be done - artificial sweeteners are very concentrated" pointed out Shelagh. "Lemon sorbet is supposed to have a tang to it - that has got to be it! Malcolm - let's do a bit of experimenting tonight – in the kitchen!" she added seeing the men exchanging glances with a grin.

"Okay I'll rephrase that. Malcolm and I can try it out a special sorbet recipe tonight. With his medical knowledge and my cooking I'm sure we could manage it. We've got her!"

"Who? Everyone made one dish for that party and let me see... yes...Karen Matherson made the desserts. Do we arrest her now? What possible motive could she have?" Steve pointed out.

"God knows! Anyway..." George slumped back in the chair, his previous elation vanishing. "If they all discussed the menu, as they obviously did, any one of them could have substituted that pudding. Still, at least we know how it could have been done!"

"Are you going to re-open the case?" Shelagh asked quietly.

"I don't see how we can - we've got no evidence - it is still only a theory. No - I guess she is going to get away with that one."

"It may help us with the next one though - who would want to see Debby Sherman out of the picture?"

"Presumably Bobby Collins and Joanna Baines," pointed out Malcolm, finally in on the whole picture.

"What about the rest of the group? I agree it is more likely to be a woman, but that still leaves.... let me see, Mel Knight and Karen Matherson. Did they know about the affair, sorry make that affairs plural?" George rationalised.

"Well Bobby certainly knew about it - the first time I met her she was extremely angry with the late Debby Sherman. Oh she tried to hide it, but I can tell you it was obvious. I thought at first Debby Sherman had been fooling around with Simon Collins, his wife was so angry!" Steve remembered.

"What about the others?" persisted George, well aware that Steve had already got Bobby, tried and found guilty, in his mind.

"I think they were both well aware of it. Neither seemed particularly upset about it though. There has been no suggestion at all that either of them was in any way involved with Jim Baines. They were both more concerned with his wife's feelings as I recall."

"Strike one for Bobby Collins then. However, if Joanna Baines did know about her husband's affair, she had just as much motive. We can't rule her out of this one."

"Everyone agreed that she didn't know," argued Shelagh.

"Doesn't mean a thing - what woman would admit to knowing her husband was having an affair? No, I think we give them equal billing on the first one."

"This brings us to the second victim - Simon Collins. We know that he was killed by a mince pie, which any one of them could have given him, no clue as to who did though. The only thing we can go on is motive. That is where, with all due respect sir; I think your suspect is out of the picture. If Joanna Baines is a murderous jealous wife there is no way she would kill her rival's husband and leave the path clear for them."

"Unless she didn't know about the second affair?"

"She still hasn't any motive. Why kill her friend's husband? It doesn't make sense. Likewise for the other two, they both definitely knew about that affair."

"Okay strike two for Bobby Collins then. She kills off the other girlfriend, and then kills her own husband to free herself." George mused.

"I really think that is more like it sir. She is on record as saying she doesn't approve of divorce, she knows financially she will lose out, it has got to be her," Steve insisted.

"What about the third one then? She has gone to all this trouble for him - only to murder him next? What is it? Habit forming?"

"We know he ditched her - that has got to be the oldest motive of all – 'Hell hath no fury...' etc."

"If Joanna Baines found out about Bobby Collins she would have the same motive remember - we can't rule her out," George argued.

"Granted sir, but that still makes Bobby Collins chief suspect, it's still three to two. Besides Bobby Collins had the means and the opportunity. We know she gave him the pastry containing the mushroom mixture from the end of the meat - she told us so herself."

"Would she volunteer that information if she had put the poison in that piece?"

"Maybe she thought someone else would tell us. Besides, what harm could it do telling us herself? We can't prove it and she knows it. By volunteering the information she makes it look as if she has nothing to hide."

"Joanna Baines had means and opportunities too, remember - she could have given him mushrooms on toast when he got home. We have only got her word for it."

"The stomach contents would have shown up the bread. Anyway the stomach contents were all accounted for," George pointed out.

"True, but if we are going with the Paracetamol theory, I wouldn't put it past the murderer to find a way around that - God knows how! After all, she appears to have got away with one post mortem! No disrespect Malcolm," George nodded at Malcolm.

"Sorry George. Well I feel a bit of prat now but it is just so bizarre," Malcolm apologised.

"Well it is still only a theory and even so that still leaves us with the plain fact that Joanna Baines had no motive to kill Simon Collins - she really liked the guy. She told me herself. I take it we are assuming we are only looking for one murderer," Shelagh defended Malcolm.

"I should think so - this is too strange to be the work of two separate murderers. Maybe Simon Collins made a pass at her or something? Perhaps having murdered once she found it easy to do again? No, I guess you are right - I can't think of another motive there. Unless of course he witnessed something."

"How could he? The poison was in the lemons, and they were already made before the party - anyway, I interviewed him myself, and he certainly didn't seem to be harbouring any suspicions. I can't see that theory panning out," Steve said thoughtfully.

"Let's explore your 'scorned woman' theory. We know, or at least, we have strong suspicions, as to why it was done - the spurned mistress. We definitely know how it was done - the mushrooms in the pastry, and we have a pretty good idea who had the strongest motive - Bobby Collins." George thought deeply, finger tips together, resting his elbows on the desk, a worried frown on his face.

"This still leaves us with the problem of proving it though sir." Steve pointed out the obvious, he groaned, "Haven't forensics come up with anything?"

"Not a thing. That's the trouble with all this media coverage these days - everyone knows how to destroy evidence. I blame all those police specials on the telly!"

"Surely the circumstantial evidence would be enough to charge her with?" Shelagh asked.

"With a good solicitor, and I don't mean that wimp she has been bringing along so far, no, with a good solicitor, she'll laugh in our faces. We have got to get a confession or some sort of solid evidence. You never know - she might even confess to all three."

"I'm afraid I really can't see what sort of solid evidence we can get. We've explored just about every avenue open to us, and it also would seem we haven't got much chance of a confession sir, she is as hard as nails."

"So far Steve, so far. We know we haven't got a chance of making it stick, but let's hope she doesn't. I want you to go around there very early in the morning, before she has a chance to get dolled up to face us - no warning. No one is at their best half asleep. Get her before she has the time to get her act together. Go around there in a squad car, sirens going - the lot, arrest her and formally charge her. Lay it on thick and put the fear of God into her. It's the only chance we've got!"

Chapter 30

*I*t was coming to an end. She knew she couldn't carry on much longer. Jim's death had really brought home to her the enormity of what she had done - she didn't know how much longer she could maintain her silence. If the police put even the slightest amount of pressure on her, she felt sure she would crack. She pictured herself telling the dour, senior policeman. Then what? Trial? Media circus? She imagined her mother - she couldn't handle this. Her friends? After what she had done? No, she shook her head; she couldn't believe they would ever forgive her. She was beginning to feel like a rabbit, trapped in the headlights of an approaching car. Every instinct was telling her to run - but where? As soon as she made a move they would be on to her... there had to be another way. She sighed deeply - there was only one way.

While the police were deciding their next move, Bobby Collins sat alone in her elegant lounge. She looked around the familiar room, picturing them all standing there. Debby and Nick - bickering again, Mel handing around drinks, Darren cracking jokes. She smiled; he was a good man, lots of fun. Her smile died as her memory moved on, and she thought of Simon, standing behind the bar, pouring drinks and playing the congenial host to perfection - God she missed him! Wasn't there a song line somewhere which said 'You don't know what you've got till it's gone'? It was certainly true. She forced herself to move on. Karen and Terry, Karen trying to coax Terry into cheering up, then suddenly she pictured Jim. A thousand memories crowded into her mind, secret assignations, quiet lunches and then.... what? He dropped her like a brick when the going got tough. Her expression hardened, how could she have been so stupid? And Joanna - what about her? She had treated her badly, she knew that.

Joanna sat in her kitchen, a cup of tea slowly growing cold as she stared into space. She felt so alone, she had plenty of friends but everyone felt so embarrassed around her and she felt uncomfortable for them. She missed Jim dreadfully, but she also missed her friends. She wondered what Bobby was doing. She decided she should face up to Bobby. Realising that she had been fooling herself, she decided it was time she grew up and accepted reality. She didn't want their next meeting to be across a courtroom - with everyone watching them to see how the two 'love rivals' faced each other. Despite everything she felt a grudging admiration for Bobby, she had certainly handled Simon's death well, obviously a strong woman, and not given to histrionics, Joanna felt she could learn from her. Maybe she should go and see her, try and have a last private talk together before it was too late. She knew Bobby would have to pay the price for her actions, but she wanted to see her one last time to tell her she understood.

Bobby wandered in to the kitchen, she ran her hand along the gleaming surfaces, should she telephone Joanna? It might be the last chance she got. She was pretty sure the police were going to charge her. She paused by the telephone - she had to ring her, try and see her, try and explain. The shrill ringing of the telephone interrupted her reverie. She jumped, startled, and grabbed the 'phone. She prayed it would not be another reporter, the police had arranged for her number to be changed twice to thwart the press, and although the new number was unlisted, somehow they had managed to get hold of it. Bobby herself had only given the number to a few very close friends and relations.

"Hello," she whispered, giving nothing away.

"Bobby? Bobby it's me – Joanna."

"Joanna! Oh thank God! I thought it might be one of those awful reporters," she paused, "how are you?"

"I don't even know how I am any more - I expect you feel the same."

Bobby gave a brief, bitter laugh. "You are so right.... look..."

"We should talk," they both spoke together.

"You first," Bobby said quickly.

"I just thought.... I just thought maybe we should sit down together and talk...the police said...no...not on the 'phone. Let's meet. Do you want to come here?"

"Why don't you come here? I feel the whole world is watching me at the moment. You can't see our house from the road and I couldn't bear to sit with you while everyone tries to stare in. I know I'm being paranoid but this whole thing is just so awful. That is if you feel you can bear to come round here?" Bobby added hesitantly.

"Of course. I'll be there - when?"

"Tonight? Come round and we'll have a bottle of wine and spend the evening together. To hell with it - we've been friends a long time - I think we should clear the air in private before the whole thing becomes too public."

"Tonight then, about eight?"

"Fine."

There was a silence, then they both quickly said goodbye and hung up. In their separate houses they stood, long after they had replaced the receivers, staring thoughtfully at the 'phone.

Tonight, thought Bobby, tonight I will tell her everything - she deserves the truth for once. Tonight I will tell her - I hope she can take it.

Tonight. thought Joanna Tonight I will tell her everything I know. I have pretended long enough. It was not her fault. I was blind. Tonight I will tell her.

That evening Joanna walked around to Bobby's house. It was not very far and she needed the time to think of what she would say. As she walked up the driveway she couldn't help but remember all the happy times she had spent in that house. She steeled herself, took a deep breath, and firmly rang the doorbell.

Bobby opened the door and both women stood for a moment staring at each other. On a sudden impulse they hugged each other fiercely.

"Oh Joanna, what is happening to the world? Come in, come in by the fire. Did you walk? I didn't hear a car - you must be freezing!"

"I needed the walk. Besides, I didn't think I'd be able to drive - I thought we could use this!" She held up a large bottle of wine, and smiled at Bobby.

"Snap!" replied Bobby as she showed Joanna in to the lounge, on the coffee table in the centre of the room stood an equally large bottle, and two glasses.

"Oh what the hell - let's drink them both!"

"Joanna! I am surprised at you - is this the new tougher Joanna?"

"It's going to have to be isn't it? I'm going to have to either grow up or give up - and I am not quite ready to give up."

They sat down together and started on the wine to ease the initial awkwardness. For a while they talked about everything and nothing until the wine started to take effect.

"Maybe this will make me sleep," declared Joanna, pouring yet another glass of wine.

"You too?" asked Bobby sympathetically. "Dr Armstrong gave me some horrible little pills - I try not to take them, they make me feel like a zombie the next morning."

"Me too! I mean he gave me them too. Why do you think men always think we won't be able to cope without their help?" she asked belligerently, conveniently forgetting that she had asked for the tablets.

"Because they know they couldn't cope without us and our help. You see, Joanna," slurred Bobby, "Men...all men, are basically weak. Women have to be strong - that's why we have the babies - men couldn't handle it!"

"You're right!" giggled Joanna, then suddenly her face crumpled, "I never had a baby!"

"Neither did I," pointed out Bobby, "Mind you - I've had quite a few big babies!" she exploded with drunken laughter.

Joanna started to laugh too. "I had the one I suppose."

"Joanna.... I..." Bobby began, suddenly trying to sober up.

"Don't say it!" Joanna said quickly, she didn't want to hear it after all. "Let's go out!" she declared abruptly, before the conversation became too deep.

"Out? What.... now? Where?" asked a startled Bobby.

"Out on the prowl, out for a good time, just out! I've never done that," giggled Joanna.

"Are you serious?" asked Bobby, struggling to make sense of what Joanna was saying.

"I don't want to ever be serious again! Let's go.... Oh! I haven't got a car."

"I have - but I don't think I should drive!" slurred Bobby.

"Bobby - pardon me for mentioning it but - you are about to be arrested for mass murder - what else can they do to you? Come on!" Joanna rose unsteadily to her feet and headed towards the garage.

"All right - I owe you this much at least," agreed Bobby, fumbling for her keys.

They stood in the garage and peered owlishly at the car.

"It is a fast car Bobby; do you think you'll be able to manage it?"

"Of course I can," declared Bobby. "Men have big cars! Have you noticed that? Men seem to think they need big cars..."She broke off giggling, "because...oh! I have forgotten what I was going to say!" She giggled again. "You open the garage doors - I'll drive." She was starting to feel incredibly woozy. I'll open the windows once I'm on the road she thought. That will wake me up a bit.

Chapter 31

*T*he following morning, at first light, Shelagh, Steve and George drove around to Bobby's house. As they approached Steve switched on the siren and lights.

"This will wake her up!" he grinned to his boss, who sat grim faced, beside him.

"Let's hope it shakes her up!" he replied sternly.

The car pulled to an abrupt stop in front of the house and the three officers got out. Steve rang the doorbell repeatedly and rapped loudly on the door. A few minutes passed - nothing.

"You don't think she's done a runner do you?" Steve asked anxiously.

"Could be." George shrugged, "That would certainly indicate guilt though. If she's run - we'll catch her!"

Steve tried again - he rang the bell, knocked loudly on the door and shouted to Bobby.

"Mrs Collins - this is the police." He always felt rather foolish saying that part - who else would it be in a police car with sirens and blue lights?

"Check the garage - see if her car has gone," George snapped out the command. "I'll get on the radio - don't worry - we'll find her!" He turned and strode purposefully towards the police car.

"Sir! Sir - I think we've found her!" Shelagh had opened the garage door. Bobby's car was still warm - it must have only recently run out of petrol. A length of hose led from the exhaust pipe to the front window - Bobby's body was slumped in the driver's seat - she was obviously dead.

The three of them stood still momentarily, looking at the scene; clearly there was nothing they could do. George walked up to the car and peered in through the passenger window. He could see an envelope lying beside her, using a handkerchief he carefully opened the door and removed it. It was addressed to Joanna. Using the minimum of contact with the paper, he opened the envelope and took out a letter. The others stood beside him and they read Bobby's final note.

Dear Joanna,

By the time you read this I will have gone to join Jim. I'm sorry. I never meant to hurt you, but I can't go on living like this. I hope one day you'll find it in your heart to forgive me. I can't help it - I really love him. Believe me though he was never good enough for you. He did have an affair with Debby, I can never be truly sorry about her death, but I could forgive him, she threw herself at him - she didn't love him - not like I do.

You know I would never have divorced Simon, but now he is gone and I have to get away from all this. I never wanted to hurt Simon you know, I did love him, I don't suppose you'll believe that now, but it is true. Please don't think too badly of me. I know I took Jim away from you, but honestly - he would have broken your heart in the end. Perhaps this way you will be able to make a new start - you deserve to find real happiness, and I truly hope you do.

Love

Bobby

"I guess that is it then, sir." Steve said flatly.

"Saves the tax payer I suppose," shrugged George, philosophically, "I'll wait here for the forensics and the ambulance. Do you want to go and break the news to Mrs Baines?"

"I think I had better sir, can I take the letter?"

"In an evidence bag, are you both going?"

"I think that'll be best – she's got quite friendly with Shelagh. I'll arrange for someone to stay with her later, and meet you back at the station then."

"Fine," George replied. He felt cheated somehow, as if she had won in the end after all. He reached up and closed the garage door. A small crowd had gathered at the entrance to the drive and he didn't want to attract any more attention.

"It will all come out soon enough, " he thought with a sigh.

They drove directly around to Joanna's house. The curtains were drawn back and the light in the kitchen was on, shining brightly through the grey early morning gloom.

Steve hesitated briefly, and then knocked at the back door that he knew led into the kitchen. He could see Joanna moving about inside.

"Hello Steve, Shelagh, you're early birds! Come in, but please, close the door quietly, I've got a bit of a hangover I'm afraid." She smiled sheepishly. "I'm ashamed to say I rather disgraced myself last night - oddly enough I feel better for it though - apart from the sore head!"

Steve entered the room and sighed, she looked the happiest he had seen her for a long while, and he was about to spoil it all.

"Come on, sit down - would you like some breakfast? I'm baking at the moment. I woke up this morning and just felt like it. I love the smell of baking, don't you? I'll put the kettle on, won't be a moment." She bustled about.

"Joanna" Steve said quietly, "Joanna, come and sit down - leave the tea, I want to talk to you."

"Pardon?" said Joanna brightly, turning round to face him, then seeing his expression she sank down on the chair.

"What is it?" she whispered, the colour draining from her face. "Tell me what has happened."

"It's Bobby Collins I'm afraid - I'm sorry Joanna. I have to tell you, she is dead."

"Bobby?" echoed Joanna thoroughly dazed, "Bobby dead? She can't be - I saw her last night. We...we got drunk together. She can't be dead."

"You were with her last night? How did she seem to you?" Shelagh asked quietly.

"To be honest, we were both blind drunk. She invited me around, she said there was something she wanted to talk to me about." She paused, remembering how warmly Bobby had greeted her the previous evening. "I walked around there - I took one of those great big bottles of wine and so I thought I had better walk home. Anyway we sat around talking and drinking until quite late."

"Did she tell you anything significant?" queried Steve.

"No," Joanna said softly, "She started to, but I stopped her - I didn't want to hear it. I think I know what she was going to say, and I'm afraid I chickened out - I just couldn't bear to hear it. Towards the end of the evening she got quite maudlin - kept going on about how sorry she was..." Joanna stopped talking and sat gazing into space.

"Joanna, Bobby was the murderer. She killed Simon and Jim." He decided not to mention Debby for the moment. "She left a note telling us, well - telling you, and then she took her own life. I'm sorry."

"Bobby? Bobby a murderer? What do you mean 'telling me'. What note? I haven't got a note. You are wrong - you must be. Why are you doing this?" Joanna looked confused.

"We found the note; it was beside her .... beside her when we found her. It was addressed to you - but we had to open it," Shelagh said gently.

Steve took out the note; it was opened out in the plastic bag and clearly legible through the clear film. He watched as Joanna stared at it - a dazed expression on her face, and wondered if she was even capable of reading anything at the moment.

"I'll leave you read it in private - I'll make that tea now - I think we could both use one. I'm right here if you need me." Shelagh went over to the kitchen counter. Steve walked over to help.

Shelagh turned to the sink and began to lay out cups and saucers. Although Steve kept his back to her, he was aware that Joanna was still sitting motionless at the table. He wondered what she was thinking.

Joanna was glad they couldn't see her - she didn't need to read the note, she knew what it said. She had known for a long time, ever since the day she found it in Jim's pocket just after Simon's death. That was why she had killed him. She had been sorting out his suit for the cleaners and found the letter. It was addressed to her so she had read it, and suddenly everything became so clear. They were obviously planning to run away together, they were just going to leave her to face everything alone. She remembered Jim muttering about starting another branch, it must have been part of their plan, he would leave, then after a while Bobby would join him, and Joanna would be left to pick up the pieces of her life. Calmly she had put the letter back in his pocket and put his suit away, she wouldn't send it to the cleaners. She had been a good wife long enough.

She had always been a good wife - right up until she killed her husband. Despite their row after Bobby's dinner party, she had still made him an omelette when she got home, a very special omelette. After all, he had asked for one in the car on the way home hadn't he? A lot of women would have made him go to bed hungry, she thought bitterly, but not her, despite her anger at how he had humiliated her that evening, she still played the loving, dutiful wife - it was what she did best - after all. Everyone said what a wonderful wife she was, even Bobby had said it, and she was right - Joanna was too good for her husband.

Shelagh made the tea and brought her over a cup. Joanna sat staring in to space silently. They respected her silence and sat quietly waiting for her to speak first.

Shelagh watched her anxiously, she seemed quite calm. She knew from experience that sometimes shock can bring on calmness as much as hysteria. Perhaps she had just had too many shocks to fully comprehend this latest one. They waited while she took time to absorb the news, watching her face they each imagined her remembering her friends who had died.

Joanna was indeed remembering. She thought back to Debby's death, it had been so simple really. The Russian Lemons were a favourite with everyone, they had swopped the recipe and it had been easy to slip one into the freezer the morning they had all gone to Bobby's to prepare for the dinner party. They each brought cool bags with the chilled wine, no one had looked into Joanna's, and it had just been so easy. Naturally she had helped Bobby throughout the evening, clearing the plates and bringing in the next course - they all helped each other - that's what friends were for. She felt very sorry for Nick of course, but still, he was young, he would be able to start again.

She didn't like to think about Simon's death, it was really such a shame, but sadly necessary. She justified herself by thinking how devastated he would have been over Bobby, really, she reasoned, she'd saved him from a lot of suffering. Jim's death was simply poetic justice - she had devoted her life to him and so she had taken his, which seemed fair. Then of course, there was Bobby. For a while she had been almost ready to forgive her. She felt sure Bobby would be going to prison for life, and that seemed enough of a price to pay, but when Bobby was not charged with the crimes, Joanna had realised what she had to do. Really Bobby not being charged with murder had been Joanna's only failure - she thought the plate swopping incident would certainly have convinced them. Shame really, I should have planted a bit of evidence, I suppose they just couldn't prove it.

Actually, the fact that the police had not charged Bobby had really tipped Joanna over the brink; it convinced her she was not invincible after all. She was not sure how much longer she could keep up the pretence, and she knew that if she were interrogated by the police she might break down completely, and that would ruin everything. She decided it was time for her to go and see Bobby. It had not been difficult to slip a couple of Dr Armstrong's wonderful sleeping pills into Bobby's wine, and the rest had been simple. Once Bobby passed out in the car, Joanna had fixed up the hose, wearing her trusty rubber kitchen gloves of course, and left the carefully saved letter lying beside her. It was over.

Steve eyed Joanna thoughtfully as he sipped his tea. He wondered if she could finally accept that it was all over now and start to build a new life. She seemed to have developed a sort of inner strength recently, and he hoped that would see her through the forthcoming formalities so that she could resume a normal life. He fervently hoped she would be able to put it all behind her.

Joanna eyed Steve thoughtfully as she sipped her tea. She wondered if he had fully accepted Bobby's note. She glanced over at Shelagh. Would they believe that it was all over now, and let her start to build a new life? Were there any lingering doubts in their minds? She really hoped they would accept that it was all finished, and put the whole thing behind them. She'd actually grown to like them both; it would be such a shame if anything had to happen to them.

Steve sat down opposite Joanna and gave her a sympathetic smile.

I wonder what she is thinking? he thought, I hope things work out all right for her.

I wonder what he is thinking? she thought, I do hope he lets things work out all right for me.

"Something smells nice," Shelagh said, smiling encouragingly. "What are you making?"

"It is a special recipe actually - it's a seed cake."

THE END...?

Epilogue

Jt was a bitterly cold day. An optimistic winter sun tried in vain to penetrate the gloom but was quickly dismissed by the foreboding grey clouds that blanketed the tiny village church. William Owens, the parish rector, shivered in his robes as he stood at the doorway greeting the mourners.

He mentally pictured the deceased. Young, vivacious and quite beautiful as he recalled. He sighed deeply. How could she possibly have done such a terrible thing as to take her own life?

He turned his attentions to the approaching group. There was no mistaking their obvious grief. One poor soul seemed almost on breaking point. Her shoulders heaved as she clutched a handkerchief to her face and openly sobbed.

"Try to be strong my dear," he murmured. "Remember her suffering is over now. Try to imagine her looking down on us all from a far better place."

The woman merely nodded and, supported by her friends, she moved into the welcoming gloom of the old village church.

Terry Matherson stared at the coffin. He glanced with embarrassment across at his sobbing friend and awkwardly patted her hand.

"Umm she wouldn't want you to remember her like this." He murmured.

I'll bet she wouldn't! She thought triumphantly. I'll bet she's looking down and reaching for the thunderbolts at the injustice of it all. Everyone thinks she killed herself. Everyone thinks she was barking mad and finally cracked. It's just amazing no one knows it was me. I killed her and no one knows. It's all just so incredible! She pressed her handkerchief into her face again to smother her laughter.

But I got away with it and now it is over. Life will eventually return to normal, and Linwood will once again become, just a nice quiet village. Not for me though. I'll always be that poor woman whose husband screwed around. I am going to leave. Make a fresh start. Somewhere warm, Spain maybe. I'm really looking forward to a quiet life.

Biography

Christine Brooks lived in the Caribbean before settling down to married life in a small Berkshire village. She now divides her time between her home there and her adopted home in Spain where she writes for a Costa Blanca magazine. She is married to Paul and they have two grown children Kate and Tim and a daughter in law Emma.

Lightning Source UK Ltd.
Milton Keynes UK
29 October 2009

145592UK00002B/7/P

9 781449 024611